MW00989711

Slated for Death

ALSO BY ELIZABETH J. DUNCAN

Never Laugh as a Hearse Goes By
A Small Hill to Die On
A Killer's Christmas in Wales
A Brush with Death
The Cold Light of Mourning

Slated for Death

A PENNY BRANNIGAN MYSTERY

Elizabeth J. Duncan

Minotaur Books

A Thomas Dunne Book

New York

This is a work of fiction. All of the characters, organizations, and events portrayed in this novel are either products of the author's imagination or are used fictitiously.

A THOMAS DUNNE BOOK FOR MINOTAUR BOOKS.
An imprint of St. Martin's Publishing Group.

SLATED FOR DEATH. Copyright © 2015 by Elizabeth J. Duncan.
All rights reserved. Printed in the United States of America. For information, address St. Martin's Press, 175 Fifth Avenue, New York, N.Y. 10010.

www.thomasdunnebooks.com
www.minotaurbooks.com

Library of Congress Cataloging-in-Publication Data

Duncan, Elizabeth J.
  Slated for death : a Penny Brannigan mystery / Elizabeth J. Duncan.—
First edition.
    p. cm.
  "A Thomas Dunne Book."
  ISBN 978-1-250-05521-7 (hardcover)
  ISBN 978-1-4668-5838-1 (e-book)
  1. Brannigan, Penny (Fictitious character)—Fiction.   2. Murder—
Investigation—Fiction.   3. City and town life—Wales—Fiction.
4. Wales—Fiction.   I. Title.
  PR9199.4.D863S58 2015
  813'.6—dc23

2014042141

Minotaur books may be purchased for educational, business,
or promotional use. For information on bulk purchases, please contact
the Macmillan Corporate and Premium Sales Department at 1-800-221-7945,
extension 5442, or write to specialmarkets@macmillan.com.

First Edition: April 2015

10 9 8 7 6 5 4 3 2 1

For Sylvia and Peter Jones

Acknowledgments

There's an old saying in Wales that you're born under a slate roof, spend your life walking on slate floors, and are finally laid to rest under a slate tombstone.

Slated for Death is set against the backdrop of what remains of the great Welsh slate industry, which played a huge role in the country's way of life for two centuries, especially in the north. (Coal mining was more predominant in the south.)

Many of the old slate mines and quarries are now worked out and the few that remain are used primarily for tourist and teaching purposes. The mine described in this book is Llechwedd Slate Caverns, in Blaenau Ffestiniog, and although I have taken liberties with its layout and operations, I hope I captured its mysterious black beauty and majesty of scope. It is well worth a visit, as is the National Slate Museum in Llanberis, North Wales.

Thank you to Sylvia and Peter Jones of Conwy, North Wales, whose e-mail with stunning photographs of abandoned, overgrown slate quarries suggested the slate theme. My time in Wales is always enriched by our excursions, picnics, and dog walks.

I am grateful to Eirlys Owen, of Llanrwst, for accompanying me down the mine—twice!—and for her excellent suggestions that moved the plot forward. Sean Copsey, Customer Services Manager, Llechwedd Slate Caverns, and his team provided much behind-the-scenes information, and I thank them for their warm hospitality.

Thanks, as always, to PC Chris Jones, North Wales Police Service, for advice on police procedural. Any errors or assumptions are mine.

To Bob and Christina Sykes, for getting me out of an accommodation predicament and making available their Summer Hill flat in Llandudno, thank you.

Grateful thanks to my agent, Dominick Abel, St. Martin's Press editor Toni Kirkpatrick, and her assistant, Jennifer Letwack, for bringing this book to life. And bouquets of appreciation to Toronto artist Doug Martin, whose whimsical, stylish paintings have graced the covers of all the books in this series.

I appreciate the contributions and corrections of Madeleine Matte and Hannah Dennison, who helped improve the manuscript when it was a work in progress.

And finally love to Riley Wallbank, for her support during an especially violent storm, and to Lucas Walker for a memorable visit in beautiful North Wales.

Abandoned slate quarries are dangerous. Rock is slippery, tips can move, falls can and do occur, portions of structures can collapse. There may be hidden and unguarded precipices and shafts.

—Alun John Richards, *Slate Quarrying in Wales*

Slated for Death

One

Glenda Roberts was having a good day, but that was about to change; things would soon take a definite turn for the worse. She had about six hours left to live. But right now, she had some errands to run.

"Hello, Penny," she said with a broad, practiced smile as she pushed open the door to the Llanelen Spa, letting in a frosty blast of January air. "Just dropping something off for Victoria. Is she in?" Glenda brushed a few stray silver wisps from her forehead. She had always thought her hair her best feature and now, although she'd gone grey, it was as sleek and glossy as it was when it had been the colour of a burnished chestnut. A lengthy session with stylist Alberto every six weeks in the hair salon of the Llanelen Spa saw to that. A meticulous trim kept her one-length bob sleek and deceptively simple while an artful silvery tint gave her the distinctive look of a young person with premature grey hair.

Penny Brannigan shook her head. "No, sorry, she's away for the day. Not expecting her in until tomorrow."

"Oh, well, no problem. I'll just leave this with you, if I may." She held out a large brown envelope. "It's her sheet music for the concert."

"Right," said Penny, taking it from her. "The concert."

"Yes," said Glenda. "The St. David's Day concert. March first. We're holding it down the Llyn Du mine this year. It's going to be brilliant, and you won't want to miss it, I can tell you." She waved her arm in a sweeping, circular motion above her head. "The acoustics! You've never heard anything like it. Why, Pavarotti himself performed there a few years ago." She smiled again and took a step back. "I'll drop by in a few days with the posters. Victoria said you'd put up a couple in the Spa."

"Oh, right. Posters. Well, we'll make sure Victoria gets this." Penny handed the envelope to receptionist Rhian Phillips and turned her attention back to Glenda. "How's your mother, by the way? I haven't seen her in ages."

"Oh, you know Mum. Just keeps ticking along. I keep telling her she'll outlive us all." She shrugged. "Mum says when you get to her age, all your friends are either in care homes themselves or they're no longer with us. She misses them all terribly and it does get a bit lonely. She doesn't get many visitors outside the family. If you get the chance, do pop in and see her. She'd like that."

She pulled out her mobile and checked the time. "Oh, where did the morning go? Must get on. These concerts don't organize themselves, unfortunately, and I've got a few more stops to make before lunch. Thanks, and we'll see you later. And don't forget to buy your tickets for the concert. Seating is limited—only about a hundred tickets available. Seriously, don't miss out. There's going to be a special guest singer and a ticket will get you into the reception afterward. Or the after-party, as I like to call it. You can rub shoulders with all the VIPs."

A moment later, with a swish of her mid-length tailored red coat with its smart row of double-breasted black buttons, Glenda was gone.

"A St. David's Day concert down the mine," said Rhian. "Whoever heard of such a thing? My grandfather used to work there." She nodded at the door. "He'll be gobsmacked to say the least, when I tell him they're holding a concert in that miserable place. 'What the hell are they playing at?' is how he'll put it."

"I'd heard that people actually get married down there, which really amazes me. But the concert thing is new to me. I hadn't heard that before. And who are these VIPs she's expecting?" said Penny. "And Pavarotti? Really?"

"If she says so." Rhian shrugged. "I wonder how much the tickets cost."

"And think about the logistics. How on earth will they get all the instruments and performers down there, never mind the audience?"

"Oh, and about the posters, Penny. I'd be very surprised if Victoria said we'd put them up here in the Spa. Put them up where? We don't clutter the place up with advertising."

Glenda dropped off a couple more packets to other musicians, ducked into a couple of shops and then decided to treat herself to a coffee and maybe a slice of walnut cake at the local café. The air was fragrant with the distinctive, welcoming aroma of freshly ground coffee as she settled into a corner table to enjoy her brew and check her e-mail. She pulled out her phone and a slow, troubled frown spread across her face as she read the first message. She massaged her arm gently as she deleted it and then moved on to the next one.

The shipment she'd been expecting would be delivered that afternoon. Great!

She replaced the phone in her bag and pulled out the spreadsheet that recorded all the details of the concert. It was going to be wonderful and so was the reception afterward. A special musical guest had signed a performance contract and although this singer would take careful handling, she should prove worth it. Tickets were selling well, even though they were priced beyond the budget of most citizens of Llanelen, and all in all, the St. David's Day concert promised to be a night to remember.

She leaned back in her chair and cupping her mug in both hands, took a warm, comforting sip. She might have taken a bit more comfort in it had she known she had about five hours left to live.

Two

A dozen or so people stood motionless in the semidarkness, reflecting on what they had just seen and heard. And then, as the recorded music faded away leaving only the ambient sound of trickling water, a few bright lights came up a few metres away, lighting the path to the next stop on the self-guided tour of the Llyn Du mine. As the unofficial leaders of the group shuffled forward, ducking their heads as they entered the low, narrow tunnel that led to the next stop on the tour, treading carefully and slowly along the damp, uneven ground, the lights behind them where the group had just been dimmed and died.

A few minutes later the group emerged into a cavernous room, a cathedral of slate. They gazed up in wonder at the vast, soaring ceiling, many metres above them, and marvelled at the men and boys who had created this space, by candlelight, using only manual tools, over a century ago. And then their attention was drawn to the small lake, lit in alternating red and green lights, the national colours of Wales, and fed by a waterfall that cascaded down the rear of the chamber. The surface of the lake was still and the lake itself surprisingly deep and clear. The group stood in awed silence that bordered on reverence, taking it all in. It was this lake that the mine was named after. *Llyn Du.* "Black Lake."

After a few more minutes they walked on, and found themselves back at the starting point of the tour where the little yellow train was waiting to return them to the surface. With happy anticipation that they were only moments away from being deposited safely aboveground, they clambered into the train. The doors clanged shut and a few minutes later, after a noisy ascent, the train juddered to a stop in the winch house. The passengers disembarked, and exchanging smiles of relief, spilled out into the reassuring, cold brightness of a late January afternoon. They dropped the red, green, or yellow hard hats mine visitors were required to wear in the large box, and chattering as they went, made their way toward the exit.

As the last visitors of the day filed past him, Bevan Jones turned to his colleague stationed beside the box of hard hats and raised an eyebrow. "All right?" he asked.

His colleague shook his head. "No. Not all right. We're two short."

"Two! Well, one of them is that fellow who panicked and we had to bring him up early. So he's accounted for. As for the other one . . . sure you got the count right? No one could have slipped past you?" When the colleague shook his head to indicate the count was accurate, Bevan called out to the operations team to let them know the train had to make one more descent.

When the group of mine workers reached the starting point of the tour, several hundred feet below ground, Bevan spoke.

"We'll go this way." He switched on a powerful torch. "The missus is making shepherd's pie tonight. I hope this won't take too long."

The men set off, raking the ground with the bright beams from their torches, occasionally pointing them down the chained-off side tunnels that were not part of the tour.

One of them stopped to pick up a gum wrapper and a little further on, a business card and then a glove.

Suddenly, Bevan stopped and held up his right hand. "What's that?" he asked in a low voice. A silence fell over them.

"I don't hear anything, said one of the men. Bevan pushed his hand forward in an impatient, halting gesture and then slowly lowered it. "Wait. Listen," he whispered. A faint, eerily moaning sound drifted down the tunnel toward them. "The lake," said Bevan. "It's coming from the lake chamber. Come on." They hurried down the uneven passage and entered the large chamber. The silence was broken only by the gentle, pleasing splash of the waterfall. Bevan used his torch to slowly scan the floor of the chamber and as its bright beam reached the steps near the lake, a crumpled splash of red was revealed.

The men raced toward it. As they got closer the splash of red came into focus as the still form of a woman wearing a red coat.

When they reached her, one of the younger workers kneeled down and gingerly touched her shoulder.

"Are you all right, lady?" he asked.

He rolled her over slightly; her silvery hair fell to one side, revealing her face.

"Hey, isn't that . . . ?" said one of the men.

When the woman did not respond, the crouching worker looked up at the others, his face a mask of shock and fear.

"Fetch the box!" yelled Bevan Jones.

Three

*D*CI Gareth Davies had been to some bad accidents and crime scenes in his thirty years with the North Wales Police. He'd seen the aftermath of horrific killings that defied belief. Scenes where the violence had been so shocking, so gruesome, that the flashbacks that jolted him awake just as he was drifting off to sleep left him sitting up in bed, sweating, and wishing there was some way he could delete the unspeakable images from his memory. But he'd never had a case where a body had been found in such a deep, dark place.

The call for an ambulance had come from the mine just after six o'clock and, unsure of the nature of the call, the dispatcher had requested police assistance. By the time Davies and his team arrived, there was no doubt that Glenda Roberts was beyond help. He stepped back from the body and looked around. Bevan Jones and his assistant stood in the shadows just outside the pool of intense, focused beams cast by the emergency lighting that had been set up near the body.

After examining the body, Davies walked over to them. "Which one of you is in charge?" he asked.

Bevan took a step forward. "I'm the operations manager."

"Right. Can you tell me how all this works?"

"Not sure I follow you. How all what works?"

"Well, the tour. The mine. I've driven by lots of times, but I've never been here before."

"That's the way of things, isn't it? We go where life takes us. I've driven by police stations lots of times but can't say I've spent much time in them."

Davies decided he liked this blunt-speaking Welshman in the bright-red boilersuit, with his large, capable hands. He appeared to be in his mid to late forties, with pale blue eyes set in an open, somewhat weathered face.

"Describe to me what happened in, say, the last hour of your day." Davies gestured in the direction of Glenda's body, which had been cordoned off, awaiting the arrival of the pathologist.

"Well, we bring the people down the mine on the train. The same one that brought you down. It's a self-guided tour for the most part that lasts about forty minutes, but we do have employees stationed down here available to help if required and to do the demonstration of Victorian mining techniques. We count the visitors in and out on each tour. This lady was on the last tour of the day and one of the lads told me we were two short when the group she was in returned up top. One was a fella who panicked, so we brought him up earlier. As soon as the tour count totalled one short, we came down looking for the other person who was unaccounted for and there she was. That's just how we found her."

10

"You've got CCTV, I assume?" Davies asked.

"Just aboveground. Not down here. It's too dark."

"We'll need to see whatever you've got."

"No problem," said Bevan. "We'll make everything we've got available to you."

"I guess it would be too much to hope for that you'd know any of the people who were on the tour with our victim."

Bevan shook his head. "Sorry, no. It's like any other tourist attraction. Anyone can buy a ticket and go."

"Well, I'll need the names of all the employees who were working today. We'll need to interview them. And I'll want to know more about this fellow who panicked and was taken up early. When you say early, do you mean before the tour ended?"

"It happens sometimes. Folks think they'll be okay but once they get down here the claustrophobia they didn't know they had reveals itself . . ."

"I can see why it would take some people that way." Davies checked his watch. "I'm sorry, but we could easily be another couple of hours. We'll need to station someone aboveground to bring the pathologist down and then you'll have to tell us how we can get the body out."

Bevan shrugged. "Well, I better call the missus and tell her to keep that shepherd's pie warm." He thought for a moment and then spoke directly to a young mine worker. "On second thought, you go up top and see if the canteen manager's still on site." He turned to Davies. "She may have stayed behind to set up for tomorrow as she likes to have everything ready to go when she comes in of a morning. That way, she's not so rushed." Turning back to his colleague, he continued, "Ask her if she'd be so good as to make up a tray of sandwiches and a large pot of coffee. I'm sure we could all do with something to eat. And tell her to keep the heat on. It's bloody freezing. And reassure her there'll be over-time."

Davies liked him even more.

"You know, I wouldn't mind going up top myself," Davies said. "I'm finding it . . . down here, it's . . ."

"Oh, I know what you're trying to say," Bevan said good-naturedly. "I've heard it all before. Many times. Dark, cold . . ."

"I admit I do find it dark and cold," Davies said, "but there's something more." He raised an arm. "It's almost as if I can feel the weight of all that slate above me, and to be honest, it makes me a little nervous. How far down are we, by the way?"

"Deeper than you think, I'll bet. At this level, we're about five hundred feet down."

"This level?"

"Yes, sir. There are lots of levels. This mine is sixteen floors or levels deep with over three hundred chambers. Our largest chamber is twice the size of St. Paul's Cathedral. Remember, the mine's been worked for over a century. There's been a lot of slate carved out of this mountain."

Davies reflected on all those hollowed-out chambers held up by pillars of slate and the backbreaking work it would have taken to create them.

"Most of us don't have that much to complain about, when you think about it," said Bevan, as if reading his thoughts. "About the kind of work we do. Driving to work, sitting at a desk, using a computer. Twelve hours down a mine, now that's real work. And they would have walked a couple of hours each way just to get here. And in Victorian times, there would have been no electric light. All this would have been worked by candlelight. Imagine!"

12

"I can't," said Davies.

"And you wouldn't have been a grown man, either. You'd be working down here from dawn to dusk as a lad only twelve years old. But of course, it would have been so dark you'd have no idea of dawn or dusk. And with your lungs full of slate dust, you'd be an old man at forty."

And then, after giving Davies a few moments to absorb that, he drove home his message. "And there'd have been no safety equipment, either. Just regular clothes. No proper boots, no hard hats, no eye protection, no harnesses . . ."

"I expect there were a lot of accidents," said Davies. God, I hope this turns out to be just an accident, he thought. If it's a crime scene, it'll be a nightmare to process.

"I don't suppose you know who she is?" he asked Bevan.

"As a matter of fact, I do," Bevan replied. "That's Glenda Roberts. She was organizing a concert down here."

"Concert? Down here?" Davies expressed the same surprise Penny had. Bevan reassured him that that mine was, in fact, a desired special-events venue with a major wow factor. Bevan then added, "But of course Glenda's well-known to us here at the mine."

Before Davies could respond to that, a mine worker in a high-visiblity jacket approached, followed by a tall man carrying a large holdall. Both were wearing hard hats, as were Davies and Bevan Jones.

"This here's your pathologist," the worker said.

Davies led him to the body and then returned to Bevan. "Let's leave them to get on with their work and take the train back to the surface."

On the way up, Davies said, "I'm curious. Mines and quarries. What's the difference?"

13

"Slate lying close to the surface is quarried," replied Jones. "That's a relatively straightforward operation. But when the rich slate veins run deep underground, they have to be mined. It's a much more complicated, risky, and labour-intensive process."

Four

Victoria Hopkirk took her first sip of morning coffee in her flat on the top floor of the Llanelen Spa. She thumbed through her diary, made a few notes on the day's to-do list, and then reached for the envelope Glenda Roberts had dropped off the day before. She slit it open and pulled out a few pages of sheet music. She read the sticky note attached to the first page:

V—Here's your music for SDD concert. First rehearsal
Tuesday 7 pm. Will call you. G.

And then she glanced at the song titles. A couple she knew well and expected to see as they were old standards at events like this, one she knew a little, and one was new to her, although she thought she'd heard of it. She read the music and heard herself humming a vaguely familiar melody. That sounds like an old '80s pop tune, she thought, but the name of it eluded her.

She and Penny had opened the Llanelen Spa the year before, but Victoria had not always lived in North Wales. She'd lived for many years in London, where she was well-known and in demand as an accomplished harpist at sophisticated gatherings. But during a somewhat messy divorce, she'd returned to Llanelen on a break to stay with relatives, met Penny who was operating a manicure salon, and the two had decided to pool resources and start a business together. So far, their venture, the Llanelen Spa, had been a success. They were providing employment and offering a service that women wanted. Their business was growing and they had recently launched their own brand of hand cream, the first in a planned series of in-house products.

It had been some time since Victoria had played the harp in public and she was looking forward to performing in the concert, especially here in Llanelen, which at one time had been home to a vibrant harp-making industry. She replaced the sheet music in the envelope, pushed it aside, then got up and walked to the kitchen to prepare her breakfast.

Just as she finished slicing a banana on top of a bowl of muesli and was about to pour milk on it, a knock on the door interrupted her. That's odd, she thought, glancing at her watch. No, she wasn't late. It was only eight thirty.

"It's me," called a muffled voice through the door.

Victoria opened the door. "What are you doing here so early?" Victoria asked. "Is something wrong? What's the matter?"

"Can I come in?"

"Yes, of course. Come through." Victoria stood to one side to allow Penny to enter.

"Oh, sorry, am I interrupting your breakfast?" Penny asked, pointing to the milk carton in Victoria's hand.

"Yes, you are, actually. I was just about to pour it on my cereal, but never mind." Victoria gestured toward the kitchen. "Coffee?"

"That would be great, thanks."

"So," said Victoria when they were seated at the table. "What brings you up here so early? You never come up here unless it's important." She raised a spoonful of cereal. "Or you're locked out. Or you need a nap in the middle of the afternoon. Or you're hungry. Oh, that must be it. Have you had your breakfast?"

"Yes, I have, thanks." She accepted the mug of coffee Victoria held out to her. "No, it's just with your concert coming up, I thought you'd be interested to know there's been an incident at the Llyn Du mine," Penny began. She took a sip of coffee. "I heard on the radio that they found a body down the mine yesterday. It's nothing to do with us, of course, but the police are investigating."

"Oh, that's terrible!" exclaimed Victoria. "What on earth could have happened? Was it an industrial accident do you suppose? Somebody fell, maybe. Dangerous places, mines. There's a lot that can go wrong and I would imagine if someone's hurt, getting them to the surface would be a real challenge. They could die in the length of time it takes to get them out."

Penny made a little noise that indicated she'd heard what Victoria said but wasn't going to comment on it.

"Anyway, thinking about the concert reminded me that Glenda Roberts was here yesterday. She dropped off an envelope for you and I wanted to make sure you got it. Did Rhian leave it in your box?"

"It was slipped under my door and waiting when I got home. The sheet music for the concert. It's right here." Victoria patted the brown envelope on the table.

"She talked a little about the concert, Glenda did," Penny said. "About it taking place down the mine. I've been wondering about that."

"Oh? Why?"

"Well, I was thinking about my old friend Emma Teasdale and how much she loved music. And there must be lots of elderly people who'd love to go to the St. David's Day concert but they couldn't possibly make the trek down the mine." She thought for a moment. "And certainly anyone who's claustrophobic couldn't make it, either."

"So what are you saying?"

"I guess what I'm saying is why the mine? Why is the concert being held down the mine of all places?"

Victoria set her spoon in her bowl and pushed it away.

"Well, now that you mention it, holding the concert down the mine was Glenda's idea. She said it was the fortieth anniversary of the mine closing and this would be the perfect way to honour the memory of all the men who worked there. To tell you the truth, the rest of us weren't too keen. Such a lot of palaver getting all the instruments down there. Do you know how big a harp is? Do you know how much it weighs? And why risk transporting an instrument that costs £6,000 down a mine for a one-off concert, for heaven's sake?"

"I have some idea about the size of them," Penny said, "but you'll know more about harps than I do, since you play one. To me, they look big and heavy, but fragile and delicate at the same time. Cumbersome. I suppose they come in some sort of case? They probably require a lot of care when you're moving one."

18

Victoria nodded. "Big and heavy is right." She thought for a moment. "I wonder if the concert will go ahead now. I know it's still a few weeks off, but I wonder if this accident or whatever it was will affect that."

"Oh, I'm sure the concert will go ahead," said Penny. "The show must go on and all that. But maybe they'll have to hold it in a different venue. Somewhere sensible. And accessible. The church, maybe. That would be good." Penny licked her lower lip. "Anyway, when Glenda was in yesterday, she mentioned her mother and I thought I'd slip out for an hour or so and stop in for a little visit with her. I haven't seen her in a long time or even thought about her, to be honest. She's in the nursing home and Glenda said she'd welcome a visitor."

"Sure. Why not?" Victoria said.

"Right, well, I'll get started downstairs. If things get quiet about midmorning, I'll slip out for a half hour or so."

The large grey stone building that is High Pastures, formerly known as the Llanelen Home for the Aged, crouches over the road that runs alongside the River Conwy. Built in the early years of the twentieth century, the property had once been the summer home of a wealthy Liverpool merchant. In the 1970s it had been converted to a nursing home, its large, spacious rooms divided and divided again. Its formal garden at the rear, once lovingly maintained by a team of gardeners, now abandoned and overgrown with thick bushes and rampant weeds, had featured a walled vegetable garden, slate pathways, and even a small maze for children's amusement on sunny afternoons. No one visited the garden now except for staff who huddled outside the back door on smoke breaks and then tossed their cigarette ends into the shrubbery.

Penny walked up the pavement leading to the front door with mixed feelings. Many years ago, newly settled in Llanelen as a young Canadian fine arts graduate, she had made a bit of extra money by giving manicures to the residents of the home. All those ladies, she thought. Been gone a long time. But there would always be more taking their place. There's a lot of money to be made in dying.

She pushed through the set of double doors and was met by the distinctive smell of a nursing home. A combination, maybe, of urine and industrial cleaning fluid. And something else: a strong swirl of fear—fear that that visitor herself might one day end up in a place like this. The reception area was painted a pale turquoise with a flowered wallpaper border near the ceiling. A couple of sturdy burgundy chairs had been placed near the window and a dark-coloured desk positioned so any visitor must pass it before venturing further into the building.

Penny walked over to the reception desk.

"Hello," she said to the receptionist. "I've come to see Doreen Roberts."

The receptionist asked her to sign in, and then pointed down the hall. "I expect you'll find her in the lounge," she said.

"How's she doing?" Penny asked.

"As you'd expect," the receptionist replied with a dismissive shrug.

The turquoise colour scheme carried over into the lounge where some of the residents spent most of their days. A television played in one corner, its volume so low that Penny doubted anyone could hear it. Faded silk flowers in cumbersome vases took up space on side tables and windowsills. Overhead fluorescent lighting cast harsh shadows into the corners of the room; what natural light there was came from tall, graceful windows whose beauty was hidden behind outdated balloon swag curtains.

A few pairs of eyes with a little life still left in them turned in Penny's direction as she entered the room, but most of the residents ignored her. They sat motionless, propped up in their chairs, looking like dessicated husks of the people they once were. And then spotting an elderly woman seated near the window, her deeply lined cheek resting on a hand that resembled a brown speckled egg, Penny made her way over to her.

"Hello, Doreen."

The woman looked up and a smile steeped in sadness flashed across her face.

"Oh, hello, Penny, love. Long time, no see."

Penny sat down and placed a small bag of lemon drops in Doreen's hands. "I brought your favourites."

Doreen ran a heavily veined hand across the bag in a smoothing motion. "They are my favourites. You remembered. Thank you."

As Doreen's eyes filled with tears Penny placed her hand delicately on top of the older woman's. The skin was so thin the hand was almost blue and felt cold. She looked years older—greyer and paler from the last time Penny had seen her. Penny looked around the lounge for tissues and spotting a box on a small table in the corner, picked it up and held it out to Doreen.

Doreen plucked a tissue from the box and dabbed her eyes. Penny waited.

"What is it, Doreen? What's the matter?"

"I haven't been told how she died," Doreen said, "but something very bad must have happened down there."

Penny's eyes narrowed in confusion and she leaned forward.

"Who died, Doreen? What's happened? Who are you talking about?"

"Why, Glenda, of course. They found her body down the mine last night. I thought you knew. I thought that's why you've come."

"Oh, God, Doreen. Glenda! I'm so sorry. No, I didn't know it was Glenda. We heard this morning on the radio that a body had been found down the mine, but they didn't say who it was. We thought perhaps there'd been an industrial accident."

"Something very bad must have happened down there," Doreen repeated.

"Yes," agreed Penny. "Something very bad."

"Bad things do happen down there. I should know. My husband died down there many years ago. But he was the mine manager, so at least he had a reason to be there. How did she end up there, I'd like to know? What on earth was she doing down there in the first place?"

"They're planning to hold the St. David's Day concert down the mine this year and Glenda was organizing it so she was on a site visit. Apparently it's the fortieth anniversary of the mine closing. Well, not closing exactly—ceasing production. Now it's a popular tourist attraction, of course. But I was wondering why the mine would have been chosen as the concert venue. There are other places that are accessible and not so, well, forbidding," Penny replied.

"The mine is important for preserving our heritage and teaching young people about their history," Doreen said.

"Yes, of course it is. I expect school groups go down there all the time. But it doesn't seem like the right place for a concert, that's what I'm saying."

Doreen turned her watery, unfocused eyes to Penny.

"Who else was down there at the same time as Glenda, that's what I'd like to know?" Doreen said. "Someone must have seen something." She raised one shoulder in a helpless shrug. "I wonder if she fell or tripped over something. It's so dark down there."

"She could have, I suppose." A silence settled over them and Penny allowed herself another look around the room. "I'm curious," Penny said after a few minutes. "How did you find out she had died?"

"A policeman in a suit came to see me last night and he had a woman officer with him. Family liaison support or some such thing. I can't remember what they called themselves. They said a body had been found down the mine and from the identification in her handbag they were pretty sure it's Glenda. But the body hadn't been formally identified. I haven't seen it." She made a vague gesture at the room. "How could I see it? It's very difficult for me to get out." After a small sigh she gazed at Penny. "Take my advice. Whatever you do, don't get old. It's bloody awful." She checked her watch. "And speaking of bloody awful, they're going to come round with a cup of indifferent tea any minute now. Be sure to say no thanks. Me, I'm used to it. I drink it. What else is there?" She had barely finished speaking when a passing care worker in a purple uniform thrust a Styrofoam cup into her hands and without saying a word, moved on to the next resident. "The problem with this tea is that it has to be barely tepid so people don't burn themselves," Doreen said. She took a sip and made a little moue of distaste. "*Pfft.* What this needs is a nice tot of rum to get it up on its legs." She raised the cup slightly to Penny in a vague sort of toasting motion and then took another small sip. "I don't know why they bother."

"About Glenda . . . when was the last time you saw her?" Penny asked.

"Oh, I guess that would have been about a week ago, maybe. She popped in on her way somewhere. I expect she told me about the concert and I forgot about it. She was always busy, was Glenda. Always on the go. Meeting someone or picking something up in Manchester or wherever. She came to see me every few days but didn't stay long. And before you ask, she seemed fine. Excited, even. The police asked me that, too. When was the last time I saw her."

Doreen rested her head against the back of her chair and closed her eyes. Penny sat with her a few minutes longer and then, after a glance at Doreen's pale, drained face, reached for her handbag and stood up. As she did so, Doreen's blue eyes fluttered open.

"Sorry, Penny, I seem to nod off . . . so tired. On your way, then, are you?"

"Yes. I have to get back to the Spa."

"Right. Well, thank you for coming." Doreen reached out with her right hand, then brought it back and set it in her lap.

"I don't have a good feeling about any of this, Penny," she said. "If I need you, will you come back and see me?"

"Yes, of course I will."

"Then please leave your phone number with the receptionist on the way out. Ask her to put you down as a contact for me, so she can ring you if I need you."

Five

I was that surprised you could have knocked me over with a
feather." Evelyn Lloyd settled herself in the client chair in the
Llanelen Spa manicure salon and held out her hands to Eirlys,
Penny's young assistant, who was to give Mrs. Lloyd her weekly
manicure. "I've just heard the body of Glenda Roberts was found
down the mine. It comes as such a shock when someone dies suddenly. And she was only just young, Glenda was. Well, youngish." Mrs. Lloyd leaned to one side to peer around Eirlys at Penny,
who was pulling nail polishes from the display for Mrs. Lloyd's
approval.

"How old was she, do we know?" Mrs. Lloyd thought for a
moment and then answered her own question. "Mid-forties? She
couldn't have been much more that."

"That sounds about right," Penny agreed. "She came here regularly to get her hair done. Took good care of herself. And she

was in here just yesterday dropping off papers for Victoria. For the concert."

"That's right!" said Mrs. Lloyd. "I heard she was organizing the St. David's Day concert. Well I guess someone else will have to take that on now." She peered at Penny. "Do you think Victoria would be up for it?"

"I have no idea," said Penny, "but I expect she's got enough to do with being one of the performers." She held up a bottle of burgundy-coloured polish. "How about this? Too dark?" She held up another one. "Do you like this one better? A nice cappuccino?"

Mrs. Lloyd looked from one to the other. "I'm not really crazy about either. And I think I've had both of those before. But it's hard to tell from here. I'll get up in a few minutes and choose one myself."

She turned her attention to her hands, one of which was soaking in warm water and the other whose nails Eirlys was shaping with an emery board. "Or Eirlys can choose a colour for me. She knows what I like, since she does my nails now. Most of the time, anyway."

Penny couldn't help but smile. Mrs. Lloyd was one of her oldest customers and although her occasional lack of tact could be hugely annoying bordering on infuriating, she could also be oddly endearing with her kind heart and honest openness. For many years she had been the village postmistress and she took as keen an interest in local comings and goings now as she had when she'd stood behind the counter with her weigh scales and stamps. Not much got past her, she liked to think. Not then and not now.

"I haven't heard yet how Glenda died," Mrs. Lloyd went on. "Was it an accident? I suppose all kinds of dreadful things can happen in a mine." She brightened. "Has that nice policeman of yours said anything to you?"

Penny shook her head. "Now, Mrs. Lloyd, we've been through this before. You know he's not my nice policeman, although he is a policeman and very nice. We're just friends, that's all."

"Well, yes, all right. I know you've told me that before. I was hoping things had changed. We all had such high hopes for you and him, Penny. But never mind that now. Tell me, did he mention anything to you about how she died?"

"No, he didn't because I haven't spoken to him. I expect the investigation is just getting started. I wondered about the logistics of dealing with a body found down the mine. I expect that'll be causing lots of problems for them."

"Well, the policeman in charge, the senior guy that Penny knows, he's going to talk about it on the telly just before lunch," Eirlys said. "So maybe he'll explain everything then." Both Penny and Mrs. Lloyd turned their attention to her.

"He is? Where did you hear that?" Mrs. Lloyd asked.

"Twitter." She reached in her bag, pulled out her phone, gave it a few clicks, and after a bit of scrolling, held it out so Penny could read it.

"You follow the North Wales Police on Twitter?" Penny asked.

Eirlys shrugged. "I follow lots of North Wales people on Twitter. Don't you?" Penny's eyes widened. "And at the very least, Penny," Eirlys continued, "if you don't personally, you should have a Twitter account for the Spa. It's really easy. You can get followers and promote specials to them. And do you know that the biggest users of Facebook are women over forty-five? Have you been on Facebook lately?"

"You're absolutely right, Eirlys," said Penny. "We should do more with social media. You carry on with Mrs. Lloyd while I go and speak to Victoria."

"Before you go, Penny," said Mrs. Lloyd, "Florence asked me to be sure to get more of your hand lotion today. She goes through gallons of it, especially this time of year. Says she's never seen anything like it, it's that good. Well, I say good. It must be extraordinary, to get Florence so excited."

Penny gave Mrs. Lloyd a quick smile. "I'll get some for you." She returned in a few minutes and set a small box on the table. "There you go. Rhian's added it to your bill."

"Put it on my slate, as we used to say." Mrs. Lloyd picked up the box and admired its simple yet striking black on white design.

"Very nice. You've done a lovely job, Penny, with your own product line. I believe I was the one who suggested to you a while back that you should develop some brands of your own, but you have made rather a good go of it, I'll give you that."

"The lotion is amazing. It really does wonders for your hands, especially in winter. We were lucky to get that formula from Dilys. Oh, by the way, we're about to launch a new product that I think you'll also like. It's a lavender linen spray made from locally sourced lavender grown right here in Wales. It's heavenly."

"Oh, I love lavender. When will it be available, do you think?"

"In a few weeks. We're just signing off now on the packaging design. It's also being made from a formula we licenced from Dilys. There's a special ingredient in it that adds a subtle scent of something deeper." Penny smiled. "I'm enjoying learning about the fragrance world."

"Well then, Penny," said Eirlys, "you'll be wanting to get your Twitter account up and running so you can use it to get the word out about our new linen spray."

"Yes," agreed Penny. "I'll have a word with Victoria about it. I have an idea about who should run the Twitter account." She placed a hand on Eirlys's shoulder and was rewarded with a broad smile from a young, upturned face.

"Twitter?" Mrs. Lloyd asked Eirlys as Penny was leaving. "'I've heard about that. Would I like it, do you think? Tell me all about it."

Six

"Let's go up to the flat," Victoria said a few minutes later. "We can have our sandwiches up there whilst we watch the news conference."

Just over a year ago Penny and Victoria had bought and restored a decaying stone building beautifully situated on the banks of the River Conwy. Reopened as the Llanelen Spa, the building included a spacious flat on the third floor, which Victoria called home. Beyond the obvious advantages of living above the shop, the flat featured striking views of the ever-changing river and the green hills beyond.

Penny now walked over to the window in the sitting room, pulled back the curtain, and peered out. The river sparkled in the winter sunshine as it splashed its way through the town on its journey to the Conwy Estuary and from there into the Irish Sea. She let the curtain drop and turned back to Victoria.

"There's something about living near water, isn't there?" she said. Victoria nodded. "It's always the same, and always changing, that view," Victoria replied.

Penny plunked herself down in a comfortable armchair as Victoria took her place at the end of a love seat.

"Have you heard how Glenda died?" Victoria asked.

Penny shook her head. "Mrs. Lloyd just asked me that. I haven't talked to Gareth. Until they know for sure how she died I expect he's leading the investigation. But I should call him to let him know that she was here at the Spa yesterday morning. The detectives are always keen to track the last twenty-four hours in the victim's life. If she was a victim, that is."

Victoria switched on the television and a few moments later the familiar figure of Penny's friend DCI Gareth Davies filled the screen. He stood in front of a backdrop that showed the logo of the North Wales Police Service and although he appeared businesslike and poised, his eyes betrayed anxiety and concern. His face looked lined and he looked tired.

He glanced at the sheet of paper in his hand and then began to speak in short, strong sentences.

"It's been a long and difficult night. A body was discovered yesterday just after closing time deep in the Llyn Du mine. Although formal identification of the body has not yet taken place, we are confident the body is that of Glenda Roberts. Her family has been notified. And although the cause of death is yet to be determined, we are treating her death as suspicious."

A large photo of Glenda appeared on a screen beside him. He paused for a moment and tipped his head toward it.

"We are appealing to anyone who saw Glenda yesterday to contact us as we are anxious to retrace her steps. We especially want to hear from you if you were one of the visitors to the mine yesterday. You may feel that you do not know anything or have any information that may be useful to our inquiry, but if you saw her, we need to hear from you, no matter how trivial you think your information is."

"See?" said Penny. "Told you he'd want to know she was here. Trivial as it may seem."

He gazed steadily and confidently into the camera and gave the phone number to call if anyone had information and then referred viewers to the police Web site for more information. After a moment, the scene faded and the newscast resumed.

Victoria switched off the television and the two sat for a moment in reflective silence. And then Victoria spoke.

"Well, there we have it. So, yes, you do need to call him. You know, I've been thinking a lot about Glenda. This St. David's Day concert was the second event I'd worked on with her. She liked to run things. She was a good organizer and put on a good show, but she could be abrasive. And on each project she seemed to need to find someone to hate."

"What do you mean, 'hate'?"

"Well, last time it was the Jubilee concert. Remember that? You were there. Outdoors, at the cricket ground? Music through all the decades of the Queen's reign? Well, Glenda really took against Ifan Williams for no reason that I could see. Seemed to positively loathe him. Or at least, she unleashed all her frustration on the poor man. Constantly berating him. As if everything that went wrong was down to him. He's the conductor, for heaven's sake. It wasn't his fault if people didn't show up on time for rehearsal. Or that it rained on the morning of the concert and the ground was wet! And yet she kept having a go at him, and in front of everybody." She made little snapping motions with her fingers. "Pick, pick, pick, if you know what I mean. And talked about him behind his back to the others. Really awful, that was. Small and mean-spirited." Victoria thought for a moment.

"And yet it was all done in a rather sly manner. Nothing overtly critical, just little nasty digs."

"And this time? Was there someone this time she didn't like?"

"Oh, yes."

Penny raised an eyebrow.

"Me. She was starting to have a go at me." She made a little moue of distaste. "I could see where she was going and I wasn't looking forward to it. In fact, I wasn't going to have it. I was prepared to stand up for myself and tell her exactly what I thought of her."

Victoria took a sip of water.

"But generally, though, she was well-regarded in the town, as far as I know," said Penny. "I didn't know her at all, besides seeing her in here every now and then, but I never heard anything bad about her."

"Oh, yes," replied Victoria, with an edge in her voice. "Except for the part where she could start a fight in an empty room, she was a real pillar of the community, that one. Making Llanelen a better place for us all to live. Doing good deeds all over the place. Glenda always had more pies than fingers to put in them. In the queue somewhere for an OBE, I shouldn't wonder."

"Oh, dear," said Penny. "You really didn't like her, did you?"

"I saw her differently than the others did, I guess. All fur coat and no knickers, in my opinion. I hated all that false humility. And yet she seemed to take in everybody else with it. They thought she was wonderful. Always giving so freely of her time to organize wonderful events for the community. Running this, finding sponsors for that. She seemed to know a lot of people. And if there were people who didn't like her, I never heard. I think people were afraid to criticize her."

"Why?"

"She just had some sort of power. I don't know what it was. Connections? Success? I don't know." Victoria shrugged. "I always felt a bit like the kid in 'The Emperor's New Clothes.'" She gave Penny a level look. "As if I saw through her somehow, and others didn't.

"And you know, people who matter did take notice of her," Victoria continued. "Yes, she dined occasionally with the lord lieutenant himself." She glanced at her watch. "Or so I heard." She stood up. "We'd better get to work. The afternoon clients will be arriving."

Penny reached up and gently touched her arm. "We can be a few minutes late. Please sit down. I want to hear more about her."

"Well, what were your impressions of her?" Victoria asked. "She was in the spa every six weeks or so to get her hair done. You saw her."

"I don't really remember her that well," Penny said. "I knew her to see, of course, but I didn't take that much notice of her. She got her nails done occasionally, but Eirlys did them.

"It's funny, that. You see someone occasionally and then, when something like this happens and you try to remember everything you can about that person, you find you can't remember very much at all. I never even knew she was Doreen's daughter."

"One of them," Victoria said.

"Doreen had two daughters?" Penny asked.

"Rebeccah. But I gather she and Glenda were chalk and cheese. Very different. Our Glenda had aspirations and Rebeccah didn't do much of anything at all. Sold cheap tat down the local market, apparently."

"Well, I guess that's a job of some sort."

"Speaking of jobs . . ."

Seven

"What do you make of the bite mark?"

Sgt. Bethan Morgan kept her eyes on the road as she and Det. Chief Inspector Gareth Davies drove along the A55 North Wales Expressway from Bangor to Llandudno. They had just attended the postmortem examination of the body of Glenda Roberts and had been shown a clear and recent bite mark on the inside of her right forearm. The area had been swabbed for DNA and close photographs taken. The pathologist wasn't optimistic, though, that they'd get any DNA from the wound. It was a day or two old and Glenda had most certainly showered or bathed since the bite had been inflicted.

"I've been thinking about that," Bethan replied. "And asking myself, who would bite another person. And the only answer I can come up with, really, is a child."

"A frustrated child who is also very angry," Davies replied.

"Or frightened?" Bethan suggested. "But the pathologist said the size of the bite indicated an adult, not a child."

"That's troubling," commented Davies.

The pathologist recorded cause of death as blunt force trauma. "I know what you're going to ask me now," he had said to Davies. "Could she have fallen? And the answer is no. The head injuries are not consistent with a fall. Someone delivered several blows to the back of her head with something sharp and flat, I would say. You wouldn't have seen the extent or nature of the injury while the body was in situ at the mine and especially in the darkness; we needed to get her up on the slab to get a good look at it. I can't say exactly what kind of weapon or instrument caused the injuries, but the blows were delivered with strength and intensity. The assailant certainly meant to inflict great harm, or more likely, to kill." The pathologist peeled off his gloves, and dropped them into the medical waste bin. "Sorry I can't be more helpful with the type of instrument. I expect determining what the weapon was will be at the top of your to-do list."

Davies sighed and glanced out the car window. The afternoon was wearing on and the countryside would soon be shrouded in semidarkness. It got dark early, this time of year, in this part of the world, and the day had brought the kind of rapidly changing weather often seen here. Rain, heavy at times, had now eased off, giving way to a pale sky filled with purplish-grey clouds, some of them tinged with pink along the tops. The waters of the Menai Strait, which separates the mainland from the island of Anglesey, pounded the shore in white-capped waves. His thoughts returned to the question of the weapon when his phone rang. He checked the caller ID and then pressed the button.

"Hello, Penny." He listened for a few moments. "She did? We'll need a statement from you, then. And can you ask Victo-

ria to gather up everything for us. Envelope and all the contents."
He peered out the window. "We're just approaching Conwy, so
we could be in Llanelen in about forty minutes. Are you still at
work?" He exchanged a quick glance with Bethan, to see if she'd
picked up that their plans were changing. She gave him a quick
nod. "Right. We'll meet you there."

He ended the call and replaced his phone in his coat pocket.

"Glenda Roberts dropped off a packet for Victoria at the Spa
yesterday morning. It's probably nothing, but it'll fill in some gaps
on the timeline. We'll talk to Penny at the Spa."

"What was in the packet?"

"Sheet music."

A light, misty drizzle was now falling so Bethan switched on
the windscreen wipers and leaned forward to turn up the car's
heater. A welcome warmth soon wrapped itself around their legs.

"Ever think about retirement, sir?" she asked.

"Retirement? Why, are you after my job?"

She laughed. "From DS to DCI? Not likely. No, I was just
thinking how good it would be to go somewhere sunny. Get away
from this awful wet weather. It's endless, this time of year."

"I would like to see you sit the inspector exam, though," said
Davies. "You have a wonderful career ahead of you and you're
ready for promotion."

Bethan smiled her gratitude.

"Thank you, sir. That means a lot to me."

They rode the rest of the way in silence broken only by the
soothing, rhythmic sound of the windscreen wipers.

As they entered the market town of Llanelen, Davies's chest
constricted in a familiar tightening that was a pleasurable mix of
anxiety and anticipation. He'd been in love with Penny almost
since the moment they'd met a year and a half ago, and for a while,

it had seemed that his feelings were reciprocated. But gradually he'd come to accept that the romantic feelings of the early relationship had run their course and given way to a deeper underlying friendship marked by respect and admiration on both sides. Although he knew that part of him would always love her in a gentle, undemanding way, he wished their relationship could be more.

Bethan parked the unmarked police car on a side street and they walked across the cobblestoned town square. The black wrought iron gate that separated the path leading to the Spa from the pavement squeaked in protest as Davies pushed it open. "Every time I come here I tell myself we need to put some oil on that thing," he remarked as he held the gate open.

"Do Penny and Victoria not have a handyman to take care of things like this?" Bethan asked as she passed through.

"Only me as far as I know, and based on results I'm not really up to the job, am I?" He closed the gate behind them and they made their way up the path.

The door opened and Penny smiled as she held it open for them. And his heart felt a little lighter and fuller.

Penny was glad to see him. She'd always liked and respected this handsome police officer and for a brief time those feelings had teetered on the brink of becoming something more, something deeper. And then, as sometimes happens, the romance had stalled and on her part, flamed out. Whatever it takes to turn feelings of friendship into romantic love just wasn't there and she wasn't the kind of woman who could pretend to feel something she didn't. She'd agonized over her feelings, but in the end, stayed true to herself. You don't want to marry someone if you have to talk yourself into it, she told herself. She had been honest with him and hoped he didn't feel she'd messed him about.

She handed over the brown envelope Glenda had dropped off the day before. "There was just sheet music in it," she said. "Victoria asked if you could return it to her as soon as possible because she needs it for the concert."

Bethan tucked the envelope under her arm and took out her notebook.

"How did Glenda seem?" asked Bethan. "Agitated, upset?"

Penny gave a little shrug. "No, she seemed fine. Normal."

Bethan asked her what time Glenda had left and if she'd said anything Penny found unusual or interesting.

"Not really. Said she had a couple more places to go and errands to run. I think she was dropping off those envelopes for other performers."

"Right, well, get in touch if you think of anything else," Davies said, with a knowing look. "Or if you hear anything else. Or think of anything else that might help us."

"I will. What happens next?"

"We'll pursue the usual lines of inquiry. Talk to people, check out CCTV footage, look at her phone records—the usual things. I have a feeling that our killer was either very lucky or very clever."

"Or," said Penny, "maybe a bit of both."

Eight

"Florence," said Mrs. Lloyd the next afternoon, "these biscuits are absolutely delicious. What are they called? And where did you get them?" She held up the little shell-shaped shortbread biscuit. "And more importantly, can you get some more?"

"They're called Aberffraw." Florence spelled it out. "I'm probably not pronouncing it correctly. Anyway, they're made on Anglesey. They're a little dearer than our usual biscuits, but as we like to support local businesses I thought we'd give them a try. Thought they'd be just the thing with your afternoon cup of tea."

"Indeed they are! Where did you get them in case I want to pick some up when I'm out?"

"I got them a few days ago when I was in Llandudno at that fancy food place. The shop where they have all the special jams and strange cooking utensils you'd use once a year, if at all."

"Oh, right. Well, maybe I'll pick up some more the next time I'm in town. That'll be tomorrow, I expect."

Mrs. Lloyd popped the rest of the biscuit into her mouth and then looked thoughtfully at her friend. The two had been living together for over a year. Although Florence was technically a lodger, Mrs. Lloyd thought of her as a lady's companion and Florence, who had been eking out a mean retirement in a Liverpool bedsit, was grateful to live in a large, comfortable house. The two rubbed along together well enough, with Mrs. Lloyd's waistline enjoying all the benefits of Florence's cooking and baking skills.

"I've been thinking, Florence," Mrs. Lloyd said thoughtfully. "Someone said to me the other day that I must have seen a lot of change in the town over the years. And I have. I've heard lots of interesting things, too. When you're stood behind the counter in the post office you hear the most amazing things. People either forget you're there or don't realize you have ears. They take no notice. And that's just while they're talking in the queue. You also talk to people while you're handling the post. Of course, in those days there was lots more of it. Post, that is."

Florence said nothing, but stood there with her arms folded.

"Yes, well, anyway, I always used to think of the stories I could tell! The married man sending a St. Dwynwen's card to his mistress. The lady keeping up appearances when she's actually getting bills with FINAL NOTICE splashed across the envelope. The mother sending a letter to her daughter who's gone to live with an aunt for a few months. Of course we all knew why she'd had to leave town. Anyway, what would you say if I told you I'm going to write my memoirs?"

"Your memoir," Florence corrected.

"Yes," said Mrs. Lloyd, her voice eager and excited. "I've been thinking about this for some little while and now seems like the right time. I've no doubt there'll be a real market for my book. After all, if the memoirs of a midwife in the 1950s can be so popular on television, why not a post office clerk in the 1960s?"

"I'm sure the film producers will be falling all over themselves to snap up the memoir of a post office clerk in a small Welsh village," said Florence with her usual dour expression.

"Exactly!" enthused Mrs. Lloyd. Irony and sarcasm had no place in her world. "I knew you'd love the idea. And the 1960s were such an interesting decade, weren't they? A great time to be young, Florence."

"Young?"

"Well, youngish. 'Never trust anyone over thirty!' Remember that, Florence? Thirty! Imagine. How foolish that sounds to us now." She cast a critical writer's eye around the room.

"Now, we'll need to sort out a workspace for me. Might be best if I work on the dining room table so I'll have lots of room to spread out my bits and pieces. And the morning light is very good there, too. Now it's important that when I'm working, Florence, when I'm in the zone so to speak, that I mustn't be disturbed. Of course, you could bring me a cup of tea and a little something every now and then, if you felt so inclined. I wouldn't say no to that."

"When are you going to start?"

"Tomorrow. It's getting a bit late for today. I'll just start thinking about it whilst I have another one of those delicious biscuits. What did you say they were called? My memory isn't what it used to be, sometimes."

"They're called Aberffraw. I might try baking them myself. And how will you write your memoir, then, if your memory isn't what it used to be?"

"Oh, that won't be a problem. I've got tons of scrapbooks.

Letters. Photographs. That sort of thing. Remember when girls used to keep scrapbooks, Florence? You'd get a big book from the stationery shop and cut out things and glue them into it. And anyway, I remember all the important things. Just not little details. That's why we have to make lists as we get older, Florence."

"I'll leave you to it, then." Florence slipped from the room as a slight grin began to form at the corners of her mouth. Mrs. Lloyd's new project should keep her happily occupied for the next few days, until she either lost interest or realized how much work was involved.

Nine

"I'm cold and I don't want to be here."

"I know, Peris, love, but tell you what. Just give me a hand setting this lot up and then you can be off. I can manage on my own for today but I need your help to get up and running."

Rebeccah Roberts smiled at her nephew, then took a long drag on her cigarette, let it drop to the pavement, and stamped it out under the toe of her boot. She wore a beige woolen hat with a ribbed knit pattern pulled down over brown hair just starting to turn grey and a green anorak that looked as if it had seen better winters. If her sister, Glenda, had taken good care of herself, Rebeccah had let herself go. Her lined face had a worn, leathery look, perhaps from a combination of outdoor work and smoking; a casual observer might think she looked older than she was. She pointed at a cardboard box sitting on the frozen ground and the boy lifted it onto the wooden display area of her stall.

He reached in his pocket for a box cutter and quickly and expertly slashed the box open. He pulled the flaps apart and then reached down for another box.

"What's in these, anyway?" he asked.

"Lavender sachets." Rebeccah began arranging the sachets into neat rows. "Your mother got this shipment in, just before she . . ." her voice trailed off.

"Do you think we should even be here today?" the boy asked. "It doesn't seem right, somehow what with Mum only just . . ."

"Well, I think she'd want us here," Rebeccah replied. "She'd want us to carry on as usual, surely. She went to a lot of trouble to get this stuff made and delivered and it can't sit around. We've got to shift this fast, you know that. We don't want the trading standards people getting wind and snooping round, asking nosy questions." She glanced at the sky and then looked back at the boy. "It looks as if the rain's going to hold off so we could do a good trade today. Let's hope so, anyway."

Peris Roberts, who looked about eighteen, wiped his nose on the sleeve of his coat, sighed, and opened another box. Rebeccah placed a hand, encased in a fingerless glove, on his coat sleeve. "And maybe, love, it'll take your mind off things for a bit." He pulled his arm away with a light but clear gesture and carried on with his work, his head down so she couldn't see his face.

"All right, I reckon that's enough for now," said Rebeccah when the contents of two boxes had been displayed. She pointed at the two boxes at her feet. "Leave these and I'll put out more sachets myself when I've sold off some of this lot. You get off now, and unless you've got something better to do, drop in on your *nain* and see how she's doing."

The boy shoved his hands in his pockets and looked around in a dull, uninterested way. Most of the market traders had finished setting up their stalls and the regular crowd of early morning bargain hunters was starting to wander into the square, not looking for anything in particular, but hoping to find something they wanted at a hard-to-resist low price.

The market was held every Tuesday and Saturday and attracted a good crowd no matter the weather. Traders rigged up awnings and tarpaulins over their stalls to protect themselves and their goods; it was the customers who had to face the wind, rain, and sometimes even snow. Stalls featured every kind of product from cushions to clothing and jams, bagged sweets, small electrical appliances and pet food, household products and underwear.

"Well, if you're going, off with you, then," Rebeccah said when Peris did not move. She was about to say something else but stopped when a woman with permed grey hair in a burgundy coat caught sight of the stall and made a beeline for it with a bit of hustle in her step.

"Oh, Rebeccah," said Mrs. Lloyd as she approached. "Fancy seeing you here today. I was so sorry to hear about your sister. Awful shock, that was." She acknowledged Peris and then asked, "Have there been any developments? Have the police told you anything more about what might have happened?" Rebeccah shook her head and Peris shifted his weight from one foot to the other, never taking his eyes off his aunt. Mrs. Lloyd inquired about funeral arrangements, and then, as if realizing how awkward it would be to leave without buying something, turned her attention to the products on display. She picked up an item with a manicured hand and peered at it.

"All our products are sourced locally," Rebeccah said. "That lavender was grown almost within walking distance."

"How much are you asking for it?" When told the price Mrs. Lloyd opened her handbag and handed over a banknote, commenting, "Better make it two. I expect Florence will want one, too." She accepted her change and then dropped the little sachets into her bag and snapped it shut. "Well, again, I'm very sorry for your loss. I expect I'll see you at the funeral."

They watched as she moved on to the next stall, took cursory note of a display and walked on.

When she was out of earshot, Peris let out a low laugh.

"'Walking distance'! Yeah, right, if you don't mind walking to China."

Rebeccah gave a tight, wan smile.

"Be off with you," she said. "And don't forget to drop in on your *nain*. You don't have to stay long, but she'll be glad to see you, I'm sure." The boy made some sort of snorting noise that was meant to signal he was leaving. "Oh, and Peris, it's just occurred to me and I'm sorry I didn't offer sooner. I should have realized. If you don't feel like going home just now, because of what happened to your mum, you're more than welcome to stop with me for a few days. Or as long as you like, really."

For the first time that day he smiled.

"I'll go home and get a few things, and be back to pick up the key to yours," he said. "It's been awful at home. Thanks!"

"Welai di yn fuan," said Rebeccah.

"Yeah," said Peris. "See you soon."

A few moments later his lean figure rounded a building at the corner of the square and then disappeared from view.

Rebeccah turned back to her stall. She wasn't that familiar with death. The last person of real significance in her family to

50

die had been her father and that was so many years ago she could barely remember him. Her memories of him were hazy and no matter how hard she tried to bring them to the surface they remained indistinct, like something lost and forgotten at the bottom of a river, seen through fast running water, in wavy, out-of-focus lines. She could dimly recall bits and pieces of family life when her father was alive. She remembered the shouting downstairs that woke her up and her big sister, Glenda, wrapping her arms around her, holding her close, providing a little comfort. Soon the sound of their mother crying would set off the two little girls and they'd cry as well, although they tried to do it quietly, so their father wouldn't hear. They trembled at the sound of his boots mounting the staircase, pulling their mother behind him when the fights were going on. Most nights he just went past their bedroom without looking in to speak to them. They held their breath until they heard him close the door of the room he shared with their mother.

And then one day something bad happened at the mine and he never came home again. People dressed in black gathered in their rarely used front room and women passed around plates of little sandwiches and biscuits that were really very good. Gallons of tea were drunk and everyone spoke in hushed voices.

Her mother never mentioned him again. Life went on. She and Glenda went back to school and to make ends meet, their mother started selling goods from a stall every market day. This stall. This market.

Rebeccah knew her mother was drowning in a tidal wave of grief over the loss of her daughter, but she didn't know what to say to her. What do you say to a mother who has lost her favourite child? What words of comfort are there? Especially when the

51

unspoken words between them are, "Why her? Why couldn't it have been you?"

"Hello, *Nain*." Peris approached his grandmother, placed a hand on her bony shoulder, and bent over. He hated the feel of her papery cheek beneath his lips and the distinctive unpleasant smell of her breath that he couldn't describe, but his mother had always insisted that he greet her with a kiss. And then, when he realized his mother wasn't here anymore to tell him what to do and then watch while he did it, he straightened up without touching her with his lips.

His grandmother raised red-rimmed, sunken eyes to meet his. He was startled by the change in her appearance since he had seen her just a few days ago. Her white hair looked thinner and she seemed to have lost weight. He turned his attention to the woman sitting with her.

"Peris, this is Penny Brannigan. She owns the Spa. She knew your mother, a little. I asked her to come and see me this morning." The two exchanged nods and Penny told Peris how sorry she was for the loss of his mother. He shifted from one foot to the other, unsure what to do. "Oh, for heaven's sake, sit down," said his grandmother.

"Sit here," said Penny. "I was just leaving."

"You don't need . . ." began Doreen, but stopped. She was looking over Penny's shoulder, toward the corridor that led from the front desk into the lounge. Her eyes seemed to brighten and widen and her mouth opened slightly. She sat forward in her seat and started to raise her right hand, but instead touched her chest. Her hand then slowly lowered and for a moment she gripped the arm of her chair. She then put her hands together and began shredding the tissue she had been holding in her left hand.

"What is it Doreen?" Penny asked. "Are you all right?" Penny followed Doreen's gaze, but saw only a uniformed carer walking down the hall, her back toward them. Penny turned her head quickly and looked behind her, but saw nothing unusual about the residents scattered about the lounge, reading, talking quietly amongst themselves, or nodding off in their chairs. She leaned closer to Doreen, and met her dazed eyes.

"It's nothing," Doreen said in a halting voice. "I'm fine. But if you don't mind, I think it might be best if you left now, after all. I'm feeling a little tired."

"Of course. I'll see you soon."

"They're having a little birthday do for me tomorrow afternoon. There'll be cake. Drop in about two if you can."

"I will," said Penny. "See you tomorrow."

She took one last look around the lounge before leaving, but saw nothing unusual. As she walked toward the exit, a familiar voice in the hall made her turn around.

"Whoa, missy, not so fast."

"Jimmy, how good to see you! How've you been?"

"Oh, you know. Mustn't grumble." He pushed his wheelchair a little closer to her. "Haven't seen you in awhile. Been busy?"

"Sorry, Jimmy. Haven't been out much. I did pop in a couple of days ago to see Doreen. I guess you heard about her daughter."

Jimmy nodded. "We were all very sorry to hear about it. She's taking it really hard, as you'd expect."

In his younger days Jimmy Hill had been a small-time thief and fence. Now, although his legs no longer worked as well as they used to, his mind was sharp and not much got past him.

Penny had met him when he'd been living in a seniors' home in Llandudno but he'd been lonely there, so he'd moved to High Pastures in Llanelen to be closer to his friends, and Florence Semble in particular. Penny liked and trusted him.

"Jimmy," she said, lowering her voice, "I think Doreen just saw someone who startled her. Have you noticed anyone around here who doesn't belong?"

He shook his head. "No. But I'll keep my eyes open."

"Why don't you come along to reception with me? There's something I want you to do."

So while Jimmy, who was very good at that sort of thing, distracted the receptionist, Penny read the sign-in sheet on the reception counter. Doreen's grandson, Peris, had been the last person to sign in.

"I'm telling you, Victoria, she looked like she'd seen a ghost." Penny took a sip of tea and reached for a biscuit. "I've heard that expression before but never actually seen it. Now I have."

"Could she have remembered something that startled her?"

"She was looking in the direction of the doorway and I got the feeling that she saw someone."

"She saw someone. Okay. So, someone who didn't belong there? Someone she wasn't expecting to see."

"Someone who didn't make himself . . ."

"Or herself," interrupted Victoria.

"Right," continued Penny. "So this person looked into the lounge, but didn't make herself known to Doreen. Maybe she didn't see Doreen? Maybe she wasn't there to see Doreen but there to see someone else and Doreen knew that person and was surprised to see her."

"Surprised to see her . . . after all these years, maybe? Some-one from her past she never thought she'd see again?"

Penny nodded slowly. "That would make sense. Someone from her past she wasn't expecting to see again." She thought for a moment. "Or the past. Someone from *the* past, not neces-sarily *her* past that she wasn't expecting to see."

"And didn't want to see," Victoria said slowly.

Penny thought that over. "Yes, of course, because if it had been someone she'd wanted to see, she would have smiled and waved and said something like, 'Oh, look, there's so-and-so. Haven't seen her for ages.'"

Victoria made a noncommittal kind of noise.

"In fact," said Penny, "seen in that light, I think now the look on her face had a flash of fear in it."

"So whoever this person was, Doreen did not want to acknowl-edge her and might even have been afraid of her," Victoria said.

"Exactly. She might have been afraid of her in a 'here comes trouble' kind of way, or . . ."

"Or, maybe the trouble's already happened."

"You mean Glenda?" Penny asked.

"Maybe."

Florence Semble turned the little sachet over, noted the border of lavender flowers and printed name and then gave it a tentative sniff. She then held it away from her with a look of distaste.

"How do you spell lavender, Evelyn?"

"Why do you ask?"

"Humour me, Evelyn, for just a moment. How do you spell lavender?"

"Let's see. L-a-v. Lav-end. L-a-v-e-n-d . . . I can never

55

remember if it's 'er' or 'a-r'. I get the *es* and *as* mixed up in 'marmalade,' too."

"It's 'e-r'," said Florence, spelling the word.

"Oh, right."

Florence turned the sachet over so Mrs. Lloyd could see the name printed on it. WELSH LAVENDAR.

"Oh, look at that!"

"What kind of company doesn't know how to spell its own name?" Florence asked.

"What are you getting at?"

"If this is made with authentic Welsh lavender, I'll eat my hat," said Florence. "It's the sweepings off some factory floor stuffed in a little muslin bag with a drop or two of some inferior lavender oil, if you ask me. And then a third-rate printing job."

"Are you sure?"

"Of course I'm sure. I worked my whole career at the Liverpool College of Art. Lavender is also a colour. It's many colours, actually. I can spell the names of more colours than you've ever heard of: burnt umber, sienna, chartreuse, cerulean . . ."

"All right," snapped Mrs. Lloyd. "You've made your point." She thought for a moment. "Er, what exactly is your point?"

"My point is that unless I'm very much mistaken, this lavender has about as much claim to being Welsh as the Man in the Moon."

Florence handed the little bag back to Evelyn.

"Well, here you go. Going to tuck it away in your drawer with your smalls?"

"Drop it in the bin, more like. And to think I paid good money for that, too."

"Where did you get it?"

"Down the market."

56

Ten

A few residents had gathered in a corner of the High Pastures' lounge where a small cluster of helium-filled pink and white balloons tied to the wall announced Doreen's birthday party. A small party was held to mark each resident's birthday, whether they wanted it or not, but the home's management didn't take too much trouble over arrangements, assuming correctly that people of that generation didn't want a lot of fuss. Cups of lukewarm, watery tea were dispensed in plastic cups; small slices of vanilla cake from the local supermarket served on paper plates to be eaten with plastic forks were handed round; and a quick verse of "Happy Birthday" was sung by a few members of the staff who then hurried back to whatever they'd been doing. Still, a birthday party didn't happen every day and it broke up the monotony for the residents, many of whom derived great vicarious pleasure from the little gatherings.

Penny, carrying a modest bouquet of cut flowers wrapped in cellophane from the local florist, entered the lounge and spotting the balloons, made her way over to them. She was pleased to see Jimmy and sat beside him.

"Doreen not here yet?" she asked.

"No," Jimmy said. "She's late for her own party."

"I wonder what's keeping her," Penny said.

Jimmy leaned in closer and whispered, "Her other daughter hasn't arrived yet. Wouldn't you think she'd be here for her mother's birthday?"

"Yes," Penny whispered back. "You would."

They waited a few more minutes with a growing sense of unease and then Penny stood up. "Perhaps I should have a word with someone." She looked around the lounge and seeing no staff member, turned to Jimmy. "I'll just go and check on her. See if she needs a hand with anything."

"Give me a push, Penny, and I'll come with you," Jimmy said. "Her room's just along the corridor from mine. I'll show you the way."

She wheeled him out of the lounge and down the corridor. "This is my room," Jimmy said, gesturing at a closed door. "Keep going. Doreen's is just here." They stopped in front of a green door with a narrow, lit cabinet with two shelves alongside the door frame. Displayed were a large piece of slate and a colour photo in a frame of a typical couple from the 1970s holding hands with two little girls, one a few inches taller than the other. The girls wore matching coats and small hats. A few daffodils were sprinkled across a small garden; Penny thought the photo might have been taken at Easter time.

Penny looked at Jimmy, silently asking a question.

"They have those cupboards outside the rooms," Jimmy explained. "They put familiar things in them so you know it's your room. It helps people with memory loss." He shrugged. "Well, that's the theory, anyway."

"Right, well, you wait here. I'll see how she's doing. She's probably putting on her lipstick or might even have fallen asleep after lunch."

Penny knocked on the door and when there was no answer, turned the handle and pushed it slightly open. "Doreen?" she called. "You in here? Is everything all right?" She pushed the door further and saw Doreen, fully dressed, lying on the bed. Penny turned to Jimmy. "I think she's asleep. Wait here." She closed the door and entered the room. A wave of an intense floral fragrance enveloped her. She put a hand on Doreen's shoulder and gave her a gentle nudge. "Doreen? They're waiting for you. Want to wake up and go to your birthday party?"

Doreen did not move. Her wispy white hair was slightly tousled and her mouth formed a small, frozen O. Her eyes were closed.

Penny touched her hand. It was warm, but limp. And the stillness of Doreen's body was alarming. The chest was not rising. Penny backed slowly away and then turned and opened the door. "I think she's dead," she said to Jimmy in a low voice. "We've got to get the nurse." She grabbed the handles of the wheelchair and pushed Jimmy down the hall. Just as they approached the nursing station loud voices coming from the reception desk made them stop and look back.

"What do you mean she hasn't shown up for her birthday party?" a woman demanded. "Where is she? What have you done with her?"

The receptionist held up her hands in what was meant to be a soothing gesture but it had the opposite effect. "What the hell kind of place is this? Why didn't someone go and get her before now?" the woman shouted. She turned and said something to the boy beside her.

"Who's that woman?" Penny asked. "Is that the other daughter?"

"Yes, that's Rebeccah," Jimmy said. "The younger one. She and Doreen didn't get on too well. Hardly ever saw her here. Sells stuff off a stall down the market, so they say. And the lad, that's Doreen's grandson. He helps out at the stall."

He gave Penny a sheepish look. "There's not much to do here. So we pass the time minding everyone else's business."

"There was a really strong smell of some kind of fragrance in Doreen's room," Penny said, with her head lowered. "Maybe some cheap scent from the market, then, that the daughter gave her. Market goods aren't always of the highest quality."

"And most of it off the back of a lorry."

By now, they had reached the nurses' station and Penny told her she had been unable to wake Doreen up for her birthday party. The nurse jumped up and started down the hall at the same time as Rebeccah left the reception desk and charged toward her mother's room.

"Oh, no," said Jimmy. "Looks like she's really going to kick off now."

Eleven

Unsure what to do next, Penny and Jimmy waited in the hall while the nurse had a few hurried words with Doreen's daughter and then the two entered the room. The shouting did not come. Everything was quiet and then the daughter, Rebeccah, emerged from the room, her hand over her mouth and her eyes fixed on the floor.

She glanced at Penny and Jimmy and then sped past the reception desk, pushed open the door and left the building. Peris followed her a moment later.

"What will happen next?" Penny asked the nurse.

"As her death wasn't what we call expected, her GP will have to call in as soon as he can, hopefully this afternoon, and have a look at her. He'll then decide whether or not the coroner needs to be informed. But I'm sure it'll all be very straightforward." She motioned toward the nursing station. "And now, I've got to get started on the paperwork. I'll send someone to the lounge to let her friends know. The residents at the birthday party." She gave Jimmy a light smile. "Shame about that. They were looking forward to it."

Penny and Jimmy joined the little group just as a care aide arrived to speak to them. She was wearing a pair of dark purple cotton trousers with a matching short-sleeved top and her hair was scraped back into a ponytail. She spoke quickly and several residents leaned forward and then exchanged puzzled looks.

"Did she say Doreen's died?" one woman asked the man beside her. "Is that what she said? Is Doreen dead?" As the news rippled through the group, their faces became etched with shock and sadness; the loss of a member of their little band was keenly felt.

"Now, then," said the care aide with false brightness. "Who's for some cake?"

One woman held up her hand. "Shouldn't we wait for Doreen?" She turned to her neighbour and said cheerfully, "It's her birthday today, you know."

Jimmy shifted in his chair and leaned toward Penny. "All right?" he asked.

"Thinking," said Penny.

"Yeah, I know. Me, too. Seems a little too . . ."

Penny nodded. "Exactly. A little too . . ."

"Connected?" said Jimmy. "Is that the word we're looking for?"

"Mother and daughter both dead so close together?"

"Makes you wonder, doesn't it?" Jimmy said. "Are you going to call him?"

Penny knew immediately whom he meant. Jimmy and DCI Gareth Davies went back a long way, albeit on opposite sides of

62

the law. "Yes, I am. It might just be a sad coincidence, but he should know. Definitely." She stood up. "Excuse me. I'm going to step out to make the call." As she walked toward reception a woman in what looked like a blue uniform, similar to the purple ones worn by staff, was letting herself out the front door, pulling on a jacket as she went.

"Did you see who that was?" she asked the receptionist.

The woman got up from her desk and approached the counter. "Sorry?"

"That woman who just left. Did you see her? The caregiver in the blue uniform. Do you know who she is?"

"A blue uniform? Our caregivers wear purple ones. Oh, wait, blue. Yes, that might be housekeeping or laundry. But she shouldn't be leaving by the front door. Employees are required to use the staff entrance."

"Well, thank you."

Penny left a message for Davies that Doreen Roberts had died and the doctor had been called, and then returned to the lounge. The little birthday group had broken up and only Jimmy remained, rubbing his eyes as Penny approached.

"You're tired," she said. "Shall I help you back to your room?"

"I am a little tired," Jimmy admitted. "Although how you can get so tired doing nothing all day beats me."

"Right. We'll go in a minute. First, though, let's take down these balloons. I thought a staff person would have done this, but I guess they've got better things to do. But leaving them here doesn't seem right, after what happened."

63

Twelve

Filled with disbelief, Rebeccah Roberts closed the door of the High Pastures nursing home behind her and stepped into a dismal afternoon of freezing rain. She pulled the hood of her anorak over her head as far as it would go and bent her head against the icy onslaught. She'd sent her nephew, Peris, on his way and stayed behind to ask the nurse a few questions and tidy up her mother's room.

My mother died today.

She whispered the words to herself and then repeated them, louder this time, as if she were trying to get used to the idea or practicing in case she had to tell someone. My mother died today. She felt confused and shocked; the nurse had told her that her mother's death was unexpected. But beneath the disbelief was a swirling undercurrent of other, darker emotions. She had known all her life that she could never please her mother, nothing she ever did would be good enough. Why couldn't she have nicely shaped eyebrows like Glenda, her mother would ask, with a disapproving frown. Couldn't she at least try to lose a little weight? Do something about her hair? Throughout her teen years her mother had been so disappointed in her looks. As she moved through her twenties and thirties the disappointment had given way to outright contempt and finally, a painful indifference. Her mother had given up on her. And then, like a glimmer of light breaking through clouds, Rebeccah realized that what she was feeling was the beginning of relief. She was finally free to be herself and now she could give up on her mother.

She turned the corner into the town square and remembering that Peris was stopping with her, decided to get in a few supplies. She didn't know much about teenage boys, but she did know they had huge appetites. Grateful to be out of the rain, she pushed open the door of the little supermarket and picked up a shopping basket, which she soon filled with a loaf of bread, a litre of milk, a couple of bananas, some sliced chicken, a pizza, and a couple of pasta ready meals. With one last look in her basket, she turned toward the checkout. "Watch where you're going, love," said a woman's voice, in a calm, low tone. "Oh, I'm sorry," said Rebeccah, adding silently, my mother died today. I'm a little distracted.

The woman moved on as Rebeccah's eyes followed her. Something about her looked familiar, but she couldn't place her. Of course, she saw all sorts of people at her stall, so it could be someone she'd had a brief exchange with at the market. She paid for her items and once again headed out into the driving rain.

As she hurried along Watley Street, she heard footsteps behind her. She slowed down, glanced behind her, and saw the woman she had bumped into in the supermarket. Although it was only mid afternoon, the sky was dark and she could sense, if not see, the gathering dusk. Droplets of rain stood out in stark contrast against the warm glow of lights from the shop windows. The pavement was slick beneath her feet and she could feel the rain trickle under her hood and into her hair. She pushed on, turning up a small side street, past small grey houses with withered, wintery gardens, then down a set of slippery stone stairs to the door of her basement flat. There were no lights on. She opened the door and entered a small, cold sitting room. She set down her shopping bag, closed the door behind her, and from the light that filtered through a small window, lit the gas fire. She switched on a lamp and went through to the tiny kitchen. She put the groceries away and then filled the kettle. The best thing to do when someone dies, she thought, is make a cup of tea. It gives you something to do. Takes your mind off things.

The knock on the door startled her. She opened it and seeing it was her nephew, reached out to him and pulled him toward her.

"Come in out of the rain, Peris," she said. "Give me your wet things and go on through. I've just put the kettle on."

"Are you hungry?" she asked. When he nodded, she said, "I'll make us an early tea. Or late lunch. Whatever you want to call it. There's beef with barley soup and bread and cheese. Will that do?"

The boy nodded again and then took out his phone and started scrolling.

A few minutes later he looked up and watched while she opened a tin, poured the contents into a pot, and set it on the cooker to heat. She sliced some bread into neat slices and arranged them on a plate. And then the boy spoke.

"I've been thinking about *Mam*."

67

"Of course you have, love."

"No, not like that. About something that happened last week."

Rebeccah raised an eyebrow and waited, still holding the bread knife. "Last week, you know, that day you were off to the chiropractor and *Mam* stood in for you for a couple hours." Rebeccah indicated she remembered and he continued. "Well, a man come up to the stall and started yelling at her. Really shouting, he were."

"Why?"

"Something about a dodgey air freshener that his wife bought at the stall and it made his kid sick. Went on about how the kid has asthma and how he couldn't breathe on account of the air freshener and they had to take him to A and E."

"We don't sell air freshener on our stall."

"Well, you know that and I know that, but apparently he didn't. His wife bought air freshener at the market and he assumed it was from us, I guess."

Rebeccah bit her lower lip and frowned.

"I hope he didn't report us to the trading-standards people."

"But the funny thing is, I think they knew each other. Because when he left, *Mam* said something like, 'See you tomorrow.'"

"And tomorrow was . . ."

"The day she died."

The two said nothing and Rebeccah carried on with the meal preparation. She quartered a small tomato and picked up a wedge of cheddar cheese.

Peris looked up from his phone. "How much do you think we'll get?"

She set down the knife and faced him. The wind rattled the

windowpane and fat raindrops, barely visible through the con-
densation, raced in rivulets down the glass.

"'Get'?"

"Well, yeah. First *Mam* and now *Nain*. They must have left
something between them and it'll come to us now, won't it? How
much do you think we'll get?"

"Do you know, Peris, I haven't given that a thought. I'm
still trying to get my head around the fact that my mother died
today."

Thirteen

"Right, well, thanks for letting me know. Yes, I'll tell him."
Sgt. Bethan Morgan pressed the button to end the call and looked at her supervisor, DCI Gareth Davies.

"Sir," she said. "We may have a problem."

He waited.

"The GP went to the nursing home, examined Doreen's body, and saw nothing that indicated further investigation would be necessary. He's signed the death certificate and notified the coroner."

Davies raised an eyebrow. "And?"

"And whilst he was examining her, he found a small piece of slate in her left hand. Of course, he didn't think anything of it. Why would he? Just thought it was something she was holding when she died. He often sees people clutching something that meant something to them—rosaries, or a photo, even a bit of clothing."

"Oh, God, no," said Davies, rising from his chair. "Call the nursing home and tell them not to move the body and not to disturb anything. Tell them we're on our way."

"I already did that. We're too late. The body was removed from the room as soon as the doctor left and all her things have been packed up and the room's been cleaned and readied for the next occupant."

Davies sank back in his chair.

"We'll have to talk to Penny. She saw the body. Let's see what she remembers. See if she can tell us anything. I'll talk to her and you go to the nursing home and go through the belongings. If the piece of slate is still there, we'll need to find out where both of them came from."

"Yes, sir."

"I know that'll be a big task; there are so many old quarries around here, but a geologist at the University of Bangor may be able to help."

"Sorry to bother you, but we've had a setback with our investigation into the death of Glenda Roberts," Davies said as he sat down on the sofa in Penny's comfortable sitting room.

"I'm always glad to help," Penny replied. "You know that."

"I do." Davies smiled at her. "This is official, I'm afraid. I'm going to have to ask you a few questions."

Penny raised her hands in a go-ahead gesture.

"I need you to tell me everything you can about what Doreen Roberts looked like when you found her. The position of

72

her body. What your first thoughts were. Start with the run-up to finding her. Put that in context for me, please."

"She hadn't shown up for the little birthday party they had planned for her. So Jimmy and I offered to go to her room to see if she was on her way. Jimmy knew where her room was. I left him in the corridor—in his chair, you know, in case Doreen was still getting dressed or whatever."

Davies nodded. "Right. So Jimmy didn't go into the room?"

Penny shook her head. "No, just me."

"Okay," said Davies. "Now tell me exactly what you saw."

"Doreen was lying on top of her bed, fully dressed. It looked as if she had got herself ready for the party, and then, maybe because she was a few minutes early or maybe she felt a little weak or dizzy, or something like that, had laid down again."

"Where were her hands? Were they folded over her chest like this?" Davies linked his fingers together and placed them over his chest.

"No," Penny said slowly. "They weren't. They were more like this." She clenched both hands into loose fists and set them on her upper chest, fingers curled downward, so the knuckles were almost under her chin. "They were like this."

"Did you notice anything in her hands?"

"Like what?"

"Like anything."

She shook her head. "No, I didn't see anything. I touched her hand, though, and it was still warm."

"Now for the hard part. I'm sorry to have to ask you to do this, but can you describe her face?"

Penny looked away for a moment and then started to speak. As she spoke, she gradually turned her gaze back to him.

"Her head was turned toward the door. Her mouth was open. Her eyes were closed. She looked peaceful enough, I guess. The bedcovers were smooth. There was no sign of a struggle, if that's what you're asking."

Before he could respond, a knock on the door signalled the arrival of Bethan. Penny let her in and she sat beside Davies on the sofa.

"Well?" he asked. Bethan nodded and gave him a quizzical look. He hesitated for a moment and then held out his hand. In it, she placed a small evidence bag. He flattened to make the contents more visible and then held it out to Penny.

"The doctor found this in Doreen's left hand when he examined her body. It's a small piece of slate. This is what's got us so worried."

Penny knew that police officers are not permitted to discuss details of a case so she wondered why he was telling her this.

She reached out for the bag and looked at the small object, then stood up and walked over to a small bowl on the mantelpiece. She retrieved something and then held it out to Davies. It sat in the palm of his hand, smooth and cool with a matte blue-grey lustre. He examined it from all angles. From a side view, tiny striated lines revealed it was made in layers. It was like a block of slate in miniature.

"Where did you get this?" Davies asked.

"At the Dorothea Quarry," Penny said. "Near Penygroes. I've been there many times to sketch and paint. The buildings have been abandoned and are falling into ruin as nature reclaims them. It's a strange kind of beauty. Desolate and decaying, but romantic, too. If you try, you can just about imagine what used to be. And you wonder how and why it happened. It's better to go this time of year when the trees are bare. In the summer you can barely see the buildings for the foliage."

"Well," he said to Bethan. "See if our slate ties in with that quarry or the mine. It must come from somewhere around here."

"I know you're not supposed to discuss your case with an outsider," Penny said, "but can you tell me why the slate is important? Doreen's husband worked in the slate mine, I understand, although not the quarry operation, so might she have had an emotional attachment to it? Could the explanation be as simple as that?"

Davies hesitated. "In any investigation police often withhold information or evidence that only the killer knows from the media. It can help later to establish if someone is telling the truth."

"Penny, we withheld that the body in the mine—Glenda Roberts—also had a piece of slate in her hand," Bethan picked up the conversational thread. "That one was dark grey and we're looking into it, but we're pretty sure it came from the Llyn Du mine itself."

"The two pieces of slate would seem to be more than a coincidence," Davies finished. "It's likely that they tie the two deaths together somehow, but we aren't sure exactly why or how. We didn't realize the doctor had found something in Doreen's hand and of course he had no idea it might be significant in that a piece of slate had also been found in Glenda's hand."

"In that case," asked Penny, "what about the other sister? Rebeccah? She was shouting at the receptionist just as Jimmy and I were leaving Doreen's room. Is she a suspect? Or is she next?"

The two police officers exchanged worried glances as they stood up.

"Is there anything you want me to do?" Penny asked. "Can I help?"

"Keep your eyes and ears open and if you think of anything that might be relevant, get in touch. And be alert at the Spa to anything suspicious or unusual."

"The Spa?"

"It's a gathering place for women. Does Rebeccah go there, by the way?"

"No."

She closed the door behind them and returned to her chair. After a moment she cupped her cheeks in her hands. She was sure she'd left something out, but it was escaping her at the moment. Oh, well. It would pop into her head later and when it did, she'd give Davies a ring.

Fourteen

"How are the concert plans coming along?" Penny asked Victoria the next morning.

Her friendly query was met with an unfriendly moan. "Awful. The whole thing is in chaos. We can't decide whether to keep on with the plan to hold it down the mine or try to change the venue. We can't agree on a program. People suddenly have other plans on rehearsal nights. And it's only four weeks away! Say what you like about Glenda Roberts, at least she managed events well and pulled them off."

"Maybe you should just scrap the whole thing, then," said Penny.

"I suggested that, but they all said, no, we must carry on. Glenda would want us to. As if that's reason enough."

"It sounds to me as if the will just isn't there," said Penny, "and if it isn't, the whole project is doomed. People have to want it to happen and be willing to pull together."

Victoria looked at her with surprise and admiration. "Now that's leadership talking," she said. And then her face lit up. "Hey, I don't suppose you'd be willing to take over the concert, would you? What we really need is someone who isn't directly involved, but who'll take charge and tell us what to do. Really, Penny, there's no one else."

"If I tell them what to do, are you sure they'll do it?" Penny asked.

"Yes. I'll tell them this is the only chance we have of bringing off this concert and if they don't pull together as a team, it won't happen."

"Give me a day to think about it," Penny said. "And in the meantime, tell me the names of the sponsors, who's printing the tickets and program, and everything else you can think of. Oh, and is it orchestra only, or will there be singers?"

"There will be a couple of singers, a few musicians, and a special guest singer. I wondered about the program when I first got the sheet music, but it turns out the singer is Karis Edwards."

"Karis Edwards . . ."

"Bit of a has been now, but she was pretty big way back in the '80s. Remember that girl group The Characters? She was one of them."

"Oh, right."

"There were six of them. According to Google, some have done better than others since the band broke up and everybody went their separate ways. One died, in New York, I think it was. And Karis; well, somehow Glenda got hold of her and she's going to be the musical guest."

"Are there files or background information on all the concert arrangements?"

"We could ask her sister or her son. I don't know if she worked
from paper files or if it's all on her computer. Or maybe it was
all in her head."

"Right."

"But there is one important thing you should know."

"And that is . . ."

"If Karis has already signed a contract, which I expect she has,
it'll include a stipulation that she will be paid whether the show
goes ahead or not. As the artist, she's set aside this block of time,
prepared a repertoire, made arrangements for her personal life,
and so on. She'll have to be paid, so that's why it's really important that the concert goes ahead. There's not only her fee to be
paid, but there's the venue, too. If Glenda didn't arrange cancellation insurance, and I doubt she did, this could be a big loss."

"How would the expenses be covered, then? Who would
pay?"

"That's just it. I have no idea. I guess we'd have to put on a
fund-raiser to raise money to pay off the debt from the concert
that never was."

"Well, when you put it like that . . . Mrs. Lloyd's always telling me that I should do more in the community, so maybe this
is my chance. As I said, give me a day to think about it. But from
what you've just told me, if there's no one else, I guess I'll have
to take it on," Penny said. She removed her glasses. "If you're
absolutely sure no one else can do it, or wants to, that is."

Victoria shook her head. "No, you're our last, best hope, I'm
afraid."

Penny rubbed her hands together. "If I do agree to take on

the concert, it's on one condition. I don't like the idea of going down the mine. I don't think I'm claustrophobic, but the idea of tons of rock above my head frightens me. So if I do it, it'll be on the understanding that I go down only twice—once for a site visit and then again on the evening of the concert."

"What about the dress rehearsal? You should be there for that."

"Don't push your luck."

Before Victoria could reply Rhian stuck her head around the door.

"Oh, Victoria and Penny. I'm glad I caught you together."

She leaned back into the corridor and made a little waving gesture at someone, then stuck her head back in the door.

"It's Florence Semble. She's got something to show you and you're not going to like it. Not one bit."

She stepped aside to usher in Florence, who was well wrapped up against the cold.

"In you go, Florence. Show them what you bought." Rhian looked at Victoria. "I'd better get back to reception."

Florence set a plastic bag on Victoria's desk and removed her gloves. With a grimace, she pulled a small white box out of the bag and handed it to Penny. Victoria leaned in closer for a better look.

LLANELLEN SPA HAND CREAM read the label. "Oh, God," said Victoria, "it's a knockoff of our hand cream! Who would do such a thing?"

"An idiot who can't spell," said Florence. "Llanellen with two ells?"

"Where did you get this?" Penny asked.

"In Colwyn Bay. I took the bus to the library as that's where the CD collection is housed. Evelyn's working on her memoir and we thought some music from the time would be helpful to her, so off I went. Whilst I was there I thought I might as well have a look at that market they have, and I found that." She pointed with distaste at the box. "The neck of some people! I mean, selling that rubbish so close to home. I knew as soon as I saw it that it wasn't yours."

"Why would they try to sell it so close to home?" said Penny. "They were bound to be found out."

"Because," said Florence, "someone is cashing in on the buy-local movement. Evelyn came home from our market with a sachet of what someone was trying to pass off as Welsh Lavender. It was no such thing, in my opinion. Lavender spelled 'a-r.'"

"What do we do?" asked Victoria.

"Well, first," said Penny. "We'll ask Rhian to reimburse Florence out of petty cash." She smiled at Florence. "We don't want you paying for this stuff out of your own pocket. And then, as a thank-you, we're going to give Florence a jar of the real stuff. And then we call the police."

Fifteen

Although she'd known for years that the best days of her singing career were behind her, forty-two-year-old Karis Edwards couldn't quite bring herself to believe the dream was over. As a member of the hugely popular girl band The Characters, she'd made it big, enjoying all the perks that come with that rare kind of stardom. Back in the late 1980s, when the group's popularity was at its peak, in what she referred to as her "carry your bags" life, staff took care of everything. Louis Vuitton trunks filled with stage wear were packed and transported; vanity cases and personal luggage were hand-carried by assistants. Hotel suites were booked, clothes were cleaned, limousines— one for each Character—arrived on time to take them to the airport, and before long they made the transition from first class to private jet. At that point, the lifestyle was beyond any of their wildest dreams: shopping extravaganzas for designer clothes, handbags and shoes that beggared belief, white mountains of cocaine, media begging for interviews, nights out costing thousands of pounds, bodyguards and paparazzi, and huge entourages. Of course, when you've got money, the entourages just materialize and when the money goes away, so do they.

When you're young and the money is rolling in, you don't think about financial investments, rainy days, or what'll happen when the music stops, as inevitably it does. Or at least Karis didn't. But one Character did and her prudent investments now enabled her to live a more-than-comfortable, quiet life in Surrey well out of the spotlight with her husband, children, dogs, and horses. Another had made millions as a celebrity chef, cooking for the rich and famous, launching her own line of expensive cookware, endorsing products, and writing hugely popular cookbooks. Karis hadn't even known this one could cook, but then how could she? They'd had their own personal chef, hired by their manager, who travelled everywhere with them and whose job it was to keep the girls slim.

Another performer who hadn't done so well for herself after the band broke up at least managed to land a role every year as the fairy godmother in a Christmas pantomime in Birmingham or Llandudno and get almost top billing on the posters that were plastered all over the town.

And then there was the bass guitarist, who'd died of a heroin overdose in a bohemian New York apartment hotel where several other celebrities had died before her. Her death had merited a few paragraphs of print and minutes of airtime for a day or two and had revived nostalgic interest in the defunct group. Karis had picked up a few bookings in the wake of that, but they'd soon dried up.

Karis had never really moved on and found a solid new way

to earn a living and be in the world. Singing was all she knew how to do and all she wanted to do. And now it had come to this: she was to perform a few songs as the special guest artiste in a St. David's Day concert to be held down a worked-out slate mine.

She blamed her agent who was worse than useless. If he'd been on top of things, if he'd put her interests first and promoted her properly, she could be enjoying the same kind of success as the last of her bandmates, who'd gone on to a brilliant, chart-topping career as a single artist. After all, she didn't have any more talent that Karis did; she'd just been luckier, that's all. She might have been better-looking, Karis would give her that, and in the shallow end of the entertainment pool, looks and youth are all that matter. Once you turn thirty you're on the slippery slope to oblivion, turning up only in the pages of some downmarket tabloid under the mean-spirited headline: WHERE ARE THEY NOW?

She thought that especially cruel. Showing a former celebrity on her way to the shops in a sloppy pair of sweatpants and baggy sweater, with no makeup and her jowls and turkey neck on show for all the world to see. Thankfully, apparently she didn't even rate that.

She leaned over and examined her face in the mirror above the sink, smoothing her neck and turning her face slowly side to side. She'd changed so much since those Character days. In fact, people rarely recognized her and when they did, it was usually a woman who squinted at her in a, "Do I know you?" kind of way. "Did you used to be somebody? Are you somebody I should know?"

She tilted her head to examine the centre part that divided her hair and noted the roots were starting to show. She'd always hated her grey hair; she'd pick up a bottle of hair dye at the chemist and get that sorted as soon as she could. One of the perks she missed most about the performing days was the grooming. Hairdressers and makeup artists travelled with the group to ensure everyone was ready for the next concert, promotional appearance, or store opening. Or even just a quick run to the shops on the rare occasions when no one was available to go for you.

She scowled as she added a sweater to the pile of clothes in her suitcase. At least her contract for this mine concert had stipulated she'd be put up in a decent hotel for the rehearsal and performance nights, not in some draughty B&B with 1980s flowered wallpaper borders. Rather like the one she was just leaving.

She didn't really want to, but she'd have to spend a few days with Mum. Or a few weeks, more like, if she was going to be honest about it. The concert was still a ways off and she had no bookings between now and then. She'd been given a rehearsal and performance schedule for the St. David's Day concert and really, all she needed to do was decide what to wear, what to sing, and show up on time. She sighed and tossed a few unwanted clothes, including a pair of blue cotton trousers, into the bin, remembering a time when she'd spent thousands on clothes that hung in the wardrobe with the tags still on them and then given them away. The one smart thing she'd done with her money was buy Mum that little house in Swansea so she'd always have a roof over head. Who could have known it would turn out that sometimes that roof was over her head, too? Mum was always glad to see her and knew enough not to ask too many questions. And she was always good for a "payday" loan that both knew would never be repaid as real paydays were few and far between.

Karis Edwards took one last look around the room to make sure she had everything, then picked up her bag and carried it to her car.

Sixteen

The fields that surround the town of Llanelen, green even in midwinter and segmented with dry stone walls, gradually give way to a more rugged terrain as the A470 passes through the Valley of the River Conwy, heading deeper into Snowdonia National Park. Steep hills, brown and barren now, but emblazoned with yellow gorse and purple heather in summer, tower over the two-lane asphalt road as it climbs higher, twisting and winding higher until it reaches the Crimea Pass.

"Your ears might pop," Victoria said.

Penny took a deep breath and continued looking out the window.

"You're very quiet."

"I'm really not looking forward to this. Going down the mine." She glanced at Victoria. "Have you ever been down there?"

"Once, more years ago than I care to remember. I was looking after my nieces during the half-term holiday and it seemed like a fun day out. It's actually rather interesting. The sense of history is powerful and it's certainly unique." She took her eyes off the road for a moment to check her rearview mirror. "And safe. Much safer for us today than it would have been a hundred years ago when it was a working mine."

Penny shuddered. "I can't bear to think of it. The conditions must have been horrendous."

As the sun struggled to emerge from behind the clouds that blanketed the tops of the hills, many scarred with deep grey slashes that marked the sites of former quarrying operations, huge mounds of slate waste came into view. For every tonne of usable slate extracted from the earth, approximately nine tonnes of waste—dust, rubble, unusable chips, and small pieces—are generated. Wherever slate was mined or quarried, the operation was surrounded by vast tips of by-product, now glowering over the landscape as constant reminders of what was once a great industry and a long gone way of life consigned to history.

"Here we are," Victoria announced a few minutes later as they pulled into the parking lot of the Llyn Du mine.

They entered the reception area and after introducing themselves to a helpful woman in the gift shop, were asked to wait. A few moments later a man in a red boilersuit approached them, holding out a welcoming hand.

"Good morning, ladies," he said, smiling broadly. "I'm Bevan Jones, the operations manager. Pleasure to meet you. I'm here to take you down and show you where the concert will take place." After Penny and Victoria introduced themselves Bevan led the way out of the reception area, along a covered walkway past the café, or *caban* as it was originally called, and then past a large, open-fronted shed where slate-splitting demonstrations were held.

"Here's the train that will take us down," he said when they reached the winch house, pointing to a bright yellow conveyance that did not look like a conventional train, but rather like a set of large metal boxes staggered on a track. "But before we go down, you must put on one of these." He handed each woman a coloured hard hat. "Make sure it fits tightly." When Penny hesitated, he gave her a reassuring smile. "You can't go down without one and you wouldn't want to. Visitors think they're just a touristy gimmick, but believe me, before this is over, you'll be glad you're wearing it." She put it on. "You'll ride in the front car with me. Ladies first. Mind your heads."

Victoria ducked her head and climbed in the first car. As Penny followed, her red helmet hit the top of the entrance into the car with a resonating clang. Bevan and Victoria laughed. "Oh," said Penny, raising her hand to touch the helmet, "I did think these were a touristy thing, but now I get it."

"Brace yourselves! It'll be a bit noisy," said Bevan as he sat beside Victoria in the guard's seat. He pushed a button inside the cab and an alarm sounded. A moment later the train lurched forward, then chugged and rattled as it entered a tunnel, leaving daylight behind and descending deeper and deeper into an all encompassing darkness. For a few minutes they travelled through an unknown place between worlds, the earth above and what lies beneath.

"This is the steepest passenger train in Britain," Bevan remarked. Penny took a deep breath and cleared her throat. After what seemed ages, the train juddered to a stop and they climbed out.

"This way," said Bevan. "Follow me. Stay close now and don't wander off. It's easy to get lost down here if you don't know where you're going and it could take us a while to find you. We don't want that." He switched on the lamp attached to his helmet and the three set off, stepping over small, grey, chalky puddles that seemed to ooze out of the uneven path. Although electric lights were positioned along the slate walls, the lighting was dim and the darkness, deep and impenetrable, felt close and confining. Penny ran her fingertips along the sides of the tunnel, feeling the jagged roughness. The air smelled damp, with a tang of earthy loaminess. A few moments later they emerged into a cavern and Bevan opened a small gate in a metal fence. "This," he said, "is where the concert will take place." The chamber was massive, with an open space in front of a stage area made entirely of slate.

"And the chairs would be here?" Penny asked as she gestured at the open area. "How many can we seat? A hundred or so?"

"Well, yes, that's about the seating capacity. When we do weddings, that's what we plan for."

"Do you store the chairs down here somewhere, or bring them down?" asked Victoria.

"We store them aboveground, where it's dry," Bevan replied. "It's too damp down here. They'd be okay for a night or two, but anything longer and they'd soon be ruined. There are a lot of underground springs and streams as we are so deep in the earth."

Penny looked around and above her in wonder. The vast, soaring underground space, resembling a villain's lair in a James Bond film, carved and blasted out of a mountain by the hard, dirty work of generations of men who spent their entire working lives breathing in slate dust, left her speechless.

"It's moving, isn't it?" commented Bevan. "It takes everyone who comes down here like that. Well, thoughtful people, anyway."

"It's too bad the word 'awesome' has become so overused that it's lost its true meaning," said Victoria. "Because this is truly awesome."

"The other lady who was planning the concert," Bevan said, "Glenda Roberts. She felt that way, too. Friend of yours, was she?"

"Well, I knew her because she was a customer of ours," said Penny. "But Victoria is a harpist so she knew her on a more professional level. Did you know her?"

"Well, when you say 'know,'" Bevan replied cautiously, "not exactly know. I wouldn't use that word. But I knew who she was and I knew of her. I'd seen her around and about and at the market. And I was in the group that found her body. In fact, I was the one that yelled, 'Fetch the box.'"

"'Fetch the box'?"

"Yes. In the old mining days anyone who was injured and needed carrying to the surface went up in a box. To this day, whenever anyone's hurt down the mine the code is, 'Fetch the box!' That's what you shout if someone's injured or even if you think they might be dead. We've got a box on display in one of the caverns. I can show it to you on the way out. Many bodies transported in that."

"So where did you find the body?" asked Penny.

"In front of the lake, she was. I'll show you that, too, in a few minutes, if you like. The mine was named after that lake. Llyn Du. Black Lake."

"Tell me," said Penny. "What do you make of this? Of Glenda's body being found down here in the mine."

"Well, we were all very sorry it happened, of course, but sadly, this place is no stranger to death. Many men died down here or were so badly injured that they died because of injuries they got here." He leaned back a little and pushed his hard hat a little further back on his head. "I heard she was murdered. Glenda Roberts."

He paused for a moment, as if weighing his words.

"I can tell you one thing for sure. If she was murdered, no one who works here did it."

"Why do you say that?" asked Victoria.

"Because there are about three hundred caverns down here, on sixteen or seventeen levels. The public only sees about ten chambers. So anyone who knew their way around here wouldn't have left the body where it was found." He shook his head. "No. Someone who worked here would know about all the unused caverns and warrens of tunnels. Twenty-five miles of tunnels. In fact, we're getting ready to backfill an old unused tunnel right now. So anyone who works down here, me for example, would know that. I'd have put the body in the tunnel and once it had been backfilled and sealed, her body would never be found." He took a step toward the fencing to indicate that it was almost time to move on and then turned to look back at them. "Never be found," he repeated.

"Would you like to see more of the mine—the lake, maybe?—or would you like to go back to the surface now?" he asked when they were back on the path. Victoria and Penny exchanged a quick glance and reached an unspoken agreement.

"We'd love to see the lake, please."

"Before we go, then," said Bevan, "I always invite people to reflect for a moment in the silence. You have to remember that when this mine was operational, it would have been filled with noise. Men pushing heavy wagons filled with slate up to the surface, calling to each other, winching, digging, blasting, shouting . . ."

"Do they speak to you?" asked Victoria. "The miners?"

"No," said Bevan. "They talk only to one another. We're only observers. They don't know we're here."

The trio stood silently, listening. But all Penny heard was the soft, steady dripping of water, trickling down the walls.

As they followed Bevan to the subterranean lake, stooping when they came to a low entrance to another tunnel, Bevan turned to Penny.

"And since you were asking, there's another aspect of this business with Glenda Roberts that I can't get my head around."

"What's that?"

"Why here? I mean, if you're going to murder someone, there must be lots of better places to do it than down a mine."

"I agree with you," said Penny. "That's what I thought. Why here?"

They stood in front of the lake, admiring its cool, dark beauty. The surface was still, with large slabs of slate visible below the surface. "Her body was just here," said Bevan, pointing to a place in front of it.

Penny and Victoria gazed at the spot, trying to picture Glenda lying there. As if reading their minds, Bevan helpfully supplied a colourful image. "She was wearing a red coat."

He gave them a few more moments of contemplation and then asked if they were ready to return to the surface. They were, and the three set off for the train. Many small rectangular pieces of slate, about an inch long and an eighth of an inch thick, were scattered along the pathway and Penny bent over to pick up a couple.

"I guess lots of people pick these up," she said.

"They do," said Bevan, "but we'll never miss them. So we don't mind if they take them home as a souvenir."

Twenty minutes later Victoria and Penny were back on the surface and on their way.

"He said some pretty interesting things about Glenda," Victoria remarked as they drove out of the car park.

"Yeah," Penny agreed. "What did you make of the bit about it couldn't have been someone from the mine? Did you think there was an element there of . . ."

"Methinks he doth protest too much?"

"Something like that. I read somewhere that people volunteering too much information can be lying or fabricating."

"I don't think he was lying, but it seemed oddly out of context. He just said that out of nowhere."

"True. But now, we'd better talk about the concert while the visit is fresh in our minds," said Penny. "It would have been helpful if we'd had a chance to review Glenda's files before we spoke to Bevan. Still, I guess we can put it together our own way."

"I asked Rebeccah to take a look for the file," said Victoria. "Why don't you get my mobile out of my bag and ring her now while we think of it. Her number will be there. Just scroll for it."

Penny reached behind her for the bag on the backseat and placed it on her lap. She scrabbled about in it, pulled out the mobile, and placed the call.

"Hello, Rebeccah. It's Penny Brannigan here," she began and then stopped to listen. She held the phone away from her ear so Victoria could hear a loud voice coming from it. "That's terrible," said Penny, when she was allowed to speak. "I'm so sorry to hear this. Yes, you stay where you are and don't touch any-

94

thing. I'll call the police for you." She ended the call and turned to Victoria.

"What is it? What's happened?"

"Glenda's son, Peris, has been staying with Rebeccah since his mum died, so her house has been empty. He went back to get a few things and discovered a break-in. The house has been burgled, and now, on top of everything else, it looks as if Glenda's jewellery's been stolen."

Seventeen

I don't suppose you've got photos of her jewellery? Do you know if any of it was insured?" Sgt. Bethan Morgan, her pen poised over her open notebook, looked at the small pile of glass shards under the broken bedroom window. Rebeccah Roberts, standing in the doorway, shook her head as her nephew, Peris, peered over her shoulder.

"I don't know. Some of it was Mum's and some was Glenda's. I don't really know anything about Glenda's jewellery. But Mum's pearls were here, I think, and her engagement ring. The pearls had earrings with them and the ring was a rather nice amethyst with diamonds. Gold. She was wearing her wedding ring, *Mam* was, but she'd given her engagement ring and pearls to Glenda for safekeeping when she moved into the home. She didn't trust the other residents." She pointed to the bureau drawers that had been upturned on the bed. "Who do you think could have done this?"

"Couldn't say," Sergeant Morgan replied, "but break-ins like this happen all the time. They know what they're looking for. Money and jewellery that can be sold on quickly. Sadly, it's often to get money for drugs. But we know places where stolen property like this often ends up, so I hope we can recover at least some of it for you.

"Actually, I was going to ask you the same question. Can you think of anyone who might have done this? Did anyone know Peris was staying with you and that the place was likely to be empty?" Rebeccah shook her head. "What about you, Peris?" said Bethan. "Did you mention to any of your mates that you were stopping with your aunt for a bit?"

"No, I didn't." He blinked rapidly several times and stroked the back of his neck.

Sergeant Morgan pointed her pen at a little pile of necklaces and earrings that had been left behind. "I'm not an expert, but it seems to me they took only the most valuable pieces." She took a step back. "Rebeccah, did your mother leave any of her jewellery with you?"

Rebeccah frowned. "No, Glenda had it all. I'm not really one for jewellery, me."

"How do you feel about this?"

Rebeccah shrugged. "It happens, I guess. What can you do?"

"Well, if you notice anything else missing, get in touch with us right away. And please check for her passport and any other important documents like that—birth certificate, driving licence, national health insurance card . . . that kind of thing." Sergeant Morgan handed Rebeccah her business card just as her phone rang. She listened for a moment and muttered a thank-you. "The fingerprints people are outside. Hopefully they'll find a print or two that matches something we have on file." She looked from Rebeccah to Peris. "They'll need yours, too, of course, for elimination."

"Both of us?" asked Peris.

"Well, yes. Especially yours. You live here, don't you?" Peris looked at the broken glass.

"Right, well, I'll be on my way and leave you with the forensics people. You'll find them very thorough so they may be some time."

Once in her police car Sergeant Morgan rang Davies to update him.

"The forensics team has just arrived. But what bothers me is Rebeccah's and Peris's reaction to the break-in. Rebeccah didn't seem that bothered and the lad, Peris, seemed very bothered. One of them might know something."

Eighteen

An ominious line of low, slate-grey clouds assembling along the tops of the hills blanketed the early morning in an unnatural, eerie darkness that gave the streets and houses a dreary, washed out look. A heavy stillness hung in the air, close and uncomfortable. Penny passed several acquaintances on her walk to work who commented on the gathering storm, and then hurried on about their business.

By the time she pushed open the door of the Spa, the air had an earthy, dense smell and the first drops of rain had started to fall.

Eirlys, not Rhian, greeted her on the reception desk.

"Morning, Penny. Rhian rang to say she'll be a bit late. Her grandfather's poorly and she's just going to pop into the nursing home to see if he needs anything. She'll be here as soon as she can."

"Right, Eirlys, thank you. Can you take care of reception until she arrives and I'll do the manicures? Who's first today?"

"It's Mrs. Lloyd and you know she prefers me to do her nails. She says you always make the water too hot."

"Well, she'll just have to put up with me for today and I'll make sure the water isn't too hot."

Half an hour later Mrs. Lloyd arrived. "Oh, good morning, Eirlys," she said as she entered the reception area. "Made it just in time. It's bucketing down now and the wind is starting to pick up. Looks like we've got some really nasty weather coming in." She turned back toward the door, shook her umbrella outside, and then closed the door against the rain. "What are you doing there on the desk?"

"I'm just standing in for Rhian for a bit this morning," Eirlys explained. "Penny will be doing your manicure this morning. But don't worry. I told her to mind the water temperature and she said she would."

Mrs. Lloyd laughed good-naturedly, stood her umbrella in the stand to dry, hung up her coat, and walked down the hall to the manicure room.

She settled herself in the client's chair and dipped the ends of her fingers in the soaking bowl. "Well, that's a little better, Penny," she said. "The temperature is almost tolerable. Not quite as hot as you usually make it."

"I'm glad you like it. How've you been, Mrs. Lloyd? All right?"

"Very busy, Penny. I've started working on my memoirs and if I'd known how much bother this was going to be, I don't know I would have done it. Masses of photographs and other things to go through and organize. Newspaper cuttings, dance programs, scrapbooks. But they certainly bring back a lot of memories. Events and things you'd completely forgotten about and then you read something and it brings it all back as if it just happened yesterday. You know, sometimes I wake up in the middle of the night and wonder where all the years went. How did I ever get this old, I ask myself."

"I hope the memories are mostly happy ones," Penny commented as she lifted Mrs. Lloyd's hand out of the warm soaking water and dried it with a fluffy white towel.

"Mostly," said Mrs. Lloyd, "although there are some that are not so good. Arthur's obituary from the local paper and the program from his funeral service, that sort of thing. And . . . well, other things, too."

She reflected for a moment and then took the conversation in another direction.

"Have you heard any more news about Glenda? Are the police any nearer to solving that, do you know?"

"No, I haven't heard anything."

"Well, that's not the first bad thing that's happened down that mine, let me tell you. Over the years many men died down there. In the 1800s the working conditions were horrific, and well into the twentieth century there were still the most terrible accidents. We used to hear about them when I was a girl."

"I can imagine."

"And even in the 1970s I think it was, just before the real operations closed, a couple of incidents down there really raised eyebrows. In fact," she paused while Penny switched to the other hand, "one of the accidents was so bad that government officials from whatever ministry looked after mines in those days came to investigate.

"They stayed at the Red Dragon Hotel and they sent reports on their findings to their superiors back in London. I know this because they used to come into the post office almost every afternoon with a big envelope with government franking on it, hand it over, and tell me to make sure it got to London." She laughed. "'Make sure it got to London!' What did they expect me to do? Hand deliver it myself?"

"Maybe they thought you were in charge of the Royal Mail."

"Maybe they did. Government officials. What do they know? It's always a bad sign, Penny, when the men in suits arrive. A lot of questions will be asked, a lot of money will be spent, and nothing will be done. Nothing good, anyway. All these changes haven't done much to make our lot better, if you ask me."

"What exactly happened at the mine, Mrs. Lloyd? Was there a cave-in?"

"No. Some scaffolding collapsed and a man was killed."

"Oh, that's awful."

"Yes, it was. The mine manager died."

"I believe mining is one of the most dangerous occupations." Penny began shaping Mrs. Lloyd's nails. And then a moment later: "Mine manager. Did I hear somewhere that Glenda's father was the mine manager at one time? Was he . . . ?"

"Yes," said Mrs. Lloyd. "Her father, Aled, died down that mine. I'd forgotten about that accident until Doreen died. Death always gets me thinking about the past, I find.

"Well, before we get to the polish part," Mrs. Lloyd continued, "I just want to ring Florence and see if she needs me to pick up anything whilst I'm out. If this storm comes in the way they're saying it will, we might be shut in for a day or two. Best to be prepared."

"It certainly is," agreed Penny. "While you're doing that, I'll make a call myself," said Penny. "Won't be a minute."

She stepped into her small office at the back of the Spa, picked

104

up her phone, and dialed. It went straight to voice mail. "Hi, Gareth. It's me, Penny. I've just heard that Glenda Roberts's father died in some kind of accident down the mine. He was the manager at one time. Scaffolding collapse? Anyway, not sure if it matters but thought I should pass that on to you. Talk to you later. Oh, Mrs. Lloyd just reminded me. Doreen did mention it. Bye."

Penny returned to the manicure room to find Eirlys applying polish to Mrs. Lloyd's nails. "Rhian's back, so I'm finishing Mrs. Lloyd." Both women smiled at Penny.

"Right, well, that's good, then. I'll leave you to it. See you next week, Mrs. Lloyd and enjoy your bridge game tonight," Penny said.

"Oh, I'd be very surprised if there is one," Mrs. Lloyd said. "I've just checked and apparently the storm is expected to get worse, so I expect the game will be cancelled. We're all over fifty-five you know, the bridge gang, and we don't like going out at night when the weather is bad."

"Sensible, that," said Eirlys. "No one should go out when the weather is bad."

"Really, Eirlys," said Mrs. Lloyd. "Sometimes I think you are wise beyond your years. Why can't more young people be like you?"

Penny left the room to the sound of laughter. A few minutes later Eirlys entered Penny's office.

"Mrs. Lloyd's gone but she left her phone here. I found it in the chair. I looked out the door hoping to catch her but I couldn't see her."

Penny held out her hand and said, "Here, leave it with me. Ask Rhian to ring her home and let her know that we have it and that I'll drop it off on my way home. Mrs. Lloyd won't be home yet, but Rhian can leave a message with Florence. Miss Semble."

"Okay. And Rhian says we've had a couple of cancellations for this afternoon because the weather is getting worse. The police are advising people to seek shelter and not go out unless they have to."

"Okay, Eirlys. Thanks."

A few minutes later the decision was taken, in light of the storm's projected severity, to close the Spa at noon. The few clients who hadn't cancelled their appointments for the afternoon were relieved to get a call from Rhian inviting them to reschedule.

Shortly after noon Penny waved good-bye to Victoria, who locked the Spa door behind her, and set off for Mrs. Lloyd's house. The wind was blowing harder now and a couple of times she had to clutch the top of a stone wall or lamppost to save herself from being blown over. The wind in her back pushed her forward as she lurched down the street, driving bits of litter and dead leaves ahead of her. She was relieved as she turned into Rosemary Lane to see Mrs. Lloyd's two-storey grey stone house with its slate roof loom into view.

As a strong gust buffeted her, she gripped the wrought iron gate, steadied herself, then raced up the path and knocked on the door. A moment later Florence opened it and reached out for Penny. "Oh, Penny, good, you made it. Do come in."

She closed the door behind her and offered to take Penny's coat.

"No, I can't stay, Florence, thanks. I must get home. That wind is absolutely fierce. I don't think I've ever seen anything like it. Just wanted to drop off Mrs. Lloyd's phone. The battery's low, so you might want to get it on the charger right away. They're saying we could lose power, so you'll want to make sure your phone's working."

"Yes, you're right." Florence took the phone from her. "Evelyn's just in the sitting room. She wanted a quick word with you. Go through. Don't worry about your boots."

Mrs. Lloyd looked up from the worktable Florence had set up for her in front of the window. She stood as Penny entered and pointed to a towering pile of papers, newspaper cuttings, scrapbooks, and boxes. Stacks of documents teetered on the table and cardboard boxes were stacked two and three high against the wall.

"Just wanted you to have a look at this, Penny," she said, holding out a yellowed newspaper cutting. "You never know what you'll find on these little side trips down memory lane."

Penny took the cutting from her, read the caption, then held it closer so she could examine the photograph more closely. A slow smile spread across her face.

"Oh, it's Emma!" she said. "And with the schoolchildren. On prizes day, I expect."

"Yes," said Mrs. Lloyd. "Our Morwyn won the prize for best writing. Well, no wonder she went on to become a newspaper reporter. Anyway," Mrs. Lloyd drew the curtain back slightly and peered out, "I thought now that you're here I'd show it to you. But you'd best take it with you. The weather is getting worse very quickly, so probably best if you set off now. Otherwise, you could end up stranded here with us. We wouldn't mind, of course, but if you want to see this storm out in your own home, you'd best be off. Take that with you and photocopy it if you wish. You can return it to me at my next appointment."

"Yes, I think you're right. I'd better go."

Penny tucked the cutting in her handbag, and after thanking

107

her for taking the trouble to return the phone, Florence opened the door, then struggled against the wind to close it behind Penny.

As soon she reached the pavement, Penny pulled the hood of her anorak up over her head, tucked her chin into her coat, and pushed off for home. The afternoon was now very dark as heavy sheets of rain, driven by a howling wind, assaulted her. Rivulets of water found their way into her hood and ran down her neck. Her thin trousers were soon soaked and her legs were cold and wet. She ploughed on, splashing through puddles in squelching shoes, grateful when there was not much further to go and comforting herself with the thought that she would be out of these wet things in a few minutes.

As her cottage welcomed her through the lashing rain, she sped up her pace, reaching into her coat pocket for her key as she did so. A moment later the key was in the lock, the door was open, and she was standing in her front hall, dripping, cold, but home and soon she would be dry.

She took off her coat and dropped it on the mat, then stepped out of her wet trousers and let them fall on top of the coat. She raced upstairs, pulling off the rest of her clothes as she went, grabbed a towel from the bathroom, and rubbed down her wet legs. She put on a cozy terry towel bathrobe and slippers and went downstairs where her cat, Harrison, wrapped himself around her legs while she put the kettle on.

She'd inherited her cottage from Emma Teasdale, a retired schoolteacher, a couple of years earlier and had had it modernized during an extensive renovation. The bright, modern kitchen was new, but Penny had insisted that the coal-burning Rayburn cooker and the original slate floor be incorporated into the design plans. She'd never really taken any particular notice of slate before; it had just seemed to blend into the greyness of the environment: grey stone buildings; grey slate roofs; grey, misty weather.

Central heating had been installed. When Emma had lived here, rooms had been heated by small heaters. Penny could not remember ever being truly warm when she visited in the winter, but Emma, even in her older years, seemed to cope with it. Or maybe she was just used to it, after living through a lifetime of British winters in wooly cardigans. The cottage was now snug and stylish, although as a tribute to its previous owner, Penny had had an attractive, efficient gas fireplace installed. She used it occasionally to provide atmosphere and comfort. She switched it on now, settled in her wing chair, took out the cutting Mrs. Lloyd had given her, and lifted Harrison onto her lap.

She stroked him as she read the article, holding the photo of Emma closer to the light so she could see it better and sitting for several minutes thinking about her. Her kindness. Her love of music. How she had taken young backpacker Penny under her wing all those years ago, cared for her, and in a final loving act, given her the security her own family never had. She blinked as her eyes began to fill with tears. While it had been kind of Mrs. Lloyd to think of her, she had many photos of Emma, and one beautiful painting, and didn't think she needed a photocopy of this article. She folded the cutting. As she did so, a headline on the back of the article caught her attention. MINER FOUND DEAD. She turned the cutting over and started to read.

When she had finished reading the story, she ran her hands down Harrison's soft, fluffy head and tufted his ears. "Well, well, Harrison," she said. "Do you think this death has any relevance to Glenda's? I'll bet you a tin of your favourite salmon it does. We just have to work out what the connection is." She turned the cutting over again to see the date. September 15, 1971.

Setting it to one side, she turned on the television to watch the news updates on the storm. The announcer, sounding serious, repeated police warnings to stay off the roads unless travel was absolutely necessary. Describing the storm as one of the worst to hit British coastal areas in decades, he provided updates on flooded low-lying areas, disruptions to railway service, and downed trees and power lines.

Thankful she was safely home, Penny opened the freezer and took out a ready meal to microwave for dinner.

As she set it on the worktop, her phone rang.

"Hello."

She listened while Sgt. Bethan Morgan explained that she had been asked to stay in the area overnight. As the storm was expected to intensify, she might get called out again and wondered if she could come to Penny for a cup of coffee and possibly, a little sleep.

"Of course," Penny said. "Come whenever suits you. I'm here."

There's just one thing, Bethan warned her. She was under strict orders not to discuss the Glenda Roberts case.

Penny laughed. "Oh, I'm sorry to hear that. I was looking forward to telling you what I've just discovered, but I guess I won't be able to now. Since we're not allowed to discuss the case."

Nineteen

It took every bit of Penny's strength to hold the door open against the force of the wind so Bethan Morgan could slip past her and enter the cottage.

"What a night!" said Bethan, removing her wet overcoat and handing it to Penny. "Honestly, this is the worst gale I've seen since I started the job. Just awful. Worst weather in decades, apparently. And we're getting so many reports of flooded roads. Really dangerous, filthy conditions out there. I just hope people will take our advice and stay home."

"Well, let's get you sorted. We'll hang your coat up by the Rayburn to dry out. What can I get you? Tea? Coffee? Something to eat? Soup?" Penny asked as she closed the curtains against the storm. The wind rattled the windowpane as pelting raindrops hurled themselves against it.

"What I'd really like is scrambled eggs, if you've got them in. They're my favourite comfort food."

"Not a problem. I've actually got a few eggs on hand and a bit of cheese, too. And we'll get the kettle on."

"Perfect. I could murder a cup of tea."

Penny pulled eggs out of the refrigerator and set them on the counter. "I've never been able to get into the British habit of keeping eggs at room temperature," she remarked. "To me, they belong in the fridge."

Bethan shrugged. "Doesn't bother me. They taste great either way."

Twenty minutes later Bethan was seated at the table tucking into a plate of creamy scrambled eggs with slices of buttered toast. "Mmm," she murmured. "Really hitting the spot."

She took a sip of tea. "Right. I know you've been dying to tell me what you've found out." She took a bite of toast.

"Well, first of all, is there any news on Doreen? Did the autopsy . . . ?"

"Nothing unusual there," Bethan said. "That is, nothing out of the ordinary. There was a slight mark on her neck but the pathologist didn't think it was anything to be concerned about. Could have been caused by something as simple as a tight collar."

"So her death was just an unfortunate follow-up to Glenda? Poor Rebeccah. Losing her mother and her sister so closely together."

"It happens," said Bethan. "Look at the Queen. She lost her sister and her mother really close together. About six weeks apart, I think. Something like that."

Penny nodded. "I guess. It just seemed like too much of a coincidence."

"Oh, we're thinking along those lines, too," said Bethan. "The slate that was found in the hands of each of the victims seems to tie the two deaths together." She pushed some egg onto her fork. "We're looking into that."

Before Penny could respond, Bethan went on. "You know that the DCI really values your input, but he has to follow procedures. And if someone like you got overinvolved in a case and corrupted evidence, say, the whole case could be lost, and a guilty person could walk free. We really don't want that."

"I understand," said Penny. "And of course both of you are always professional in every way."

"Right, well now that we got that out of the way, tell me what you found out."

"It's not directly related to Glenda's murder," Penny began, "but there might be something here that's of interest to you." She handed Bethan the newspaper cutting and pointed to the small article.

"There. MINER FOUND DEAD. Read that and see what you think."

" 'The body of a thirty-seven-year-old miner was found in a side tunnel of the Llyn Du mine this morning. Gwillym Thomas, who was pronounced dead at the scene, leaves behind a wife and two small children. North Wales Police are treating the death as suspicious.'

"And what's the date on this?" Bethan asked turning the cutting over. "Oh, here it is. September 1971." She thought for a moment. "Not sure if this ties in with our case, but I'll make a note of it and we can look into it." She put her fork down and looked at Penny.

"Why do you think this might be important? Have you heard of this man? Penny, this happened a long time ago."

"No, I haven't heard of this man," said Penny. "And I don't know for sure if this is important. But the mine setting may be significant in some way."

"It may be," agreed Bethan, "but I'm sure a lot of people have died down there over the years."

"Oh, they have. In mining accidents. But why was Glenda murdered there I ask myself?" She gave a little shrug. "Well, I just thought I'd pass it on for what it's worth, that's all."

"I've noted it," said Bethan. "I'll mention it to the DCI, and if he thinks it warrants a closer look, then we'll look into it."

She sat back in her chair and rubbed her eyes. "Is there any more tea in the pot?"

Penny lifted the lid and peered in. "Just about. I'll get more hot water."

Just as Bethan started on her second cup of tea, a strong gust of wind shook the cottage, lifting up the slates on the roof. They settled back down with a clatter. The two women looked at each other.

"This storm is making me a bit nervous," said Penny. "I've never seen anything like it. I've always felt safe and sheltered here, but tonight . . ." The savage wind picked up at that moment, sending a howling blast swirling around the cottage while the rain drummed harder on the windows. "I hope this storm won't prove too much for the cottage."

"This cottage has stood here for a hundred years, Penny, and it'll be here tomorrow. But there's a good chance you could lose your power. I think we'd better start charging your phone and laptop. Torches with batteries are safer than candles, but let's start gathering up whatever you've got. And make sure the Rayburn is well-stoked and you've got lots of coal in. That's the great thing about a Rayburn. They give off a bit of light but more importantly, heat. And you can always brew a cup of tea or heat up some soup when others can't cook." They got up from the table and went to the kitchen. "Oh, and just to be on the safe side," said Bethan, "let's fill some containers with water so there's some to drink or for tea making. We don't know how bad this storm is going to be or how long it's going to last."

They gathered up the supplies Bethan had suggested and checked the torch to make sure the batteries worked. "I'll leave it here on the table," she said. "And when this is over, be sure to get in some new batteries so you're prepared for next time. We could be in for more weather like this."

Penny nodded and sat down. As she did so, Bethan's phone rang. She pressed the button and listened. "Right. On my way."

Penny stood up. "No rest for you, then."

"Afraid not. The Conwy River has burst its banks and a man and his dog have been swept away."

"Oh, no!"

"Why on earth people insist on walking there in this dangerous weather I will never know. But they do. It makes me so mad. And now we have to put our lives at risk to rescue them."

"Sometimes the dog gets swept away and the human goes in to save the dog," Penny said.

"Yeah, and the dog climbs out further along the bank and the human drowns. Well, I hope that won't happen this time."

"I hope not, too."

Bethan pulled on her coat. "We weren't finished with him."

"Him?" asked Penny.

"It's Ifan Williams, the choirmaster. We had a few more questions for him about Glenda Roberts. Apparently they didn't get on very well."

She opened the door and said, "Well, thank you for dinner."

"Take care, Bethan. I mean it. Be very careful."

The police officer started her car, turned on the windscreen wipers, and started to reverse. The car's headlights illuminated the slanting rain driven by the moaning wind and then picked up the figure of Penny running toward the car, holding a raincoat above her head. Bethan lowered the window.

"Take this." Penny held her hand through the window and shouted to be heard above the storm. "It's the key to the cottage. Come back when you've finished. You'll be tired and coming here will save you the drive home. You know where the spare room is."

With a wide grin, Bethan took the key and Penny ran back into the house.

She closed the door against the night, and grateful for her cozy, comfortable sitting room picked up the phone just as the lights went out.

Twenty

As the early morning light filtering under the window blind signalled the start of a new day, Penny flicked the switch on her bedside lamp. Nothing. She picked up her phone and checked the time: 7:47. She pushed back the duvet and shivered as the frosty air made contact with the exposed skin of her bare legs. Not bothering to remove her nightdress, she pulled a heavy jumper over her head and stepped into a pair of long thermal underwear that she normally wore only on winter sketching trips. Even the clothes were cold and it would take a few minutes for her body heat to warm them to a comfortable temperature. She stepped out into the hall and at the top of the stairs, she reached for the light switch before remembering that there was no power. So holding the railing, in the dim light, she crept downstairs. Bethan's police-issue boots, caked in mud and bits of grass, sat forlornly on the mat in front of the door. She hadn't heard Bethan come in, but was glad she had. She must be exhausted. Penny had put an extra blanket on the bed in the spare room the night before and hoped Bethan had been warm enough.

When Penny had arrived in Britain over two decades ago very few houses had central heating and winters were long and cold indeed. Sitting rooms were heated with one or two-bar electric heaters or a coal fire. People huddled around the fire, and dried clothes on wooden racks in front of it. When you left the room you closed the door behind you to keep the heat in, and then hurried through an unheated hallway to get to another room. Kitchens were warm from cooking, but bedrooms were usually unheated and always freezing. Her cottage had been like that until the recent renovation. And now, with the power out, she was very glad she had kept the elderly, but still serviceable Rayburn cooker.

Penny filled a pot with water and set it on the Rayburn. With the well-banked Rayburn, she was better off than most people in a power cut. As Bethan had said, she had heat and the means to cook when other people did not.

Leaving the water to boil for coffee, she turned her attention to the refrigerator. She pulled out a half-full carton of milk that should still be okay for coffee and cereal. And thanks to the Rayburn, they could make toast under the grill.

Of course there was no television for news of the storm, which seemed to have blown itself out, and its aftereffects, but she could probably find something on her phone, which, she remembered, she had left on her bedside table. Should she go back upstairs to get it and risk waking Bethan? Bethan had had a late night, so it might be better to let her sleep. And while she was wondering what to do, Bethan herself answered the question. Footsteps overhead signalled that she was up and about and a few minutes later she opened the door to the kitchen and closed it quickly behind her.

"Oh, thank God for the Rayburn—it's nice and warm in here! Morning, Penny."

"Morning, Bethan. Did you sleep all right? Were you warm enough? I'm just organizing breakfast. There's toast and cereal. Fruit in the bowl. Coffee. What can I get you?"

"Coffee and toast would be wonderful, thanks."

"We'll eat in the kitchen where it's warm," said Penny. She handed Bethan a cup of coffee. Bethan, wearing a pair of navy cargo pants and a ribbed police jumper with shoulder patches and a crest on the left shoulder, leaned against the counter.

"Well, I expect you want to know about Ifan Williams," she said. "It's good news and bad news. He'd managed to get himself out of the river by the time we arrived, but his dog was not so lucky. He was swept downstream. There wasn't much we could do in the dark, at the height of the storm."

"Oh, no."

"Yeah, we all felt bad about that. But we mustn't give up hope. He was young and a good size, so he may have been able to climb out on his own." She gave Penny a reassuring, professional smile. "Let's hope so, eh? I told Ifan what we always say in these circumstances—try not to worry too much. But you could see that he was really distressed."

"Well, I'm glad Ifan's okay. I rang Victoria last night to tell her about him and his dog going in the river and she was beside herself because if anything had happened to Ifan, she would have had to take over the music part of the program. Choir and musicians. All the arrangements, including practices." Penny gave a light laugh. "She said all the things that are going wrong with this concert are starting to cause her to lose the will to live.

119

Because after Glenda, I ended up agreeing to organize the concert. Did you know that?"

"Can you cancel it? I'm sure people would understand."

"We discussed that, and I wish we could, but there are too many contracts already in place. So, no, this show must go on. And not because we're determined, spirited troupers and all that, but because we have no other financial choice. If we cancelled, we'd still be liable for a lot of payouts, so we have to hold the concert to cover the costs. We can't find any indication there was cancellation insurance."

"I see. Well, would it help if I bought a ticket?"

"It sure would! I've got about seventy-five more to sell. Sales haven't exactly been brisk, despite Glenda's optimistic promotion. We really need to get the word out."

"Well, I'll see what I can do. If you've got a poster, maybe I can put it up at the station. And you know, pensioners who are fit enough might like to go. Many of them, I'm sure, have long family ties to that mine. It was such a big part of the economy of this area."

"You're right about that. Rhian's grandfather worked down there."

"Rhian? Oh, right. The receptionist at the Spa."

"That's her. She said her granddad would have been appalled by the very idea of holding a concert down that mine. I guess having worked there he sees it as being nothing more than a dark, damp, claustrophobic place that sucked the life out of everybody."

Bethan looked at her watch. "Have to think about getting ready to leave. It's going to be a busy day as the storm cleanup begins. I wonder, do you have an old brush or something I can use to clean the mud off my boots? I'll do it outside."

Penny reached under the sink and retrieved a brush with stiff wire bristles. "Here, try this. I use it on my boots sometimes when I'm back from a sketching ramble."

"Great." Bethan took the brush, put on her overcoat, and then looked down at her feet in their warm woolen socks. The two women walked to the hall and Penny picked up a pair of green Wellies and handed them to Bethan. "Here. These should do," she said. She pulled on her coat and a pair of hiking books and the two women stepped outside into a damaged landscape. Her garden looked as if a ruthless giant had taken a scythe to most of the wintering bushes and trampled on whatever plants remained. Small branches littered the walkway. But the air smelled fresh and renewed.

Bethan held a boot away from her body and began attacking it with strong, swift strokes. For a moment, the only sound was the scratching, scraping sound of the wire bristles. And then Penny spoke.

"About Glenda. I can't stop thinking about the mine. I can't work out why she was killed there, of all places. Have you considered that the mine might have had a special significance to the killer? And the slate was left in her hand as a kind of calling card?"

Bethan paused, the boot covering one hand and the raised brush in the other.

"We can't go there, Penny. We can't think like that. The DCI told me about that kind of thinking ages ago, and in recognizing the dangers of it he was a bit ahead of his time."

Penny frowned. "What do you mean?"

"It's called confirmation bias and it's very dangerous in some lines of work. Like policing. Or journalism. Or intelligence." She took a half-hearted swipe with the brush. "It's a psychological thing. It means the tendency to accept evidence that confirms our beliefs and to reject evidence that contradicts them. It's a filter that we all use to make sure reality—as we perceive it—fits with our expectations. In other words, people search for information that confirms their view of the world and ignore what doesn't fit."

"Sorry, I'm not following."

"Okay. Here's an example. I saw this on telly recently. An American sheriff's deputy called 911 to report that his girlfriend had just shot herself. The evidence didn't show suicide; the evidence suggested homicide and in my opinion, led directly to him. But the police could not accept the evidence because they could not bring themselves to believe that one of their own could possibly do such a thing. So they ignored the facts that pointed to homicide and accepted the suicide theory. They twisted the facts to make them fit what they wanted to believe."

"So are you saying that people see what they want to see and disregard the rest?" asked Penny.

"Something like that. And we all do it, this confirmation bias. Sometimes we do it to hide a truth we cannot face or accept."

"Like the wife who ignores signs her husband is cheating on her."

"Quite possibly. We had to do a course on this. It's to do with perception. Perception is reality. Let me see if I can remember how it works. Because Every Person Counts. That's the little mnemonic I made up to help me remember. BEPC. Beliefs shape expectations, which in turn shape perceptions, which then shape conclusions. Thus we see what we expect to see and conclude what we expect to conclude.

"So when police officers approach a case believing something to have happened or to be true—and it's not true—under this theory, they twist the evidence to support their theory. And that leads to all kinds of problems, like the wrong person being charged, or a terrific waste of time and resources.

"Sorry this is turning into a lecture, but what I'm really saying here is I don't know if Glenda's death had anything to do with the mine. The investigation might take us back there. Or it might not. We don't go into an investigation with theories . . . we let the facts lead us to the truth." Bethan looked a little sheepish and resumed brushing the last of the mud off her boot. "Or at least we try to. We try to keep intuition and hunches out of it. They keep reminding us not to get obsessed with an idea, no matter how clever we think it is."

Penny glanced up at the winter sky, threatening more rain in the distance, and then she gazed at the hills, their tops shrouded in mist, rolling away into the distance. She then turned to go back in the house.

"I still think the murder had something to do with the mine," she said over her shoulder.

"Why do you think that?" Bethan asked.

"It's a hunch. You're not allowed to have them. But I am. And I think it would be a good idea for you to revisit the mine and ask yourselves, 'Why here?'"

Bethan raised the brush one last time and then slowly lowered her hand.

"Why do you say that?"

"Because there must have been easier places. That mine is just so . . . challenging. I think the killer chose the mine to make a point." Penny smiled. "And I think that's what the slate in the hands is telling us. But that's just my theory. You can take it or leave it."

Bethan gave her boot one last smack with the brush, picked up its mate, and joined Penny inside the cottage. A few minutes later, with a cheery wave, she drove off.

With the power still out in her cottage, Penny called Victoria and was told that the power had not yet been restored to the Spa, either, but Rhian was coming in anyway. Today would be a good day to tidy things up and sort things out and she could do that in natural light without the distraction of the day-to-day running of the business.

Twenty-one

The massive extent of the storm damage was breathtaking. Downed trees, their branches broken and huge roots clotted with dark, wet soil, blocked main roads and country lanes. Fields lay under water and frightened, bleating sheep, many of them heavily pregnant, huddled together on the highest bit of land they could find. Upstream, a huge, ancient rock formation battered by ferocious storm-force wind and waves had been reduced to rubble and hundreds of homes had been flooded.

Her feet warm and dry in Wellies, Penny crossed the town's bridge, which had fortunately withstood the storm, but instead of going to the Spa, she turned down the road that ran along the swollen river and led to the nursing home.

After a few words with the receptionist, she walked to the lounge where the residents gathered after breakfast to chat, watch television, or just sit. This morning, the televison was silent and although the curtains on the north-facing windows had been fully opened, not much natural light got in. As an artist, Penny knew the impact light has on mood and was not surprised that the atmosphere in the dimly lit room was gloomy and dreary.

She spotted Jimmy in the corner, and as she had hoped, he was sitting with Dylan Phillips.

"There aren't many men in this place," Jimmy had told her. "I get along fine with Dylan. He's good company." He was also Rhian Phillips's grandfather, a retired miner, and the man Penny had really come to see.

"Morning," she smiled at the two. "Well, look, I'll come right to the point. Mr. Phillips, I wonder if I could ask you a few questions about your days down the mine. It's about Gwillym Thomas. I don't know if you remember him, but I came across an old newspaper cutting and it mentioned that he'd been found dead down the mine. I wondered if you remembered that incident. Apparently he had a head wound. Was it an accident?"

"Well, let me see. That was a long time ago." Dylan shifted in his chair. "I honestly don't remember too much about it." He smiled. "When you get to our age, your memory isn't what it was."

"Do you remember the man at all?" Penny asked. "Can you remember anything about him personally?" She thought for a moment and then answered the question herself. "The newspaper said he was married with two small children. The article gave his age as thirty-seven."

"The thing is, see, so many of us worked down the mine back then," Dylan said. "I vaguely remember him, I guess. Big fellow. Liked to sing."

"Oh, come on. You can do better than that, surely," said

Jimmy. "Every Welshman likes to sing. This death must have been a big event in the mine. Everyone must have been talking about it."

Dylan waited a few moments before responding.

"The work was organized so that you worked with the same few men in separate chambers. We arrived together, worked together, ate lunch down there together, and left together. Most of those groups were men who were related to one another. Brothers, uncles, cousins, fathers, and sons. We didn't really mix with the others or get to know them all that well."

Dylan shook his head. "No, sorry, that's about all I can think of at the moment."

Jimmy and Penny's eyes locked as he gave her a shrewd look. Then, Penny thanked Dylan for his time and got up to leave. Jimmy watched and waited. When Penny reached the receptionist's desk, nodded good-bye, and then disappeared out the front door he turned to his companion.

"Why'd you lie to her?"

"Who says I was lying?" Dylan shifted in his chair.

"Of course you bloody were. You think I can't tell when someone's lying? I worked with liars all my life and they were a damn sight better at it than you, mate. So I'm asking again. Why'd you lie to her?"

"Because sometimes the truth does more harm than good." Dylan made a small pleading gesture with an upturned hand. "Look, all that happened a long time ago. What's the point in raking it all up again? Stirring up all those buried hatreds now won't do any good. It won't bring anyone back. Thousands of men worked down that mine over the years and they're all gone. Including the ones I worked with. For God's sake, let them rest in peace."

"Well, I think you'll find this isn't going to go away. This won't be the end of it."

Dylan shrugged. "It is as far as I'm concerned."

"No, Dylan, it isn't. See, here's the thing. When people are lied to, it just makes them more curious—more determined to ferret out the truth. And I know her. She's not going to let this go."

"And what business is it of hers, I'd like to know." The two sat in silence for a moment.

"I've got one more thing to say," said Jimmy, "and then I'm going to leave it alone. Those men who died down there, including the one Penny was on about. How do you know they're resting in peace? If there's unfinished business that needs sorting, maybe now's the time for you to . . ."

"I wish they'd let us smoke in here," Dylan interrupted.

"Why? What do you care? You don't smoke."

"Gave it up must be forty years ago," agreed Dylan. "But I'd like one now."

Jimmy said nothing and the two sat for a few minutes, each with his own thoughts. And then Jimmy spoke.

"I hear it's your birthday in a few days. How old will you be?"

"Eighty-three. But I'm not looking forward to it."

"No?"

"After what happened to poor Doreen? Of course I'm not."

Twenty-two

"Penny thinks we need to take a closer look at the Llyn Du mine." Bethan set a mug of tea on Davies's desk. He took a sip, squared the papers on his desk, took off his glasses, and rubbed his eyes.

"Does she now."

"I explained the confirmation bias theory to her and said we couldn't look at the mine just to make a theory fit the facts. I think she thought it was all a load of tosh."

"It is a load of tosh, if it prevents us from investigating something that may prove relevant. It could very well be that we do need to look deeper into the mine."

"After I'd had a chance to think about what she said, I was leaning toward agreeing with her," Bethan said. "She said we should be asking ourselves why Glenda was murdered in the mine because there must have been easier places for the killer. And she was on about the slate in Glenda's hand."

She flipped open her notebook. "Penny found a cutting about an incident that happened in 1971. The body of a Gwillym Thomas was found dead in a side tunnel. Head injuries. Police at the time described the situation as suspicious."

"Right. Well, look into it. Find out what happened there. And see if there's anything we can learn from it that will help us with the Roberts case. Sometimes revisiting an old case sheds a brighter light on a new case."

As Bethan got up to go, he added, "It happened so long ago you might need a trip to the archives. I doubt the reports going back that far will have been computerized. If you do find the files, sign them out and bring them here. I wouldn't mind a look at them myself."

Bethan had mixed feelings about old files and evidence boxes. On one hand, she liked the idea that they were complete and she liked seeing the artifacts for themselves, but on the other, there were always a lot of things in those plastic bags you didn't really want to see, never mind touch, even wearing gloves.

"Oh, and we need to reinterview the choir leader, what was his name again?" Davies asked.

"Ifan Williams," replied Bethan.

"Right. I'm not satisfied he's telling us the whole truth. Let's see if we can get him to tell us what he's been leaving out."

At first light, Ifan Williams had pulled on his anorak and Wellies and headed for the river. Where last night the water had been high and churning, in the still greyness just after dawn it was calmer, but still much higher than it should be and fast flowing.

The water level had receded somewhat, leaving the banks muddy and slippery. He walked downstream, picking his way along the top of the bank, looking down at the river and stopping every few feet to check the tall grass and call for his lost dog.

"Taff! Taff!"

After an hour, he reluctantly headed back the way he had come. He'd go home, change his socks, check his home phone in case someone had spotted Taff, and then come back to search the bank on the other side of the river.

His eyes raked the path that led to his bungalow and as he hurried up the path that led to his home, his heart pounding, he whispered, "Let him be there, let him be there." He imagined Taff waiting for him on the steps, tail wagging, eyes bright, and his lips pulled back in what Ifan thought of as a smile. But he wasn't. Ifan pushed open the door. His heart lurched at the sight of Taff's half-empty water bowl.

He threw his keys on the table, tossed his coat on the back of a chair, and slouched into his sitting room where he picked up an almost empty bottle of Scotch whisky and tipped the last of it into a used glass. He drained it in one large gulp and wiped his eyes. He feared the worst, dread clawing at his heart, but was still holding out hope for the best. His eyes, raw and stinging from lack of sleep, made him look like a warehouse rat. He'd been awake all night wondering where Taff was and praying he'd somehow made it out of the river and safely to shore. Maybe someone had found him and taken him in and was looking after him. Maybe he was injured and lying on the bank waiting for Ifan to find him and take him home. If he hadn't made it out alive, Ifan prayed the end had been quick and that poor Taff hadn't suffered. Ifan was buried under a mudslide of fear and guilt. All the bad choices he'd made. The decisions, one after another, that had led to this. To take Taff out in that weather. To walk so close to the river. To let him off his lead. He hadn't realized just how bad conditions were and that the daft dog would head for the river. He couldn't turn off the horrific images that played out in an endless loop in his mind of Taff's heroic struggles in the water. The thought of how frightened he must have been brought instant tears to his eyes.

He picked up the empty bottle. He'd have to get more whisky. But first, there was something else to sort. A choir practice was scheduled for tonight and feeling the way he was, he couldn't possibly take it. Maybe, in light of yesterday's weather, it would be cancelled anyway, but he doubted that. If it had been last night, then, yes, it would have been cancelled for sure, but there was no reason why it shouldn't go ahead tonight. The concert was in three weeks and the choir and musicians were nowhere near ready.

A flush of anger spread through him. That cow Glenda Roberts. All that misery she'd caused during the Jubilee event, blaming him for everything that went wrong when none of it had been his fault. And now, she'd gone and got herself killed. He wouldn't go as far as to say she deserved it, because no one deserved to be murdered, but still. All the disruption and up-heaval her death had caused to the concert organizing, not to mention the personal cost. Bloody typical of the selfish bitch.

The police questioning him. Telling him he was free to go but he must not leave the area as they would likely want to speak to him again.

Of course he'd been down the mine that morning. The whole point was to go over the arrangements. He'd need to see for himself where the choir would be placed, try out the acoustics, and work out how to organize everybody.

It was bad enough trying to herd everybody at a local church, never mind down a mine. Which had been Glenda's idea. For that alone, some people might think she deserved what she got. He'd better ring Victoria and let her know he couldn't make it tonight.

And then he'd get back to what really mattered. Where his heart was.

Twenty-three

"He lied to me."

Penny pulled a white towel from the stack in the linen cupboard and placed it on a tray. "Who lied to you?" asked Victoria, leaning against the wall.

"Dylan Phillips. Rhian's grandfather. I asked him if he could remember anything about Gwillym Thomas, the miner who was found dead down the mine in 1971. He was evasive. He didn't answer my questions."

"Well, maybe he couldn't."

"Oh, I'm sure he could. He's sharp enough on everything else. He lied by omission."

"Or perhaps he just chose not to answer your questions, for reasons best known to him. Like, maybe, he thought it was none of your business. And anyway, what makes you so sure he lied to you?"

"I could tell by the look on Jimmy's face. Jimmy's really good at reading people and he knew he was lying. He even tried to give him a bit of a prod."

"Maybe Dylan was exhibiting older person selective memory syndrome."

"Older person selective memory syndrome? What on earth is that?"

"Something I just made up. My gran used to do that. Ask her a question she didn't mind answering and her memory would be just fine. Ask her the wrong question, about something she didn't want to discuss, and it was, 'Oh, when you get to my age your memory isn't what it used to be.'"

"That's practically word for word what Dylan said."

"Well, maybe he was hiding something, then, but why would he?"

"Because he had something to do with the death of Gwillym Thomas himself or he was covering for someone else?"

"Did you talk to Jimmy about it?"

"No, I couldn't really and I'm not sure there was any point. I just got up and left."

Victoria sighed. "Well, I'm sorry, but we've got more important things to think about here. If the power isn't restored by lunchtime, we'll lose all our afternoon clients, too. You don't realize how much you depend on electricity until it's gone. Every two seconds I want to check something on the computer and I can't. We can't even access our bookings to know who's scheduled to come in this afternoon so we can call them. That was one good thing about the old appointment book. At least you could read it during a power cut."

"And we can't do hair without a hair dryer or give someone a manicure because we can't sterilize tools," said Penny. "It's getting close to lunchtime now. Even when the power does come back, it'll take about an hour to get everything up and running and to get the staff in."

"Well, look," said Victoria, "There's no point in both of us hanging around here. If you've got other things to do, why don't you take off and Rhian and I will hold the fort. The minute the power comes back, we'll let you know."

"That sounds sensible," said Penny. "I'll come back as soon as you ring me."

"I hope the power comes back soon," said Victoria, "or all our phones will be dead. Mine's desperate for a charge."

As Penny put her coat on, Rhian entered her office.

"Could I have a word, please, Penny?" she asked.

"Yes, of course. What is it? Is everything all right?" Rhian frowned and looked away.

"I'm sorry, but my Mum rang me. She said you'd been asking questions about something that happened down the mine a long time ago and it kind of upset my grandfather. So I just wanted to ask you to not speak to him again about that, whatever it was. He's old and he doesn't want to talk about those days."

"Oh, of course. I'm so sorry, Rhian, I didn't realize it was a bad topic. I feel terrible."

"It's all right. I know you didn't mean any harm by it."

"No, of course I didn't."

"Right, well . . ." The awkward, uncomfortable silence swallowed any unsaid words and a few moments later, Rhian left. Penny made a little grimace and picked up her handbag. Why, she wondered. Why did he find it so hard to talk about? What had happened down there?

Sgt. Bethan Morgan dropped a file on DCI Gareth Davies's desk. "There's some interesting reading in there," she said, tapping the documentation on the old Gwillym Thomas case. "Nobody saw anything, nobody heard anything, nobody knew anything. The investigation went nowhere. You have to wonder why.

"But here's the really interesting thing. The victim had a head wound and it's described in practically the same way as the wound on Glenda Roberts's head. But this pathologist back in 1971," she tapped the file, "was able to suggest what caused it."

Davies looked up.

"Now you've really got my attention. What was it?"

"A slate splitter."

Twenty-four

There's a saying in Wales that if you don't like the weather, wait ten minutes. By lunchtime, the mist had lifted from the hills and a pale but determined sun was peeking through scattered clouds. Although the powerful winds and lashing rain of the previous night had left violent destruction in their wake, the storm was definitely over and an eerie calm had descended on the valley.

Penny crossed the bridge that spans the River Conwy and spotting her friend Bronwyn Evans, the rector's wife, downstream gave her a wave. She couldn't see Robbie, Bronwyn's Cairn terrier, but had no doubt he was with her, nosing about in the long grass. You rarely saw Bronwyn without him. Bronwyn returned her wave enthusiastically. As Penny moved away, she thought she heard Bronwyn calling her name and turned around. Penny now realized Bronwyn wasn't giving her a friendly wave, but making a broad, come-here gesture with both hands that stopped Penny in her tracks and sent her hurrying along the path toward her friend.

"What's the matter, Bronwyn? Are you all right?" she called.

"No, I'm not. Look! Robbie's found an injured dog. I think its front leg is broken." Lying at her feet was a wet, mangled, red-and-white Welsh collie. His eyes were closed.

"Is he alive?" Penny asked. "Oh, Lord! I think that's Ifan's dog. I heard the two of them went in the river last night. Ifan got out safely, but this has to be his dog. What a shame."

She bent over and stroked the dog's cold, wet fur and then felt his chest. "His heart's beating, but we've got to hurry. He's probably been here all night." She stood up, took off her coat and covered the dog. "I'll run back to the Spa and get some towels and a blanket and tell Victoria to get the car ready so we can take him to Jones the vet. You stay here with him. When I get back we'll try to carry him across the bridge together."

Bronwyn crouched down to comfort the dog and as she turned to go, Penny spotted the outline of an approaching figure. He was some way off, but she could tell from the way he walked, slowly, poking the grass with a stick and turning his head from side to side, that he was looking for something. She touched Bronwyn's shoulder.

"That looks like Ifan. Call him over as soon as you can and if this is his dog, perhaps the two of you can carry him to the Spa. We'll meet you on the other side of the bridge. That'll save us some time."

Moments later she burst through the door of the Spa and without noticing that the lights were on, raced down the hall to Victoria's office.

"Oh, you're back," said Victoria, looking up from her computer. "Good. I was just about to ring you to tell you the power's back on."

Penny glanced wildly around the room. "Oh, so it is. Well, never mind that right now. We've found an injured dog and we have to get him to the vet right away. Can you bring your car round to the door? Bronwyn should be arriving any moment with Ifan and the dog. I think he's pretty bad. He's been out all night and he's probably got hypothermia. And Bronwyn thinks his leg is broken."

Victoria jumped up and grabbed her keys. A few moments later she drove into sight just as Ifan and Bronwyn crossed the bridge. Ifan was carrying the dog, wrapped in Penny's coat as Bronwyn walked beside him, leading Robbie.

Penny opened the back door of the car and Ifan laid Taff tenderly on the backseat, then rushed round the other side to get in beside him. He cradled the dog's head in his lap as Penny climbed into the front passenger seat. Victoria reversed, then drove away, leaving Brownyn and Robbie looking anxiously after them.

"A slate splitter?" Davies pronounced the words slowly, enunciating each syllable.

Bethan nodded. "Apparently it's a flat, sharp tool, used with a mallet, to split blocks of slate into thinner and thinner slices. The block would be halved, then halved again and again, until the pieces are the right thickness for a roofing slate or whatever it's going to be used for."

"Right, well, let's get back to the mine and see what else we can learn about this slate splitter. And we'll need to gather up every one they've got for DNA testing. And to show the pathologist to see if that could be our murder weapon."

Bethan parked the car and the two walked into the reception area and asked for the manager. A few minutes later, Bevan Jones appeared, his hand extended to Davies. He smiled at Bethan.

"How can I help you today?"

"We'd like to ask a few questions about slate splitting," Davies said. "And then I'd like to see the tools that are used."

"No problem," Bevan said. "Follow me." He led them out the door, past the café that Davies recognized from his previous visit, and through a large open door into a single-storey building. It consisted of one very large room with a high ceiling supported by exposed rafters. "Here we have the saw house and dressing shed combined." He pointed to a fearsome machine in the corner, sitting idle. "That's the saw used to cut the big blocks of slate. And once the slate is a manageable size, they're given to the splitter who splits them up into smooth, flat plates." He gestured at pieces of slate stacked up against a wall. "Bit of trivia for you. Although we consider slate to be the Welshest of industries because all the techniques and processes were devised here, there is no Welsh word for it. The word 'slate' comes from the old French esclater, to splinter or break off. And that's how we do it.

"Here, I'll just get Bryn to show you how it's done." He motioned to a man smoking outside. "Bryn, would you please show these two police officers how you do the slate splitting." He turned to the officers. "What Bryn Thomas here doesn't know about slate splitting isn't worth knowing."

Bryn dropped the cigarette and ground it out under the toe of his work boot. His boots were covered in a thin layer of fine grey dust as was the left leg of his denim work jeans. He wore a friendly, open expression but his dark blue eyes were guarded. A few grey curls framed his face on each side of a navy blue watchman's cap.

He sat on a low stool, stretched out his left leg, placed a rough piece of brown cloth over his thigh, and leaned a block of slate against it. He then picked up a tool that looked like a broad chisel with a short handle and a wooden mallet. He positioned the splitter on top of the slate, tapped it a few times, and then moved the splitter along. After four or five taps in different places, he was able to force the splitter deeper into the block of slate.

"Here it comes now," he said. "Almost there." A moment later, with a loud crack, the slate split in two. Each piece was the same size as the other, and half the thickness of the original piece.

"That's first-class roofing slate, that is," he said, holding up the two pieces of slate he had just split.

"Do you use your own tools?" Davies asked. "Or do they belong to the mine?"

"Oh, these belong to me," said Bryn. "They've been in my family for three generations. Handed down to me, they were. Slate splitting often runs in families, see. Some say it's more than a craft, that you need to have an instinctive feel for it. The father teaches the son, and so on."

"Did your father teach you?" Bethan asked.

"He did."

"Mr. Thomas, we're looking into the death of a Gwillym Thomas, who died at this mine in the early 1970s. Relative of yours, was he?"

Bryn bowed his head as he set the splitter and mallet on the ground. "My uncle, he was. I were just a nipper when he died.

I don't remember him." He straightened up. "My father never spoke of him. People didn't talk much about things like that back in those days. Or at least that generation of Welshmen didn't. Kept it all in here." He tapped his left chest.

"Mr. Thomas, where do you keep your tools?" Bethan asked. "When you're not using them."

He shrugged. "Well, I just leave them here in this room." He frowned. "Why? Do you think someone would want to steal them?" The guarded look returned to his eyes.

"Mr. Thomas, we're going to have to take them away for some testing. We'll try to return them to you as soon as we can."

"But what about the demonstrations?"

"Well, you'll have to discuss that with your manager," Bethan said.

"Thank you very much for your time this morning," said Davies. "We may need to talk to you again."

Bethan closed her notebook. "I was interested in what you said about fathers teaching this skill to their sons. Do you have a son you'll be teaching?"

Bryn shook his head. "I have a son, but I probably won't be teaching him slate splitting or anything else to do with the mine. He's only just young, but I expect he'll want to make his own way in life and that'll likely mean moving away. And breaking his mother's heart."

"Of course. They do that, don't they? Well, thanks again and we'll be in touch."

Bethan pulled two large evidence bags from her jacket pocket and dropped in the slate splitter and mallet. She and Davies exchanged a quick glance and Bethan nodded.

They found Bevan Jones waiting for them in the reception area a few minutes later.

144

"We need to know if there are any other slate splitters and mallets on the property," Bethan said. "If there are, we're going to need to take them away for forensic testing."

"There's a display slate splitter," said Bevan. "It's kept locked in the case in the education centre. You're welcome to take it. If you'll give me a moment, I'll get the key."

"And are there any others that you know of?" asked Davies. "We'll need them all."

"Any reported missing?" Bethan asked.

Bevan thought for a moment. "These old tools are hard to come by these days. Each splitter bought his own set of tools when he started the job, he used them all his working life, and took them with him when he retired. Or a man might use his father's or grandfather's tools. Most men took very good care of their tools because they had to last their working life or else they were inherited tools so had obvious sentimental value. And I think, too, there was a lot of pride wrapped up in them."

He paused for a moment and then spoke. "I'll get that key."

"Before you do," said Davies, "please answer my question. Has anyone reported a slate splitter missing or do you know if one is missing?"

"No. No one has reported one missing."

"And," Davies prompted. "Do you have personal knowledge that one is missing?"

Bevan shook his head. "No."

The two police officers waited until he'd gone and then Bethan turned to Davies.

"Evasion always troubles me," said Davies.

"And does it seem odd to you that Bryn Thomas would be so casual with his tools?" said Bethan. "If they've been handed down, why would he just leave them lying about where presumably any-one could take them."

"Why would anyone want them?" Davies asked.

Bethan peered at the tools in the evidence bag.

"To own a little bit of British industrial history? To kill Glenda Roberts?"

Twenty-five

"I'd better let Bethan know that Taff's been found," said Penny. She and Victoria were back at the Spa, having left Ifan with the vet to sort out his dog's care. Staff at the veterinary clinic had warmed Taff and were monitoring his vital signs carefully. Ifan had wept in the consulting room, both with gratitude to Penny, Victoria, and Bronwyn, and with relief that his lost dog had been found alive.

"But he's not out of the woods yet," the vet had warned, adding that Taff would have to be hospitalized and the next twenty-four hours would be critical. "But he's young and very fit, so he has that going for him. It goes without saying that we'll do everything we can." The vet had recommended that Ifan go home and get some sleep, but Ifan had asked if he could stay for a bit and told Penny and Victoria he'd make his own way home.

"Poor Ifan wasn't in very good shape," said Victoria. "I didn't know he drank, but you could really smell it on him. As things turned out, it was a good thing he'd already arranged for me to lead tonight's practice." She glanced at the calendar on her desk. "We've only got three weeks or so until the concert and there's still so much to do."

"Yikes!" said Penny. "You're right. Not much time. I'd better get in touch with the guest singer and make arrangements for her rehearsals and find out what she needs. By the way, I thought we'd offer to do her hair and give her a manicure here at the Spa. I'm assuming she does her own makeup, but I'll find out."

"Good idea. Oh, and when you're speaking to Bethan, ask her if there's anything new on the knockoff goods. A friend told me last night that fake Halen Môn salt has now turned up at the market."

"I wonder if there's any more of our stuff out there. I hate thinking of some crappy imitation being passed off as our beautiful cream."

"Me, too. The damage it can do to our reputation . . ."

"Right, well, I'll leave you to it."

Bethan answered her phone almost immediately and thanked Penny for the Taff update. When Penny asked about the counterfeit goods, she hesitated. That investigation is ongoing, she said, but a new line of inquiry had revealed some interesting information.

"We're working on that," Bethan said. "All the fake products that we've been able to uncover so far trace back to one local distributor. But I have a question for you. Did you sell a jar of your hand cream to Glenda Roberts?"

"I don't know. I'd have to ask Rhian. If anyone would know, she would. Just hang on a second." Penny put the phone down and went to find Rhian.

"Yes, in fact I sold her two. She said she wanted one for herself and one for her sister."

"Her sister doesn't strike me as the hand cream type."

"And I'm not sure Glenda strikes me as the thoughtful type who'd buy a jar of relatively expensive hand cream for her sister." Penny returned to her office and resumed her conversation with Bethan.

"Do you think Glenda was the distributor of these goods?"

"We'll know more once we've audited her bank accounts. Financial forensics. Apparently she had some good jewellery and apart from organizing events and just generally being useful in the community, we can't find that she had a real job of any sort. So she must have been getting her money from somewhere. We'd like to know where."

As Penny rang off, Rhian poked her head round the door. "Oh, good. You're off the phone. Just wanted to ask you . . . my grandfather's birthday is on Friday, and we're hoping you'll join us."

"Are you sure?" asked Penny, avoiding any reference to their previous exchange.

"Yes," said Rhian. "There's no hard feelings you know, Penny. We all know what you're like. Asking all the questions, like."

"Well, I'm sorry again that I upset your grandfather, Rhian, and I'd like very much to go to his party. We'll walk over together, shall we?" Rhian nodded and returned to her desk. Penny made a mental note to let Jimmy know she was coming. He'd asked her to always let him know when she was coming. "Old people don't like surprises," he'd told her. "A surprise robs us of the pleasure of anticipation and our days can use a little more pleasure."

Twenty-six

"Right, you lot," said the High Pastures' recreation director, also known as the third housekeeper, with false cheeriness. "Time to get ready for Dylan, today's birthday boy." She looked at the few people in the lounge. Two or three were asleep in their chairs after lunch and the rest seemed only vaguely interested.

"We need someone to sort the balloons. Who'd like to volunteer?"

"I'll do it," said Jimmy. "I've done it before and I know where they're kept." He wheeled himself down the corridor and into the crafts room. Shelves filled with neatly stacked rolls and sheets of coloured paper, plastic boxes filled with small tools, bottles of glue and glitter, rulers, artificial flowers, ribbons, and small embossing machines lined one wall. Miss Owens, an elderly resident seated at a table, did not look up as he entered, but kept her eyes on her work. Her scissors made little snipping sounds as

Jimmy opened the door of a cupboard and pulled three balloons from a box. Then he lifted out the helium gas canister and attached a balloon to it. It gave an empty little fizz and then nothing.

What the hell's the matter with it, thought Jimmy. He fiddled with the valve and gave the canister a thump. He'd filled the balloons for Doreen's party and there'd been plenty of helium in the tank when he'd finished. Maybe the staff had used the helium for a little party of their own.

He sat for a moment with the bright red tank on his lap. A staff member would just have to blow up the balloons because he doubted any of the residents had enough puff left in their lungs for the task. Unless there was another tank hidden in the cupboard somewhere. He bent over but didn't see another tank on a lower shelf, and it would be hard to miss. But something did catch his eye. He pulled out a large plastic bag with an adjustable Velcro strip around the opening. When he'd worked out its significance, he looked at the tank in his lap and regretting he had touched it, held it under the bottom and placed it back on the shelf. He set the plastic bag beside it, closed the door, and returned to the lounge where he waited for Penny to arrive.

He turned his head each time someone entered the lounge and finally, he saw her, entering with Rhian. She smiled and made her way over to him.

"All right, Jimmy?" she greeted him, giving his hand a friendly pat.

"Good, thanks Penny. But before things get started here, I've found something I want to show you. Come with me." Penny took the handle of Jimmy's wheelchair and pushed him toward the door of the day room.

"Where are we going?"

"Down the hall, here. To the crafts room. Straight on and I'll show you." A few minutes later he gestured at a door with a faded wreath made from dried flowers on it. "In here."

He nodded at Miss Owens who smiled a brief acknowledgement and then bent her head over her delicate scissoring. "Over here," he said to Penny pointing to a worktop with storage cupboards underneath. "Right." He opened the door. "That's the helium tank and behind it, there's a plastic bag. Probably best we don't touch anything."

"What about them, Jimmy? I don't understand what you're telling me."

"Come around in front of me here, Penny." He motioned to a small desk nearby with a chair. "Bring the chair over." She did as she was told and sat close to him.

"The bag that's there. It's not an ordinary bag. It's got a Velcro strap on it so you can fasten it."

"Fasten it?"

"Yes, you put it over your head and fasten it around your neck." He let that sink in for a moment and when Penny's puzzled eyes narrowed slightly, he continued.

"The helium tank is empty. I know it was almost full on the day of Doreen's birthday because I inflated the balloons for her party myself. That's my job. I fill the birthday balloons."

Penny glanced at Miss Owens who seemed engrossed in her work as she pushed the little pieces of cut paper into a neat pile with the edge of her hand. "I'm listening. Go on," said Penny.

"Well, the empty helium tank and the plastic bag—hood, really—makes me think we could be looking at assisted suicide."

"Sorry, I'm not with you."

"Doreen Roberts. The way we found her. She might have done an assisted suicide."

Penny's eyes widened. "What do you mean?"

"It could be a suicide kit. Helium's meant to be quick and painless. You put the plastic bag over your head, attach a tube to the helium tank, and feed the tube under the hood. Then, using the Velcro, you tighten the bag around your neck and turn on the helium. You breathe it in and the end comes quickly.

"Trouble is, if you don't want the suicide to be obvious, you need someone with you. The assistant is not supposed to touch any of the equipment or provide any help with the actual process. The helper's role is just to take away the equipment when it's all over. It mustn't be found with the body, so the death looks natural. And apparently, the helium isn't detected at the post-mortem."

"Oh, Jimmy," said Penny. "How do you know all this? No, don't tell me. I can guess."

"You just have to look around you when you're in a place like this, Penny," he said. "Almost everybody in here has considered this at one time or another. To some, it seems like a better alternative than being here for years, eating up the kids' inheritance. Some people live in places like this for three or four years. Or longer. And really, after a while you ask yourself, what's the point?"

"Did you ever hear Doreen Roberts talk about suicide?" Penny asked.

"No, but it wouldn't surprise me," said Jimmy. "See, there are two types of people in here—those whose minds have gone, but their bodies are still relatively strong, and those, like me, whose bodies don't work very well anymore but who've still got it up here." He tapped his temple with a forefinger. "Doreen was like that. She was pretty sharp, let me tell you. Not much got past her. And those are the kinds of people who might contemplate suicide. The ones who've had enough, realize that this is all there is and there's no going home, and one day they just can't take any more."

He spoke so softly that Penny had to lean forward to hear him. She glanced at Miss Owens, now engrossed in adding a touch of colour to her creation and hesitating before exchanging one pastel marker for another.

"Suicide as a theory just doesn't seem right to me," said Penny. "It doesn't make sense. Why would she commit suicide just before her birthday party? Wouldn't she wait until the party was over? Or, did she want to make sure her body was found quickly? She'd know that when she didn't turn up on time for the birthday party, someone would come looking for her."

Jimmy raised an eyebrow. "Or, there's the possibility that . . ."

"Someone gave her some unwanted assistance and it wasn't suicide at all," finished Penny.

"Either way, we need to inform the police," said Jimmy. "Suicide or otherwise. Because here's the thing: if someone took the tank away, someone else was there."

"And why would they just leave the bag here in the cupboard where it would be found sooner or later?" asked Penny. "Because they were in a hurry to get away or because they didn't care if it was found?"

Jimmy did not reply, but looked in the direction of Miss Owens.

"Maybe you should ask her if she saw anything. She's in here all day, every day. Makes the most beautiful greeting cards, by all accounts."

Penny exchanged a few words with Miss Owens and then returned to Jimmy.

"She says she's only seen residents and staff in here. But she admits that she doesn't always pay much attention to who comes and goes."

"So not a lot of help there."

"No. Let's think this through. If we call the police, we'll have to inform the staff," said Penny. "We can't just have the police turning up and the staff not know what's happening."

"We'll have to be careful how we do this. If we tell the staff, one of them could come in here and remove the stuff." Penny got up and took a picture of the cupboard's contents on her phone. "They might want to remove the stuff," she repeated, "if they thought one of their staff might be implicated in an assisted suicide. I don't know the legality of it."

"Oh, that's easy," said Jimmy. "Assisting someone in a suicide is illegal in Wales."

He straightened in his chair.

"I'm staying here until the police arrive," he said. "Close the cupboard door and push my chair back against it."

When Penny sat down again, he nodded. "Right, you call the police now and I'll wait here. Then tell a staff person that you've called the police and put in an appearance at the party. They'll be wondering where you've got to."

Penny left the room and a few minutes later a staff person entered the room, and asked Jimmy to move. He refused to budge, shooing her away with his hand.

"I'll move when the police get here," he said, "and not until."

When DCI Davies, followed by Sgt. Bethan Morgan, entered the room, he moved.

Twenty-seven

Florence Semble put the phone down and joined Mrs. Lloyd in the sitting room. "That was Penny," she said. "She's going to drop by in a few minutes to return your clipping." She sat down. "Now I want to talk to you about the St. David's Day gala."

"Oh, a gala now, is it? Last week it was just a concert."

"Well, gala. Concert and reception. We haven't got our tickets yet. Are you going?"

"I don't know that I'd want to go down to a mine to listen to some music. I'd feel a little anxious being in that hollowed-out space with all the weight of a mountain above me."

"That doesn't sound like you, Evelyn. Why, you're the most adventurous person I know."

"I am?"

"Course you are," said Florence. "Born to be wild!"

Mrs. Lloyd laughed. "Well, I don't know about that." She thought for a moment. "Perhaps we could buy two tickets—just to show our support—and not go?"

"That's not a good idea, Evelyn. If everybody did that, they'd have a sold-out concert with nobody to perform for. And we'd be dogs in the manger . . . keeping two tickets we knew we weren't going to use out of the hands of two people who might have enjoyed the concert. But it is a nice thought and I know your intention was good.

"No," Florence continued. "We'd be better off to buy the tickets and give them to people we know will go. Or, we should buy the tickets and go ourselves."

"All right. I'm persuaded. Let's take two tickets and we'll go."

"Good decision, Evelyn. Penny's dropping off our tickets in a few minutes."

"You what? I've only just decided that we're going."

"No, Evelyn, you've only just decided that you're going. I'd already made up my mind to go, and told Penny to bring two tickets just in case you wanted to come with me."

"I wonder what kind of music there'll be," said Mrs. Lloyd.

"Well, loads of Welsh music since it's St. David's Day," said Florence. "And maybe a bit of pop music, too. The guest singer is Karis Edwards. Do you remember her from the 1980s? Sang with a pop group called The Characters."

"I don't know anything about 1980s music," said Mrs. Lloyd. "As far as I'm concerned, there's been no decent pop music since the Beach Boys. Remember them Florence? Oh, how I longed to be a California Girl!" She laughed. "But of course, the Beatles are probably top of the pops with you, what with your little friendship with that John Lennon."

"We weren't friends, Evelyn, as you very well know. He was

a student at the art college when I worked there, that's all. Although I've often thought it interesting that the art school's most famous student should be known around the world for his music, not his art. But never mind. We . . ."

She was interrupted by the doorbell.

"Right. That'll be Penny. I'll go."

A few moments later Penny and Florence entered the sitting room. After greetings were exchanged, Penny set the newspaper cutting down on Mrs. Lloyd's worktable.

"That was interesting, Mrs. Lloyd, thank you," she said. "How's your memoir project coming along?"

"Well, it's taking much longer than I thought it would," Mrs. Lloyd replied. "So many documents and so on to sort through. I never realized how rich and full my life has been." She laughed. "Well, not as full as yours. I never travelled much. Stayed here at home. When I was young we thought a three-day coach trip to Brighton was all the thing. Nowadays, it seems everyone's on a cheap flight to Spain to drink themselves under the table for a week." She made a little scoffing noise.

"I've been wondering about something, Mrs. Lloyd. Can you think of anyone who might have wanted to harm Doreen Roberts?"

"Harm Doreen Roberts? Why would you ask that? Why would someone want to harm her? Is there something fishy about her death? I thought she just passed away peacefully."

"Well, something new has come to light, and the police aren't sure now if she committed suicide or someone . . ."

"Now it's suicide is it? I wouldn't have thought she'd be up for that, but really how can you know what someone is thinking? She may have been feeling low enough to do that, I wouldn't know. And as for someone harming her, I can't think of anyone now who might have wanted to, but back in her younger days, well, I'm sure two or three wives would have happily had a go."

"Wives? Really?"

"Yes, really. No man was off-limits for our Doreen. In fact, the man she married, Aled Roberts, he was married when she started working at the mine and apparently it wasn't long before they were carrying on. Then his wife died and a few months later they got married. And a few months after that Glenda arrived. And it wasn't nine months after, I can tell you that." She raised her eyebrows and nodded in a knowing way. "You can imagine what people thought of that back then. There was talk. How times have changed. These days, girls see having a baby at seventeen as the way to sign on for a lifetime of benefits."

Penny ignored the last remark.

"Doreen worked at the mine?"

"Yes, she worked in the office. Not exactly sure what she did there, but she used to come into the post office almost every day with parcels and letters. I used to see her regularly. Except for the times I didn't."

"What do you mean?"

"Well, she was a little ahead of her time, was Doreen. You see, back then, most single women worked and then quit when they got married. But a few kept working after they got married, but then quit when they had a baby. Doreen kept on working after Glenda was born. Her mother looked after Glenda. And she did the same thing after Rebeccah was born. And then a year or two after that, she had another baby, but sadly, that baby died."

"Oh, that is sad."

Florence was about to say something when Penny's phone rang. She knew from the ringtone that it was Victoria, so she excused herself, saying, "It might be business. Sorry, I'd better take this." She listened for a moment and then said, "That's great news. I'm so happy to hear this. Right. See you later."

Mrs. Lloyd beamed at her. "Always glad for good news, Penny."

"Indeed, this is wonderful news. Taff, Ifan Williams's dog, was found on the riverbank this morning in terrible shape, and we weren't sure if he was going to make it. Turns out he's improving rapidly and will be going home later today. The vet thought he'd have to keep him overnight in the surgery, but now they think Taff will do better at home."

"Oh, that is wonderful news," said Florence. "We hadn't heard about Taff, but we're so glad it's all turned out well."

"Well, the thing is, though, that understandably Ifan wants to stay home tonight and look after Taff, so Victoria's going to take choir practice. I thought I'd go along and sit in." She looked from one to the other. "But first, apparently I have to get over to his place now to pick up the music Victoria will need. Did you know that I've taken over organizing the gala since Glenda died?"

"No, I didn't know that, Penny, although I'm glad to hear it," said Mrs. Lloyd. "A nice opportunity for you to give back to this community that has taken you to its bosom all these years."

"Well, yes, it is," said Penny. "But there's not much time for me to give back and still a lot of do. I've got the whole shebang to organize."

"I'd like to help you, Penny," said Florence. "If you need me to, I'd be glad to organize the food and drink at the reception afterward. Or is it before? I can't remember. Does it say on the tickets?"

"It's after. The concert's down the mine, as you know, and then afterward there'll be a reception aboveground in the café part of the venue."

"Well, I would like to help you out by volunteering to look after that reception," said Florence. "You just have to tell me how many people and what's the budget and you can leave the rest to me."

"That's brilliant!" said Penny. "And I know you'll do a great job." She checked her watch. "Look, I've got to go now, but I'll catch you later, Florence, and we'll go over all the details and sort out the logistics. In the meantime, maybe you could give some thought to what you think we should serve. Wine, of course, and . . ."

"Leave it with me, Penny. I'll sort it. And you'll like it."

"Wonderful! Thanks so much, Florence."

"I'll see you out."

Florence returned to the sitting room to find Mrs. Lloyd in a frosty mood.

"Well, when I said people should do more and give back to the community I didn't necessarily mean you, Florence," she said. "After all, you've only been here five minutes."

"And why shouldn't I help out?" asked Florence. "I'm good at catering and I want to do my bit." Seeing Mrs. Lloyd's down-cast face and suspecting she was put out because she felt left out, Florence went on, "Maybe you could do your bit, too, Evelyn. Penny's in a bit of a bad place here, and she'd appreciate every bit of help she can get. Why don't you offer to take tickets at the door?" Mrs. Lloyd brightened. "And that way, you'd get to arrive early and you'd see everybody arrive." Mrs. Lloyd brightened even more.

Twenty-eight

"Come in, Penny," said Ifan Williams, whose broad smile told her all she needed to know. "Here, let me take your jacket." Penny handed her jacket to him and then walked into the kitchen. Taff was asleep in a cozy dog bed, a small blanket draped over him, his nose just touching his pink-bandaged front leg. As Penny crouched beside his bed and gently stroked his head, the dog's cognac-coloured eyes opened and the blanket moved over his thumping tail.

"He's saying thank-you," said Ifan. "As do I." He switched on the kettle. "I hope you can stay for a cup of tea."

"Yes, I certainly can," said Penny. "I can't tell you how glad I am that Taff's going to be okay."

"The vet said what saved him was that he was found before he went into shock and the break wasn't as bad as it might have been. Never again will I complain about the cost of vet fees," he said. "You moan about the cost of a checkup or annual jabs and then you stand by, useless, and watch as that same vet has the equipment, never mind the education, skill, and experience to save your dog's life . . ." He dabbed at his eyes with his sleeve, gave Penny a sheepish smile, looked away, and then continued. "Sorry. He means everything to me, does Taff." He bent down and stroked the dog's ears. "All right, old son?" He straightened up and turned his back to Penny while he fussed with the tea things. A few minutes later he set two mugs down on the table along with a small plate of chocolate digestives.

There was something about his home, his life, and Ifan himself that put Penny in mind of Father McKenzie in the Beatles' song "Eleanor Rigby."

"Milk?"

Penny nodded.

He added a splash, then passed her the mug. He pushed a rose-patterned bowl toward her and she helped herself to a teaspoon of sugar.

"Of course I'll never forgive myself for letting him off his lead like that," said Ifan as he stirred his tea. "I don't know what I was thinking. Or maybe the point is I wasn't thinking. I can't tell you how glad I am that Bronwyn and you came along when you did."

"And then, of course, Taff had the good sense to climb out where we could find him," said Penny, "although from what Bronwyn told me, it was really her Robbie who found him. We just sorted out the logistics to get him to the vet in time. But the great thing is he's doing so much better and all that matters now is that he's home with you, where he belongs."

Ifan smiled. "Yes. Home with me. I like the way that sounds."

They sipped their tea in silence and then Penny remarked, "Well, we understand completely that you need to be at home tonight. After we've finished our tea, perhaps you could hunt out that music Victoria will need this evening. Mustn't stay too long."

"Oh, yes, of course," said Ifan. "It's just here, in the dresser." He pulled a bundle of papers held together with an elastic band from the top of a teetering pile of documents, file folders, and envelopes sitting on top of an attractive Welsh dresser that took up most of one wall in the kitchen.

"That's a beautiful dresser," Penny remarked.

"It's been in my family for generations. I've known it all my life, so I never really take any notice of it. The place is full of antiques. My parents lived in this house and my grandparents before them. It's all pretty much the way it was when they lived here."

He handed the papers to Penny. "Did Glenda drop this off on the morning she died?" Penny asked. "She came by the Spa and left an envelope for Victoria."

"No, she gave it to me when we met at the mine for the site visit," he replied. He thought for a moment and then, as if making up his mind, continued. "Look, I know you're not supposed to speak ill of the dead and all that, but I have to say I'm really glad you've taken over the management of this concert. She was an absolute cow to work with. At least she was to me, anyway. Always giving me black looks and blaming me for things I had no control over, like she did when we were putting on the Jubilee concert. I vowed then I'd never work with her again, and yet, there we were, with another concert underway.

"Working with her caused me a lot of stress. I just wanted to get on with the music and not have to listen to her, going on

165

and on about things that are nothing to do with me and getting blamed for everything that went wrong. I'm glad I don't have to deal with her anymore."

"How glad?"

"Not that glad. I didn't kill her, if that's what you're thinking, although I'm sure the police think I did."

"Why do you say that?"

"Because they've been around twice asking me the same questions. As if they think I did it and they're just looking for the answers to prove their theory right."

"I can tell you that's not true," said Penny. "See, there's this thing called confirmation bias, and, oh, well never mind. Just take it from me they're letting the facts, not theories, drive the investigation.

"But Ifan, can you think of anyone who might have wanted to hurt Glenda?"

"The police asked me that. I told them there were folk round here who didn't much care for her, including me. She was given to taunting people and with her demanding, bossy ways she wasn't popular with everyone, but I can't think of anyone who would want to hurt her. Not really. And certainly not to that extent."

"Well, someone didn't like her. Not one little bit."

Ifan shifted in his chair and took a sip of tea.

"I did hear something about her . . ."

"What did you hear?"

"Well—and I told this to the police—I heard that she was supplying counterfeit goods to traders to sell in the local markets. You know those stalls they set up once a week in the various towns. There's one here in Llanelen on Tuesdays, I think it is. Her sister operates the stall. Anyway, I heard there'd been complaints about the products. So maybe one of the traders who bought some stuff from her had it in for her. Maybe it was some kind of business dealing gone wrong."

A wave of heat flushed through Penny's body as her heart began beating faster. She remembered what Bethan had told her about the police looking into Glenda's source of income.

"Are you saying that Glenda Roberts was behind the fake goods showing up at the markets?"

"Well, that's what I heard," said Ifan. "I don't know if it's true or not. That's for the police to find out."

"Who did you hear that from?" Penny asked.

"I don't know his name. Just someone in the pub one night telling another fellow that if you want good quality knockoffs, talk to Glenda. Apparently she could get big quantities of what was supposed to pass for high-end stuff. Sunglasses, electrical goods, handbags, fancy trainers . . . all sorts. You know the expensive kind of fake goods with the big names."

"Oh, I know all right," said Penny. "And it wasn't all just big names, either. There were some local names, too. Knockoffs of our beautiful hand cream have been sold in the market and if I'd known Glenda was behind it, I'd have cheerfully killed her myself."

"Well, maybe that's it, then," said Ifan. "Maybe a business owner whose product had been counterfeited found out what she's been up to and killed her." He shrugged. "Or had her killed. From what I see on telly it's better if someone else does the job. And then you make sure you have a good alibi. Having dinner with your wife in a crowded restaurant, or something like that."

"Well, it could be somebody like a disgruntled business owner, I suppose," said Penny. "Or maybe someone who bought a counterfeit product and it didn't do what it said on the tin. Electrical goods, you say. I wonder what kind."

"I don't know," said Ifan. Penny stewed in silence for a moment while Ifan gathered up the tea mugs. He offered Penny the last biscuit and when she shook her head, he carried the plate and mugs to the sink.

"Well, about the concert," he said when he returned. "Glenda and I came up with what I think is a good program. I'll tell you about it, and if you want to make any changes, now's the time, while we've still got time to rehearse."

"I doubt very much I'll want to," said Penny.

"Right, so here's what we have. The concert has to be fairly short as there's no place for the audience to go for an interval."

"So one act, as it were," said Penny.

"Yes. No break. The choir sings three songs with light accompaniment of harp and keyboard, the guest performer does three songs, and the choir does three more. Nine songs. And then the guest performer sings one last song as a kind of encore. I don't think people are there for a full-blown concert. They're there to get a flavour of the music, see the mine, and have something nice to eat."

"Sounds good," said Penny. "And speaking of eats, when the music is over, we bring everyone back to the surface as quickly and efficiently as we can for a reception in the café. So tell me about the program. What songs will the choir sing?"

"We'll open with '*Rhyfelgyrch Gwŷr Harlech.*'"

"Sorry, Ifan, my Welsh isn't as good as it should be. English, please."

"Of course. 'The March of the Men of Harlech,' then a folk tune, then we'll wrap that section with a sing-along, '*Calon Lân*' that is, 'A Pure Heart.' Everyone in the audience will know it."

"Yes, they will. Even I know it. Everyone will enjoy singing it."

"Then the guest performer. Karis Edwards. Although why Glenda chose her, I have no idea. She'll need her own rehearsal time, then she'll need to be present for the final run-through the night before the concert. This should be held down the mine, with everyone present, so we can make sure the sound system is right and get a clear idea of the timing." Penny scribbled a few words in her notebook.

"Do I really need to know all this?" she asked.

"Of course you do. As the organizer, you need to know everything, no matter how trivial it might seem and you need to be there for all of it. You need the complete big picture and all the little pictures."

Taff whimpered and stirred in his basket so Ifan got up to see to him.

"I'm going to have to take him outside," he said. "If you'd be so kind as to open the door." Penny jumped up and opened the door while Ifan lifted the injured dog out of his bed being careful not to move the splinted front leg wrapped in a neon pink bandage. A few minutes later Ifan returned to the kitchen and tenderly placed Taff back in his bed. Penny put her coat on, said good-bye, and set off for home.

As soon as she turned the corner into the next street, she pulled out her phone and called Davies. She left him a voice mail about Glenda and the knockoffs and asked him to call her.

Twenty-nine

*I*n his office in Colwyn Bay, DCI Davies shifted in his chair and frowned. Before him was the file on the investigation into the death of Gwillym Thomas, the mine worker who was killed in 1971 with a slate splitter.

Davies had read the report thoroughly and been struck by how unhelpful the miners had been. No one had seen or heard anything. No one wanted to help with the investigation. But someone must have heard or seen something. Conspiracies of silence troubled him on many levels. There was always an element of fear and intimidation. Good people, who wanted to do the right thing and come forward to help, were sometimes coerced and threatened into doing nothing so they became part of a cover-up, which allowed the guilty to remain free. Sometimes a hard, killing glare was all it took. You say anything, and we'll hurt you. Or even more powerful and persuasive, you say anything and we'll hurt someone you love.

As he was about to close the file, the name of one of the investigating officers caught his eye: PC Tim Crawford. He'd known that name for some time, but although he'd been very curious about him, for ethical reasons had resisted the temptation to use police records to learn more about him because his interest was purely personal. Now, he felt he could just about justify it. He logged into the securest of police personnel databases and entered the name. A moment later, the file came up and he scanned the early details—the date PC Tim Crawford had joined the force, glowing performance reviews—until he found what he was looking for.

July 29, 1995. The day PC Crawford died. Written in the stilted, curiously bland language of police reports that describe events of great emotional significance in detached, flat detail, the report had been written by the officer who'd responded to the call for assistance when PC Crawford was reported in trouble in the River Conwy.

At that time I observed PC Crawford on the far side (west) of the riverbank, struggling to get out of the water. He had a young girl in his arms and with some apparent difficulty was able to push her against the steep side of the bank near the Ivy teahouse where a group of people reached down and pulled her up to safety. The girl was able to breathe on her own and did not require medical intervention except to treat a few scrapes and small cuts.

Unfortunately the group was unable to assist PC Crawford out of the water. The River Conwy at this place is fast flowing, made up of the convergence of three rivers just a short way upstream. At the time of the incident the tide was coming in, so the water was high and with the opposing forces of the tide and the normal flow of the river downstream, the water was turbulent.

PC Crawford was swept away and despite the best efforts of attending police and fire officers and citizens, we were unable to rescue him. His body was recovered downstream later that afternoon.

Interviewed at the scene was Penny Brannigan, 34, the woman in charge of the little girl. Miss Brannigan stated that she was the fiancé of PC Tim Crawford and that she had been charged with looking after the girl, Morwyn Lloyd, 11. Miss Brannigan, a watercolour artist, said she had been momentarily distracted by her sketching at the time the girl went into the water and that PC Crawford, who had accompanied the two to the riverbank, was off getting ice creams. When he heard the commotion at the bank he rushed over. The life ring, which should have been secured on the bank for such an emergency had been removed by vandals and not replaced. Witnesses said the girl was caught in the current and seeing no alternative, PC Crawford entered the water and reached the girl a few moments later. Miss Brannigan was understandably distraught and was offered medical assistance, which she declined. The child and Miss Brannigan were driven in a police car to the home of the child's aunt, Evelyn Lloyd, of Rosemary Lane.

The report was followed by details of PC Crawford's funeral and recommendations for a bravery medal.

With a pounding heart, Davies closed the file. Penny had told him about Tim Crawford early in their relationship—that they'd been engaged and that Tim had drowned in the River Conwy saving a child's life—but she hadn't told him that she'd been there. She'd left out a few other details, too: that she'd been in charge of the child and been distracted with her painting when the child had fallen in the river. He thought he knew Penny in ways that she didn't know herself. She must have spent every day since buried under a landslide of guilt and self-blame, berating herself to hell and back. He'd thought for some time that something was holding her back emotionally, preventing her from opening up to him. Had he found the reason why she was unavailable? Because she hadn't forgiven herself for what had happened on that riverbank so long ago? And now what? What should he do with this knowledge? Bide his time? Mention it during a quiet, gentle chat over lunch. He was about to reach for his phone when it rang. He listened to Bethan for a moment and then stood up as he pressed the button to end the call.

Bevan Jones had called to report that a third slate splitter had turned up in the depths of the mine. And if Bethan was right, there was a good chance that this one was the murder weapon.

Thirty

I suppose I'd better sort out Karis Edwards today," said Penny. "She sent me an e-mail with her performance requirements."

"Oh, let me see it," said Victoria, picking up the document on Penny's desk. "It's called a rider. These showbiz people can be very demanding and the riders can be quite entertaining. Does she want a huge dressing room filled with white orchids?"

"Not quite," said Penny. "Her demands seem reasonable. Fresh, clean white towels, preferably from Marks and Spencer, new but laundered once."

Victoria looked up from the paper. "We can provide good quality towels from the Spa. We don't need to buy any."

"I understand the request," Penny continued. "I'm sure if not spelled out some venues would provide threadbare, dingy old things. There's a few details on the technical requirements—amplifier and microphone and such. I'll make sure Bevan at the mine sees that. But I was interested that she sent it to me herself. Doesn't an agent usually handle that sort of thing? And I thought you paid the agent, not the performer." She pointed at the document. "Or, as she's called there, the artiste."

"'Artiste,'" laughed Victoria. "Sounds like someone about to do a turn at an Edwardian music hall, doesn't it?"

"Anyway, I told her we would do hair, makeup, and manicure for the concert, so I'll make sure Rhian schedules that with Alberto. We'll take care of her hair before the dress rehearsal and then he can just do a comb-out before the performance. Manicure the day before as well, I think."

Victoria scanned the rider, running her finger down the short list of items Karis Edwards was requesting. "Wait a minute, there's something missing here. It doesn't mention a runner, but artists usually like to have a local person assigned to them to fetch and carry. Someone who knows the area who can make sure all their needs are met. 'My zipper broke. I need a copy of *Hello!* magazine. Where's my gin and tonic? My phone's dead. I dropped my lipstick.' Whatever. And you'd be amazed at some of the demands. The whole day is one long, 'I've got a problem. What are you going to do about it?' But the thing is, I'll be busy with the concert. You'll be busy with everything. So we need to find someone who will look after Miss Edwards. And that's probably what she'll expect to be called, by the way. Someone who's tactful and good at dealing with complaints."

"Who can handle being bossed about."

At that moment Rhian stuck her head round the door. Victoria and Penny turned their eyes toward her and then exchanged sly smiles.

"What?" said Rhian, looking from one to the other. "What's

the matter with you two? Why are you looking at me like that? I just wanted a word with Penny."

"I had you down to take tickets at the concert," said Penny, "but Mrs. Lloyd has volunteered to do that. Another task has come up, which I think, that is, we think, you'd be really good at."

"Oh, yes? What's that, then?"

"How would you like to be personal assistant to our guest artist?"

"Artiste," corrected Victoria.

"Fine," said Rhian. "Whatever. Penny, I need to talk to you."

Thirty-one

P enny, it's my grandfather," said Rhian. "He's gone bad."

" 'Gone bad'? What does that mean?"

"Taken a turn for the worse. We're worried about him. The nursing staff told us he's probably getting pretty close to the end."

"Oh, I'm so sorry to hear this," said Penny. "Well, you take all the time you need. Do you need to go over to the nursing home now?"

"No, I don't," said Rhian, "Not right now. But you do, if you can. He wants to talk to you. He's become quite agitated and it seems nothing will do except he speaks to you." She pulled Penny's coat off the coatrack and handed it to her. "Please. Go now."

Penny hesitated for just a moment, then accepted the coat and pulled it on.

"Oh, and, Penny, please tell him I'll be over in about an hour."

Penny welcomed the short walk to the nursing home as a

chance to clear her mind and think about all that was going on. Now, in mid–February, the rain had let up for a few days and the freshening wind was blowing a delicious hint of the sweet scent of spring over the hills and up the valley.

Jimmy was waiting for her in the reception area of the nursing home. He pushed his chair closer to her and greeted her with a worried frown. "I knew you'd come," he said. "It doesn't look good. Still, he wants you to hear what he has to say." Penny reached for the push grips of the chair and turned Jimmy around. "Do you know what he wants to tell me?" she asked.

"I do," he said. "He told me last night and then asked what he should do. I said he should tell you and that you'd take it from there. He was comfortable with that. He doesn't want the police. Not here. Not now. Not until . . . well, after he's gone."

He led Penny to a closed door just down the hall from the nurses' station. "In here."

"Are you coming in?" Penny asked.

Jimmy nodded. "He asked me to be there."

"Is this about what he didn't want to tell me before?"

When Jimmy didn't reply, Penny opened the door and pushed his chair inside.

The small room, painted a dull, flat grey and smelling of a powerful cleaning solution, contained only a single hospital-style bed with side rails, a bedside table, and a straight-back visitor's chair. A lot of thought and effort has gone into making this room as dreary and uncomfortable as possible, thought Penny. It certainly doesn't encourage lingering, and that may be the point for it was to this room that residents were moved as death approached.

Dylan opened his eyes as Penny came closer to the bedside and he gave her a weak but sincere smile. "I'm glad to see you," he said. She started to say something, but he held out a trembling hand to silence her. Unsure if he wanted her to take it, she hesitated and he withdrew it, lowering it to his side outside the bedcovers. His hand had a slightly bluish, mottled look, which alarmed her. She cast a glance behind her at Jimmy who looked worried.

"I'm sorry I wasn't open with you the other day," Dylan began. "You see, what I am about to tell you wasn't my secret to tell. It belonged to all of us, and we all kept it. We closed ranks. But I'm the last one left, and now it's time for me to set this burden down. There's no one left to protect and I want to be free of it. I've already told Jimmy and now I'm going to tell you. What you do with it is up to you. But Rhian thinks the world of you and I trust her judgement. I know you'll do the right thing."

Penny started to speak, but he lifted his hand slightly, frowned, and shook his head.

"Please. You don't need to say anything. Just listen." She nodded.

"It was a different world back then," he began, "although it was barely more than a generation ago. We didn't have the opportunities young people have now. The class system was alive and well. Everybody knew where they belonged and those with jumped-up ideas above their station were soon put back in their place. Oh, a few lads might have escaped the town but not many. For most of us, our future was down the mine. You didn't question it; you just joined your fathers, uncles, and brothers. That's what was expected of us, and that's what we did. And it was all we had. We had no prospects of other jobs.

"Aled Roberts was the mine manager and he was the biggest bastard you could ever imagine. You see, we had to bid for the chambers to work. Some chambers had better slate than others. He used to give the good chambers to his mates or those who paid him the most. The rest of us got the poor quality slate. And we were paid by how much we produced and the quality of it.

"So a lot of us hated him. And then he found out that his wife—that's Doreen—was having an affair with Gwillym Thomas. It couldn't have been much of an affair because we all worked such long hours and were so tired at the end of our shift, but I guess they managed to steal away for a bit of time together. We enjoyed the idea that Gwillym was putting it over on him. But somehow he found out and the next thing we knew Gwillym was dead. Bashed over the head with a slate splitter. We had no doubt that Aled had killed him, even if the police couldn't find any evidence he had. So we did what we had to do."

"You mean . . ."

"We arranged a little accident. There's always a risk with scaffolding in a place like that. The floor's uneven. It's hard to see in the dark. Maybe a bolt or two wasn't as tight as it should have been." He closed his eyes and paused to catch his breath, then resumed. "We didn't care if he was dead or just injured, as long as we got him out of there."

"How many men were in on this?" Penny asked.

"About fifteen. And don't ask me their names. I can't remember all of them and I wouldn't tell you anyway. But out of them, I'm the last one still alive, and I just want this out in the open now. I wouldn't have said anything while Doreen was still alive, but she's gone now, too, so there's no one left to care."

"I'm not so sure about that," said Penny. "Her daughter Rebeccah is still alive and she might care about what happened to her dad."

Dylan made a little grimace that looked almost like a smirk. "Ah, but was Aled her dad? Who knows how long the affair had been going on? Still, he probably was. But then there was the baby that died. Everyone thought for sure Gwillym was the father of that child."

Having said that, he gave a small nod, signalling he'd said all he had to say, then, with some difficulty, turned on his side to face the wall. Penny pulled the sheet and light coverlet over his thin shoulders, just visible above the blue and white patterned hospital gown.

Jimmy placed his hands on the wheels of his chair and maneuvered himself toward Penny. "Right, well, he looks as if he could use some kip. We'd better leave him to it."

Penny pushed Jimmy into the hall and turned toward the morning room. "Shall we sit for a few minutes?" she asked. "That's a lot to take in."

When Jimmy had been arranged in his favourite spot that afforded a good view of the lounge, with Penny seated beside him, he turned to her.

"What did you make of all that, then?"

"Feeling a bit overwhelmed, actually. We've just had two murders described to us. But one thing that strikes me is how people seem so reluctant to talk about the past. 'What's the point of raking up all that misery?' they say. But wouldn't you think they'd want the truth to come out, no matter how many years later?"

"What about you?" Jimmy asked. "Surely you did things or know things that you'd prefer stay buried in your past. And haven't we all."

Penny said nothing and after a few moments Jimmy asked, "Right, well, where does this leave us? Where do we go from here?"

Thirty-two

*G*ood question, thought Penny, as she trudged back to the Spa along the familiar streets. Where do we go from here? If there was a connection between what happened in the mine all those years ago, and the murder of Glenda Roberts, she couldn't see it. And what about Doreen Roberts? Had her death been an assisted suicide? And if it was, who had done the assisting? Someone who worked at the care home? Rebeccah? But Rebeccah had apparently arrived at the home after Penny and Jimmy had discovered the body, so did that exclude her?

Had anything happened that day that was buried in the back of her mind, waiting to be recalled? As she struggled to bring to the surface something, anything, she had overlooked a friendly voice brought her back to the Llanelen street.

"Hey up, Penny! Mind where you're going!"

"Oh, sorry, Rhian. I was miles away."

"Just on your way back to the Spa, are you? How was Grand-dad? Was he . . . ?"

"He was a bit weak. He talked for a bit, and then he dropped off to sleep. My visit seemed to tire him out."

"Mum's arriving this afternoon. We're preparing for the worst. The doctor tells us it probably won't be long now."

"I'm sorry, Rhian. It's always difficult to lose someone. Look, take as much time as you need from work."

"Oh, Penny, thank you for that. I was going to speak to Victoria before I left as I really do report to her, but if you wouldn't mind letting her know that I may not be back this afternoon."

"Of course." Penny gave her a little pat on the shoulder and the two set off in opposite directions, Rhian to the nursing home and Penny to the Spa.

"Oh, you're back," said Victoria a few minutes later, as Penny entered the building and and closed the door behind her. Penny told her that Rhian would need more time away now to be with her family as it looked likely that her grandfather's death was approaching.

"Yes, I was thinking that myself, so we'll all take turns on reception. We'll just do what we have to do while she's gone and hope she's back in time for the concert. Time's flying and it'll be on us before we know it," Victoria replied."

"It will," agreed Penny. "And I for one will be so glad when it's over. How did the rehearsal go last night, by the way?"

"Not bad," said Victoria. "And I heard this morning from Ifan that Taff's doing so much better, that he'll be fine from now on to lead the choir. Oh, and he mentioned something else we hadn't thought about."

"What's that?"

"It's about Glenda. Ifan was wondering if we should do something special for her, since she contributed so much to the organizing of the concert. An acknowledgement in the program perhaps. Or dedicate a song to her? And should we offer complimentary tickets to her sister and son—Rebeccah and Peris?"

"I'm impressed he thought of that," said Penny, "especially when you consider that he didn't care for her very much. Very thoughtful of him. It hadn't occurred to me to do something like that, but Ifan's right. But we mustn't do anything without talking to Rebeccah first. I'll have a word with her. If we're putting something in the program, we need to get her approval right away. But I definitely think we should offer them tickets."

Penny then gave Victoria a broad, open smile.

"What are you grinning about?"

"Well, I've been wanting to have a little chat with Rebeccah and this is a perfect excuse. I'm glad Ifan thought of it."

"If you're going to to talk to her, you could always use counterfeit goods as an opener," said Victoria. "Honestly, just thinking about it makes me so mad. That Glenda could produce those items, ripping off people she knows, and her sister selling them."

"We don't know for sure, though, that Rebeccah did sell them. Or, for that matter, that Glenda had them made. That's just what someone overhead in the pub. Anyway, I've passed on what Ifan had to say about the knockoffs although I think the police were already looking into that. Still, it's best left to the police, don't you think?"

Victoria laughed. "That's rich, coming from you. Anyway, about Rebeccah. I heard she's staying in Glenda's house now, while she sorts things out. And Peris didn't want want to be on

his own, but he wanted to be at home, so Rebeccah moved in."
She checked the client files on her computer, scribbled the address on a piece of scrap paper, and handed it to Penny.

"Here you go."

Thirty-three

"Hello, Rebeccah."

"Oh, it's you. I can probably guess what this is about. You'd better come in, then." Rebeccah Roberts opened the door wider and stood to one side as Penny entered. She found herself in a narrow hall and the two women experienced an awkward moment as Penny squeezed past her.

"Come through." Rebeccah gestured toward a door that led to a small sitting room. The main feature was an electric fireplace with a slate surround and scrolled detailing supporting the mantel piece. Penny reckoned that the slate work was original and at one time the fireplace had burned coal. Several cardboard boxes, taped shut, sat against the walls. Two cabinets, their shelves bare, flanked the fireplace and Penny guessed that the contents were now in the boxes. Following Penny's gaze, Rebeccah commented, "Mum lived here and then Glenda moved in with her when her marriage broke up. Now it falls to me to get rid of all their stuff. I can't afford to keep this place. It'll be up for sale soon."

"I'm sorry for your losses," said Penny. "Your mother and your sister so close together. That's hard."

"Well, thank you, but I don't suppose you've come about that," said Rebeccah. "I expect you've come about the hand cream. I heard you were asking questions about it."

Penny made a small shrugging gesture with a slight turn of the head that was both dismissive and acknowledging.

"Naturally we were very disappointed and upset to find that smelly rubbish being passed off as our beautiful product. We worked really hard to get that formula and to develop our product for market. I'm sure lots of counterfeiters don't care that selling knockoff goods is just plain theft, but really, if Glenda was behind this, and I don't know that she was, I would have expected better from her than ripping off people she knows."

Rebecca glared at her with a cold contempt.

"It wasn't my doing. Mum started the stall when dad died and she had to find a way to support us. That's just how we got by. And then Glenda got involved, started ordering stuff for it, and then she became a supplier to other stalls as well. At first, it was all legitimate, but then she got in with some people in Manchester and next thing you know, the knockoffs were on offer. And I know this doesn't make it right, but everyone who goes to the market knows the place is full of knockoffs. Do people really think you can buy a curling iron for ten pounds that sells for fifty pounds in the shops? Or a pair of Jimmy Choo shoes for forty pounds? Of course the stuff is dodgey, but for crying out loud, that's why folks come to the market. They're after bargains, aren't they?

"But I don't need you coming round here to give me a lecture on knockoffs, so if that's why you're here . . ."

190

"Sorry. Didn't mean to upset you. But you can see my point, can't you? Our livelihoods depend on our reputation. Anyway, that's not why I'm here," Penny said.

She explained that the organizers of the St. David's Day concert wanted to acknowledge Glenda's contribution and described the offer to include an acknowledgement in memory of Glenda in the program.

"I can talk to Peris and see what he thinks," Rebeccah said. "Personally, I think a mention in the program would be nice. Yeah, Glenda would have liked that."

"We'd also like to give you and Peris complimentary tickets," said Penny, opening her handbag and offering them to Rebecca. "We hope you'll come. If you decide not to go, would you mind either returning the tickets to me or passing them on to someone who will go? We want to make sure every seat is filled.

"Glenda booked a rather expensive guest performer. Well, expensive for us, that is. Karis Edwards, her name is. Used to be the lead singer in The Characters. Maybe you've heard of them. They were pretty big back in the day. Apparently she's a bit of a diva and there'll be problems if seats are empty."

For the first time, Rebeccah's posture relaxed and her face softened.

"I loved The Characters! I know it was all a bit daft, but I was about the same age as a couple of them."

Sensing an opening, Penny moved in.

"Well, I'm sure we can arrange for you to meet Karis, if you'd like that," she said. "Peris, too, of course, if he wants to, although The Characters were long before his time.

"There'll be a reception after the concert in the café, but you might prefer to come to the dress rehearsal the night before.

191

There'll be more time then and fewer people about. You're more likely to get her all to yourself."

Rebeccah's face edged toward a smile. "And again I'm very sorry about your mother and sister, Rebeccah. I'm sure both deaths came as a great shock to you."

Rebeccah moved uneasily in her chair. "I knew Glenda, but not very well," Penny continued. "She used to get her hair cut at our salon." Rebeccah nodded politely. "But I knew your mother better. She was a friend of an old friend of mine who died almost two years ago. My friend left me her cottage so I had to go through all her things." She tipped her head at the boxes, "Just like you're doing. It's not easy. You rake up all those old memories and you have to deal with all of it whether you feel up to it or not. It's a lot of work and it can be quite emotionally draining. I found it easier to do it with someone who could be more objective. So I was glad when a friend stepped in to help me."

Rebeccah's eyes brimmed with tears and she looked away. She took a swipe at her eyes with her sleeve and recovered her composure. Penny leaned forward.

"They're not just things, though, are they? It's not just stuff. Objects hold memories and it can be very difficult to let go of them."

Rebeccah's face fell and she looked down at the floor.

"Not in my case," she said. "I'm glad to be rid of them. Peris and I have taken what we want and everything else will be auctioned or donated. And then this place will be sold."

"I see."

"And I'll be giving up the stall. I never particularly liked doing it and I wasn't very good at it. It takes a lot of bluffing. You've got to have a special knack for it." She paused for a moment at the sound of the front door opening. "Oh, that'll be Peris." A

192

moment later he slouched into the room, glared at Penny, then shot his aunt a questioning look. No one said anything, and Rebeccah continued. "Anyway, Glenda was quite good at it. Enjoyed chatting up people. Saw every punter as a challenge. And she didn't have any qualms about selling them knockoff goods."

"What are you talking about Mum with her for?" Peris asked.

"The stall," Rebeccah said. "I was just telling Penny here how good your mother was at selling. Had the gift of the gab, she did. But she didn't work the stall very often anymore. Busy with other things."

Peris laughed. "That's why it was so funny when that punter kicked off and started shouting at her about the air freshener!"

"Somebody yelled at her?" Penny asked. "What did he say?"

"Oh, it was nothing," Rebeccah said. "A mix-up, that's all."

"He said the air freshener gave his son a bad reaction," Peris said. "The kid had asthma or something and landed in the hospital. To hear him going on about it, you'd think the kid just about died." He laughed. "Poor Mum. She wasn't normally even on the stall and she didn't sell the air freshener. She was just on the receiving end of his big rant."

"Well, parents do tend to get riled up if they think someone's hurt their child," said Penny. "That's understandable."

"I'll be in my room if you want me," said Peris. A moment later they heard him thumping up the stairs and then the sound of a door closing with a little more energy than was required.

"I was wondering if you know anyone who might have wanted to harm Glenda," said Penny.

"The police already asked me that and I told them no."

"Did you tell them about this man who shouted at her?"

"No, I didn't. I wasn't on the stall that day. Peris told me about it later."

"Any idea who this man could be? Has anyone else complained about any of the products Glenda supplied?"

Rebeccah shook her head. "Haven't a clue who he is. We do get a complaint every now and then, but we don't take them seriously and we don't do anything about them. It's a market stall, not Selfridges. What you see is what you get. We don't do refunds or exchanges and to be honest, we don't give a toss about customer satisfaction or any of that crap."

"Really." Penny stood up. "Interesting way to do business. Well, I'd better be on my way. I'll be in touch about arrangements for the dress rehearsal and as I said, both of you would be more than welcome." She handed Rebeccah a document. "I almost forgot. Here's the acknowledgement of Glenda's contribution we drafted for the program. Can you please go over it, and let me know if it's all right. You'll need to let me know by Wednesday at the latest so we can get the program to the printer in time."

Thirty-four

"T he concert's coming up fast. Are we ready?" Victoria asked.

Penny wagged her hand from side to side.

"Almost ready, then?" Victoria continued.

"The logistics are in pretty good shape," said Penny. "At least we don't have to worry about catering; Florence has everything sorted for the reception. The food and drinks will be terrific and everything'll be within the budget. Bevan assures me that the sound system will work perfectly and the transportation arrangements are all in place. How about the concert? Everything okay with the music?"

"It's good. Our guest singer is scheduled for a run-through discussion with me and then the final rehearsal. Is Rhian's grandfather still doing a bit better? Is she okay now to act as Karis's assistant?"

"She is. I asked Rhian to contact Karis and let her know that she'll be available to her if she wants or needs anything." Penny glanced at her watch. "Eirlys is on that makeup course today, so I'm doing the manicures. My client will be here in a few minutes, so I'd best crack on."

At that moment Rhian herself poked her head around the door.

"I've just heard from Karis," she said. "She wants a hair appointment for this afternoon. She wants a colour treatment. She says she wants the color done today in case she doesn't like it and if it has to be done over there'll still be time to get it right."

Victoria covered her eyes with her hands and let out an exasperated gasp. "Oh, no. Here we go. I've worked with divas before and believe me, this is just the beginning."

"Of all the bloody cheek!" exclaimed Penny. "We didn't even offer her a colour and it was awfully generous of us to offer hair, manicure, and makeup at all. It's great that Eirlys is doing the makeup course and she'll put it to good use for wedding clients, but she's doing it now, really, just to accommodate Miss Karis Edwards. Really, expecting a colour treatment on top of everything else is just brass-necked cheek, if you ask me."

"We need to check the rider," said Victoria. "See what we've agreed to provide and we'll do that and not one thing more."

"And what about tonight?" said Penny. "We didn't agree to pay her hotel for tonight. I hope she doesn't expect us to. It was her choice to arrive early."

"First, let's get this hair colour sorted," said Victoria. "Rhian, does Alberto have any free time this afternoon to take her? We are certainly not cancelling a regular client so we can accommodate madam."

"He said he was willing to squeeze her in," Rhian said.

"Right, well, you get back to her, Rhian, and tell her that

although a hair colour treatment was not included in our offer, as a goodwill gesture we will do it for her. But only one. We won't redo it if she doesn't like it." She looked from one to the other. "I think it's important at this early stage that we let her have the colour treatment to get everything off on the right foot. Am I right?" Rhian and Penny indicated agreement, so Victoria continued. "But you should also find a way, Rhian, to let her know that going forward we can provide only what was agreed to in the rider. And if she gives you any attitude about anything, let me know and I'll speak to her."

Penny gave them both an encouraging smile. "Just a few more days. We can get through this." And then she added, "Right, well, we've all got a mountain of work to climb this morning, so let's get on with it."

Thirty-five

S hortly after three the Spa door opened and Rhian looked up from her work as a tall woman who appeared to be in her early forties entered. Her hair was pulled back and her expression was coolly neutral. "Hello," she said. "I'm Karis Edwards. I'm expected for a hair appointment this afternoon."

Rhian stood up and walked round her desk and introduced herself. "Yes, we've been expecting you," she said. "Let me take your coat and I'll show you to our hair salon. Would you like a coffee? How was the journey?"

"Have you ever driven in a car for an hour or two? It was like that," Karis replied with an icy smile as she sloughed off her coat and handed it to Rhian. "The person who's doing my hair, is she any good?"

"It's a he," replied Rhian. "Alberto. And he's very good. I think you'll be pleased with the results. This way, please." She led Karis down the hall to the hair salon and stood gracefully to one side as Karis entered. "Alberto, this is Karis Edwards. I'm leaving her in your capable hands."

Rhian hung Karis's coat in the closet and then ducked into Penny's office. "Well? What's she like?" Penny asked.

"A bit abrasive, to be honest," said Rhian. "And there was something . . . oh, I don't know."

"What? What is it?"

"I don't know. There was just something about the way she spoke to me, in that arrogant kind of way that put me in mind of Glenda Roberts. You know. As if I'm her servant or something."

"Well, you carry on and leave her to me. I'll check in on her in a few minutes and see how things are going. Did you offer her a coffee?"

"I did. She didn't say if she wanted one or not."

As Penny stood up, Rhian's phone rang. She glanced at the caller ID then threw Penny a worried look. "It's Mum." She listened for a moment, and then said to her mother, "I'd better come right away." She ended the call.

"Sorry, Penny. Wouldn't you know. Granddad's taken another turn for the worse. He hung on longer than they thought he would and they even moved him back into his old room. But Mum said it won't be long now. I really should go."

"Of course."

"What about . . . ?" She tipped her head in the direction of the hair salon.

"Don't worry about that. I'll see to her," said Penny. "You just go and be with your family. We'll be thinking of you. Take all the time you need." Rhian hesitated and Penny touched her arm. "We'll manage. Go."

"Thanks, Penny. I'll just get my things together and then I'll be on my way."

Penny opened her handbag, took out a lipstick, and applied it. She then crossed the hall to the hair salon and stood in front of the closed door. She hesitated for a moment, then made a fist and raised her hand to knock. She paused, her knuckles aimed at the door, then slowly lowered her arm and walked to Victoria's office. She peered in through the open door, then entered and sat in the visitor's chair. She waited until Victoria finished her e-mail and turned toward her.

"She's here," Penny said. "Karis. She's getting her hair done. Alberto's door was closed and honestly, I didn't know what to do. I can't remember the last time Alberto's door was closed. I thought I'd just pop in to say hello and ask if she wanted a coffee, but then I thought if she's sitting there with hair colour goop all over her head she might not be pleased at being seen like that. So I left it."

"You did right," said Victoria. "Celebrities need careful handling and it takes real tact to get on with them. They develop a huge sense of entitlement and expect to be treated with a certain amount of deference. And in a way, former celebrities are worse. They no longer command the treatment they were used to, but they can't accept that their time in the sun is over. The world's moved on to the next big thing and they're pretty much forgotten. No one cares about them anymore. It's very hard on the self-esteem. Saw a lot of that when I was in the music world. Can be very sad."

"Rhian said Karis spoke to her in rather an abrasive manner."

"She could have been a bit imperious. That goes along with it. I'm not particularly looking forward to working with her and I still can't understand why Glenda would have asked her to sing at our concert, but I do have some experience dealing with divas, so we'll just get on with it. Which reminds me. Ifan and I need to speak to her about the songs she's chosen. Do you remember a song by The Characters called 'If I Can't Have Him'?"

Penny laughed. "No. I can't say I do."

"That's my point. Karis listed that on her playlist. Completely unsuitable for our audience. Can you imagine Mrs. Lloyd and Florence reacting to that?"

"Actually, I think Florence would find it rather amusing."

Victoria gave her a sharp look. "That's my point! Songs aren't meant to be amusing."

"Anyway, I think I'll just see if everything's all right with Alberto." But just as she said his name, Alberto himself eased into the room and closed the door behind him. In his late forties, tall, and wearing expensive, well-fitted jeans, and an immaculate white shirt, Alberto had been with the salon since it opened and was well liked by all his clients. He was often booked two weeks in advance, so Karis had been lucky that he'd agreed to fit her in.

"We were wondering how you were getting on," said Victoria. "How's it going?"

"I'd forgotten how some women can be," he said. "I've done my best, but we'll have to wait and see. I gave her a nice warm chestnut with honey highlights that should really suit her. She's got a few more minutes before the rinse and then I'll give her a tidy-up trim. Her hair's not in good shape. She's been colouring it herself and those home dye jobs are so hard on hair. It should be in much better condition when I've finished with it." He sighed. "Just thought you'd like an update. Bit of reassurance, like. Going to make a coffee for her now. She wants a caramel latte with skinny froth. Glad we've got that fancy machine." He turned to go. "Oh, I noticed something strange."

Penny raised an eyebrow. "Her hair," Alberto said. "Hair is

very individual. Density, weight, curl, texture, porosity, elasticity . . . just the way it feels in your fingers. She's completely grey and because of her age I'd say she's been grey for many years. And in all the areas I just mentioned, her hair is just like Glenda Roberts. Were they related?"

Penny gave a little start with widened eyes.

"It's so strange you should say that. Rhian just told me that the way Karis spoke to her reminded her of Glenda."

Penny felt a vague churning in her stomach as she and Victoria exchanged puzzled looks.

"Well, I'd better get back," said Alberto. "Mustn't keep her waiting. Just thought I'd let you know how things are going." As he left the room he bumped into Rhian, who was wearing a waterproof coat and carrying a large tote bag.

"I'm leaving now," she said. "I've left everything tidy and a note on the desk so Eirlys or whoever's filling in will know what's happening. Oh, and Rebeccah Roberts called and she'll be here in about half an hour to drop something off for Penny."

Victoria gave her a questioning look.

"Sorry, Victoria. I thought Penny might have said. My granddad is very bad and Penny gave me permission to be with my family. I really do have to be with them. Mum needs my support."

"Of course she does," said Victoria.

"But Mum says we'll still be coming to the concert on Saturday. She said Granddad was starting to come round to the idea of it. He reckoned if it helps people remember the slate miners and all they did for the area, then he'd go along with it, so Mum says we're going."

With Rhian gone, it was agreed that Penny would take over in reception until Eirlys arrived after lunch. Penny enjoyed reception duties every now and then and was busy cleaning the glass on the front door when Rebeccah Roberts strolled up the pathway leading to the Spa. Penny opened the door for her and stood aside.

"Hello. Welcome and come in." Rebeccah looked around the calm reception area with its blond hardwood floor and pale green walls. "Nice," she said and then put her hand in her coat pocket and pulled out a piece of paper. "Here's the bit about Glenda for the program. I liked what you wrote, I just changed one small thing." As she handed the document to Penny, Karis Edwards emerged from the hair salon and in long strides, proceeded down the hall toward them. "Is that her?" Rebeccah whispered to Penny.

Penny nodded. "I haven't met her yet. I'll introduce us."

She held out her hand as Karis approached. "Hello, Ms. Edwards. I'm Penny Brannigan, coordinator of the St. David's Day concert. Welcome to Llanelen. And this is Rebeccah Roberts. Her sister, Glenda, was the original coordinator and your first contact would have been with her."

Karis smiled at Penny, shook her hand, and then turned to Rebeccah. "Hello, Rebeccah." She held out her hand. Her tone was friendly, but a flicker of something almost imperceptible passed between them. Rebeccah shook her hand, then took a step back, a microexpression flashing across her face that Penny caught, but couldn't read or understand.

"I do hope you like your hair," said Penny.

"Yes, it's fine. Just fine." Karis touched the ends of her hair and turned her gaze back to Rebeccah.

"Good," said Penny. "Well, I understand that I'm to take you to meet my business partner, Victoria Hopkirk. I believe she's giving you lunch. She's our concert harpist and helping out with the music at the concert so I'm sure you'll have lots to talk about." She looked from Rebeccah to Karis. "Ready? Shall we go?"

Karis broke off looking at Rebeccah whose shoulders then seemed to relax. Rebeccah's gaze followed Karis as Penny led her away.

After introducing Karis to Victoria in her office, Penny returned to the reception area where Rebeccah remained standing beside the desk.

"What just happened there?" Penny asked. "What is it?"

"I just felt the strangest sensation," said Rebeccah. "I've never felt anything like that in my life. When she looked at me, the way she lowered her head and then looked at me in that way, I thought I'd seen a ghost." She placed her hand on her chest. Penny steered her to a chair and then sat beside her.

"Whose ghost?"

When she didn't answer, Penny leaned closer and offered a prompt. "Was it Glenda? Does Karis remind you of Glenda?"

Rebeccah shook her head.

"No, I wasn't thinking of Glenda. My mother. She used to look at me like that. Karis reminded me of my mother."

She gave a weak, helpless smile. "To be honest, she scares me, just like my mother used to. But I don't know why."

"Victoria's talking to Karis now about her concert program and she might not be happy with Victoria's suggestions. It's probably best if you aren't here when she comes out." Rebeccah considered that for a moment, then left immediately and Penny returned to the receptionist's desk to think about what she should do next.

A few minutes later Karis entered the reception area, shot Penny a thunderous look, and left. Victoria followed a moment later.

"Your suggestions didn't go down too well, I gather," said Penny. Victoria shook her head.

"Honestly, she is the most unreasonable woman. I told her our audience is older. They don't know The Characters or their music and they don't care. I suggested that as she's singing only four songs she might want to sing something more appropriate for this audience. This is way too late to be sorting out the program. Karis and Ifan should have had all this worked out before now, but I'm guessing that when Glenda died, the song selection got overlooked.

"Anyway, I suggested she come up with some songs that might be familiar to our audience and that they might enjoy. She just sneered and said she doesn't do show tunes like 'Oklahoma!' Argh."

"What on earth have we got ourselves into?" moaned Penny. "We didn't ask for any of this. And now that we've lost Rhian, I suppose I'll have to look after her myself. But I wonder if I should ring Gareth and tell him that people have noticed something about her that reminds them of Glenda. And now, would you believe, Doreen."

"What?"

"Yes. Rebeccah said Karis reminded her of her mother."

"Three people noticing a family similarity can't be a coincidence," said Victoria. "Do you think they're related somehow? And of that family, Glenda was murdered and we're not exactly sure how Doreen died. So if Karis is somehow tied up in all this, she could be in danger."

"As could Rebeccah."

"Well, I'm sorry she took my program suggestions so badly. I was looking forward to a nice lunch. I don't suppose you . . . no, I guess not. You're on desk duty."

Thirty-six

"I'm glad you told me," DCI Gareth Davies said over the telephone. "I'd like to hear more, but I'd rather not come to the Spa. Can you get away for a half hour or so? Perhaps we could meet here at the station and go for a walk?"

After a word with Victoria, and glad of an excuse to get out for some fresh air, Penny pulled on her jacket and walked the short distance to the town's police station that Davies used occasionally as an operational base. He was waiting on the step as she walked up the short path. He liked her confident stride and thought she looked better in practical walking boots than any woman he'd ever met.

He placed his hands gently on her shoulders, bent down, and kissed her lightly on both cheeks. "How are you? Everything all right?"

She shook her head lightly as they fell into step. "I thought we might walk along the river and through the fields to Trefriw and back," he said. "See how the fields are recovering after all the rain."

They walked in silence along Station Road and then turned off onto the asphalt pathway that led to the neighbouring village. Although the patchwork fields on either side were a startling, vibrant green, the trees that graced the surrounding hills were bare.

Davies glanced down at her, wondering what she'd looked like twenty years ago. Probably not much different than she did today. Her skin was well cared for and although there was a slight slackening along the jawline, she looked fresh and youthful when she smiled. But today, her face was drawn and closed. He couldn't tell what she was thinking and then the word came to him: troubled. She had something on her mind and it was burdening her. And then, as if reading his thoughts, she spoke.

"I'm concerned for Rebeccah Roberts. She's had a lot to deal with: the death of her sister and mother and now trying to look after her nephew. Teenagers can be a handful at the best of times, so she's probably finding him a challenge."

"It's bound to be a difficult time for the lad, too," said Davies. "He's also lost his mother. But tell me more about what people said about Karis and her resemblance to Glenda." So Penny described how Rhian had commented that Karis's manner had reminded her of Glenda Roberts, that Alberto had noticed that the two women shared a remarkably similar hair structure, and that something about Karis's manner put Rebeccah in mind of her mother.

"And something unusual happened in that exchange with Rebeccah that I'm just not sure about," she continued. "From what I've been hearing, Karis has been imperious and almost

208

rude and yet with Rebeccah, she was softer and, well, quite nice really."

"That may be a rock star kind of thing," said Davies. "If you've ever done protection or got close to one of those people, you know they're different. There's them and then there's the rest of us. They live their lives on a plane that most of us will never know. When they're alone or with members of their entourage they're one person, and when they're with fans they're somebody else. They can turn it on and off like you wouldn't believe. And they live very comfortable, high-end lives with someone to do their bidding and take care of their every need."

"Victoria said pretty much the same thing. But I don't think it's like that for Karis anymore," said Penny. "She drove herself to the hotel, apparently. And I can guarantee the Red Dragon in Llanelen isn't anything like the hotels she's used to."

"She hasn't enjoyed that lifestyle for a few years, though, has she?" said Davies. "And it's got to be hard to accept that you're not the star you used to be. Still," he said, thinking of Penny's involvement in the drowning incident that had happened just a little further along the bank of the very river they were approaching, "life moves on for all of us. And Karis did a whole lot better than people thought she would."

"Did she?"

"Apparently. There was a program about The Characters on television recently. Very driven, was our Karis. Came from Swansea. She was the only musicial one in the family. The program made the point that this group paved the way for the Spice Girls in the 1990s. The big difference was that the Spice Girls had so much merchandising and marketing going on. Made millions from all the stuff—everything from watches to makeup that every little girl in the UK had to have. The Characters didn't do that, so when the music stopped, so did the income. They really missed the boat on the merchandising and lost out on a fortune."

"Well, that's got to hurt. And it's a little strange when you think about it because there was a lot of merchandising around The Beatles and that was twenty years earlier. So people in the business knew about the importance of the product sales and all about the kinds of stuff that would sell besides the records." She smiled. "Remember the Beatles' lunch boxes? It's really strange the manager of The Characters didn't insist on all the products. There must have been some negligence there."

"How have you found her so far?"

"She's only just arrived, but it hasn't been going all that well, to be honest. Victoria was supposed to take her to lunch, but she stormed out of the Spa because she didn't like what Victoria had to say about her choice of music. Victoria's rehearsing privately with her this afternoon, or at least they're supposed to, so I hope they can put their disagreement behind them and Karis will behave professionally so they can get on with it. We're all a bit anxious about this whole concert thing. I'll be really glad when it's over and I expect everyone else will be, too."

They walked on for a few more minutes, enjoying the quiet peace of the countryside against a background chorus of birdsong.

"We'll take another look at Rebeccah and the young lad to see if we can rule them out of the investigation. I will admit, this case has got messy." As if in unspoken agreement, they slowed down as they approached the modern footbridge that spanned the River Conwy and he pointed to a bench. "Shall we?" They watched the sparkling river for a few moments as it flowed peacefully on its endless journey to the Irish Sea. The fields on the other side of the river, empty now, would be filled in a month or so with ewes and their spring lambs. Many people who live in North Wales, and not just farmers, see lambing season as the real beginning of a new year and as a landscape watercolour painter with a deep love of the countryside and a keen eye for its natural beauty, Penny counted herself among them.

After they were seated, Davies picked up where he'd left off.

"We have so many loose ends to tie up on this investigation. First there's Glenda Roberts. Murdered down the mine, possibly with a slate splitter. That's still to be confirmed, but we have good reason to think so. Then there's her mother, Doreen Roberts. Died of what could be an assisted suicide in her nursing home. If it was an assisted suicide, and the empty canister and plastic hood suggest that it was, who was present when she died? And then we have the counterfeit goods that Glenda was distributing and Rebeccah was selling. Is there a connection between the two deaths and the knockoff goods? I don't know. We've heard there were some complaints about them, and we've established that the counterfeit goods come from Manchester, so we're working with the police there. They've been very helpful."

He sat back, folded his arms, and looked down river.

"I did hear something more about the knockoffs," Penny said. "Peris said that a man was yelling at Glenda about some air freshener that he thought had been sold off her stall. It was fake, and contained something hazardous. The man said it triggered a reaction in his son and the boy ended up in hospital."

"Did he say when this happened?"

"Shortly before Glenda died, I think."

"I don't suppose he said who it was."

Penny shook her head. "No, sorry."

"Well, we'll try to find out," said Davies. "I'm not surprised, though, that someone was angry. People are suffering ill effects from these counterfeit products and the problem's getting worse.

"The knockoff business is huge. And growing. There's a street in a rather rough Manchester neighbourhood that looks like all the shops are shuttered, but they actually sell every kind of counterfeit product you can imagine and some you wouldn't think of. We know Glenda went there to buy fake goods, which she sold on to the local traders to sell on their stalls, but it's hard to get any information out of the people who run the operation. They actually have lookouts posted in the street who warn shoppers and vendors when the police are coming and the goods simply vanish. And nobody's talking, of course. At least not to us, but there's nothing new about that.

"The really troubling thing is they've now moved into counterfeit wines and spirits. The vodka is made in Eastern Europe, smuggled into this country without paying duty, and the quality is so bad, it can actually cause blindness. The labels are often a giveaway, as Florence discovered with the lavender. I've seen Chardonnay spelled with an *S*! The other thing they do is create new brands. Lil Mouse vodka! Whoever heard of that?"

Penny smiled.

"Anyway," Davies continued, "we're working on several lines of inquiry and Glenda's involvement in the counterfeit industry certainly opens up a world of possibilities.

"So what have we got? Two deaths. A murder and a suicide? A murder and a natural death? Or two murders? And linked somehow with pieces of slate found in two dead hands.

"But we haven't been able to establish a clear connection between the two deaths and probable or even possible motives. Are we looking at one puzzle? Two? More than two? And then there's

Ifan Williams, who despised Glenda and admits he was on the mine tour when Glenda was killed. There are just so many persons of interest and potential persons of interest in this complicated case. I'd love to hear your thoughts."

"My thoughts? I thought your investigation had to go where the evidence led, not where some theory might take you," said Penny. "Confirmation bias and all that."

"Oh, I think there's room for some insight and speculation," smiled Davies. "A fresh point of view can be very helpful and I've always valued your input. We're not supposed to discuss operational details with people outside the case, but you've always been really helpful to the investigations and I trust you. So tell me, what do you make of all this?"

"Well, I don't have a lot of information . . . not nearly as much as you do, I expect, but I think all this is connected to something that happened down that mine a long time ago. I think that's why each of the dead women had a piece of slate in her hand. The killer was sending you a message. Old sins cast long shadows. But right now I'm more concerned about Rebeccah. I'm wondering if she's at risk. Could she be next?"

Davies seemed to take a keen interest in the sun sparkling on the river as he considered his answer. Although the air was cool, the brightness of the day spoke of long, warm days to come. A pungent tang of damp earth seemed to rise from the riverbank. The water was a deep blue, reflecting the paler blue of the sky and drawing the eye to the deep greens and dark purples of forested hills that rolled away to meet the horizon and then disappear into the mist.

"She may be. I hope not. I'll ask Bethan to talk to her."

Penny stood up. "I should be getting back. Victoria's meant to be taking Karis to lunch and with Rhian gone, I'll need to be there." Davies stood up and the two set off at a steady but comfortable pace.

"Rhian's away?"

"Her grandfather is dying. She's gone to be with her family."

"Oh, right. I'm sorry to hear that."

Penny hadn't yet told him what Dylan had disclosed about the murder of Aled Roberts down the mine all those years ago and although she would have liked to, she'd promised she would tell no one until Dylan was gone. This was not her secret to share. Not yet.

"Can you think of anything else that happened when you found Doreen Roberts?" Davies asked. "Anything at all."

Penny scanned the scene in her mind. "No," she said slowly, "I've told you everything I saw in her room."

"All right," said Davies. "Now, about Karis. It would be helpful if we ran a DNA test so we can see if there's a family connection. We'll need samples from both Rebeccah and Karis."

"Won't that take too long?" asked Penny. "If they're in danger, waiting around three months for DNA results won't help."

"Oh, we've come a long way," Davies replied. "We can fast track our request to get a result back in just a day or two."

Penny thought for a moment. "I can get you a skin sample from Karis Edwards tomorrow, if you want me to. All you have to do is send Bethan to the Spa. I'll let you know what time." She reached into her pocket for a tissue. "By the way, is it okay to collect people's DNA samples without their permission?"

"We prefer to ask them to give us a sample, and most people are willing to do that, but if we think there's going to be a problem, or if they refuse, we can get the authority to collect it."

"I suppose being unwilling to provide a DNA sample tells you something in itself."

Davies smiled. "It can. My thinking in this case is that Rebeccah would give a sample willingly and Karis would not. I'll get Bethan to ask Rebeccah for a sample when she talks to her."

By the time they arrived back at the Spa any chance Davies might have had of bringing up the death of Penny's fiancé, Tim Crawford, was gone and he wasn't sure now what mentioning it would accomplish. He placed a hand on her shoulder and bent down to kiss her cheek with the same tenderness as when he had greeted her. He loved the smell of her and drank it in. Her hair, her skin. She smiled up at him as he released her, and she then turned and walked up the path. He watched her until she entered the building, but she did not look back.

Eirlys was waiting for her on the reception desk. "Victoria's gone for lunch, after all, with the client," she said. "That Karis Edwards. She came here, asked for Victoria, and the two of them left together."

"Right," said Penny, mildly surprised. "Well, that's good, I guess. Now, I've got to talk to you about something that's going to happen tomorrow. But first, let's look up what time Karis Edwards is coming in for her manicure."

Thirty-seven

"I'm Karis Edwards, here for my manicure."

"Good morning," said Eirlys. "Penny herself will be looking after you this morning. I'll let her know you're here."

A moment later Penny emerged from the manicure room, greeted Karis, and walked with her down the hall.

"Just give me your coat and we'll get started," said Penny, pointing to the client's chair. She handed Karis's coat to a young woman in a pink smock. "This is Bethan," Penny said. Bethan set a bowl of fragrant, warm water on the white towel in front of Karis and Penny gently dipped her client's fingertips in the bowl.

"Is the water temperature all right? Not too hot, I hope."

Karis nodded. "It's fine."

"So," said Penny conversationally, "is your program sorted for your concert?"

"It's just a few songs in a small town," said Karis, with an indifferent shrug. "Not sure it rates being called a concert."

Penny struggled to contain herself. "Well, we've all gone to a lot of work to put this event on," she said. "Especially after the original organizer died. And the people in our small town have paid good money to hear you sing." She added a slightly icy emphasis to the words "small town," which Karis either did not notice or chose to ignore. Oh, man, this is going to be heavy going, thought Penny. Over the years she'd become very good at reading body language and Karis was stiff and closed. Penny had learned that sometimes the right question could really break the ice. "Do you have a pet?" worked wonders with a new client who would immediately break into a broad smile and tell Penny all about her amazing cat who kept the household in stitches with its clever antics and had its own channel on YouTube. But she suspected it would take more than cat talk to connect in any meaningful way with the woman sitting across from her.

When clients were uncommunicative Penny tried to sense if they preferred to have their manicure in silence or if they wanted to chat and just needed a bit of drawing out. She wasn't sure what Karis wanted, so grasping for conversation, commented, "That's a pretty ring." Karis pulled her left hand out of the soaking water and manipulated the ring between her middle and small fingers to centre the purple-coloured stones. "Thank you. It was my mother's."

Penny placed the hand she had been working on back in the soaking water and picked up Karis's other hand. She began shaping the nails and silence once again settled over them, broken only by the whispery sound of the emery board brushing against a fingernail. When she'd finished the filing, she looked over her shoulder to speak to Bethan, who was pretending to busy herself sorting bottles of nail polish that Eirlys always kept perfectly arranged. "Bethan, would you mind helping Karis choose her polish?"

"I think a bright red," Karis said, looking up. Bethan pulled four bottles and showed them to her. "That one, I think," Karis said, pointing at one.

Penny picked up a pair of sterile clippers and began trimming around her fingernails, letting bits of discarded skin drop onto the towel. When she had finished both hands, she rolled up the towel and handed it to Bethan who exchanged it for a fresh one. Penny arranged this over the table, running her hands over it to smooth it out, gave Karis a reassuring smile, and began applying a base coat as Bethan left the room. Bethan carried the towel to the reception area where Eirlys held open a plastic bag. She placed the towel in the evidence bag, sealed it, and initialed it in the appropriate box. She handed her smock to Eirlys, thanked her, and left the Spa. Within the hour, the towel was being unrolled in the North Wales Police Service lab and the bits of skin it contained prepared for DNA testing.

Penny applied the final strokes of top coat and then sat back as Karis held up her hands. "Thank you," she said. "They look very nice."

That's high praise coming from you, thought Penny. "You're most welcome," she said. "We'll see you tonight at the dress rehearsal."

Thirty-eight

"W e'll take the musicians and singers down first," said mine manager Bevan Jones. "And for those who don't want to wait for the train, one of our guides here will walk the rest of you down. But it's steep and there are a lot of stairs—sixty-one in all—so mind how you go."

Victoria, accompanied by Ifan, helped Karis into the yellow train that would transport them to the carved-out bowels of the mine. Penny chose the stairs and holding on to the wooden handrail followed Rebeccah Roberts step by step into the mine. When they reached the bottom, their guide led them in the direction of voices along the rough passageway until they came to the chamber where the concert would take place. Victoria and Ifan huddled with Karis, referring to bundles of sheet music. As Penny and Rebeccah approached, the conversation stopped.

"Penny, we need your opinion," Victoria said. "Even though

it's so late in the day we haven't agreed on the final song choice for Karis. I think it would be great if we went with something big and dramatic that would give Karis the chance to really show off her range. We're thinking this one. What do you think?" She held up a page.

Penny scanned the title, silently agreeing with Victoria's earlier comment that they'd left it awfully late to be sorting out the playlist. "Oh, that would be perfect. Everyone will love that."

"Karis insists that if Rebeccah is to be here for the dress rehearsal that she sit in the back row where she can't be seen," Victoria said. "She says she never allows anyone except the musicians and technicians to be present at a dress rehearsal but she's making an exception for Rebeccah, maybe because it's just so dark down here. So you, I'm afraid, will have to make yourself scarce."

"That's fine," said Penny with a puzzled frown. "I'm meeting Florence in the café to go over the arrangements for the reception and then I'm meeting with Bevan Jones to see what he suggests we do with media. Well, I say media. With a bit of luck there'll be one reporter from the local paper. So I'll leave you to it."

Before she left, Penny had a word with Rebeccah, who dutifully picked up a chair and took it to the complete blackness at the rear of the seating area.

The lights came up, showing Karis in a bright, white circle. The little group of musicians whose output would be augmented with an instrumental tape, tuned their instruments. Victoria tilted her harp into her lap, placed her ear close to the strings, and plucked them. She adjusted the tension and then plucked again. Satisfied, she nodded at Ifan, who motioned to Karis and the rehearsal began. Penny listened for a moment, then groped her way along the tunnel's cool, damp walls to the steep flight of stairs that led to the light and air of the surface. She reached the stairs, arrived at the top slightly out of breath, and then hurried to the warmth of the café.

In most Victorian mining operations, because only half an hour was allowed for lunch, the miners did not have enough time to walk up the steep incline to the surface, eat, and return to their caverns, so they ate where they worked. Their meals were usually meagre and poor: bread and dripping with cold tea or buttermilk. They would eat in fifteen minutes and in the remaining fifteen minutes sing, debate politics, or discuss the sermon they had heard at chapel on Sunday.

By the twentieth century, with mechanization and more time allowed for a midday meal, miners often gathered in the café, or caban as it was called, to study, debate, or engage in programs of self-enrichment.

When Penny entered the café the tables had been rearranged to accommodate a buffet along one wall. Above them hung large blowups of black-and-white photos possibly taken in the 1920s. The miners' stern, grainy faces, frozen in time, gazed down at her. They wore working-class clothing of frayed cloth caps and rough trousers, with white shirts, vests, and jackets as their work clothes. One man hung perilously high up the slate face, secured only by a rope around his waist, another raised a mallet to strike the chisel that would split the slate that rested against his leg. Penny gazed at their inscrutable faces. She doubted they were happy in their work. They likely loathed and resented every backbreaking, mind-numbing moment of it, as they continued to do it, day after day, year after year, to feed their families, until they were as worn out and worked out by the age of forty as the mine itself was now. But there were no benefits back then, no easy life on the dole for those who chose not to work.

A small noise behind her pulled her away from these thoughts and she turned to see Florence pushing through a swing door marked:

Staff Caffi yn Unig
Café Staff Only

"If you're here to check up on me, everything's under control, Penny," she said. "You don't have to worry about the food. It'll be all right on the night, as they say, and we're setting up here so the musicians can enjoy some refreshments during their break. There's tea and coffee, sandwiches, and tea cakes. That should keep them going."

Penny touched Florence lightly on the arm. "I have no worries about you Florence. If there's one person we can count on it's you." They both turned at the sound of approaching footsteps. "Oh, good, there's Mrs. Lloyd. She's taking the tickets so I'll just have a word with her about that. Excuse me."

"She's feeling a little left out tonight, I think," said Florence in a low voice. "Maybe if you could find a little task for her. She would insist on coming with me even though I told her there wouldn't be much for her to do here, but you know what she's like. She needs careful handling, sometimes."

Penny gave Florence a grateful nod. "Right, well, thank you Florence. I'll leave you to it." She turned to Mrs. Lloyd who was looking rather smart in a finely made burgundy wool coat.

"Hello, there," said Penny. "Everything all right?"

"Yes, I imagine so," said Mrs. Lloyd. "Fine with me. How about you? Got a lot to pull together at the last minute, have you?"

"Oh, yes," said Penny. "Everyone's been really helpful and doing their bit, so we'll be all right on the night, as they say. Now, let's have a seat over here and we'll go over the ticket taking." When they were seated Penny explained to Mrs. Lloyd that they were planning to seat her at the front entrance. Penny herself would be nearby to point the arrivals to the little yellow train that would take them down the mine to the concert level.

"Are you sure you're all right, Penny?" Mrs. Lloyd asked. "You seem distracted. Is there something else you should be doing now? You seem rather worried."

"It's not the event itself," said Penny, frowning. "But I've just seen something that's got me wondering."

"Oh," said Mrs. Lloyd, leaning forward. "What's that?"

"Well, they're rehearsing downstairs, and apparently our guest singer, Karis Edwards, never allows someone to sit in on the rehearsal. Only musicians and stage crew allowed. You know, the people necessary for the performance."

"That's understandable, I guess," said Mrs. Lloyd.

"Oh, of course it is," said Penny. "That's not the problem. The problem is, she just said Rebeccah Roberts could watch. That just seemed such an odd thing. Why would she allow her to sit in? Why would she break the rule for someone she doesn't know?"

"Oh, but she does know her," said Mrs. Lloyd. "I've seen them myself. Nattering away like old friends, they were, so maybe that would explain it."

"When was this?" Penny asked sharply.

"A day or two ago. Why? Does it matter? Is it important?"

"It might be," said Penny, her mind whirling. "Where did you see them?"

"Let me see. I'd been to the chemists and I was on my way to the post office, so I crossed the town square and . . ." Mrs. Lloyd's eyes wandered over to the black-and-white photographs of the miners as she tried to visualize. "That's right. It would have been

Tuesday. Market day. Rebeccah was running her stall and that's where I saw her, talking to that Karis Edwards woman. I recognized her from the photo on the poster."

"Well, Mrs. Lloyd, if they were talking at the stall, that means nothing. Rebeccah talks to all her customers. She has to. Karis was probably just strolling around the town, saw something that interested her, and they exchanged a few words about it."

"Oh, no, Penny, it was more than that. Glenda's son Peris was there and Rebeccah said something to him—asked him to keep an eye on things would be my guess because the next thing he's stood behind the stall—and the two women left. They didn't go far, though, just to the café. You know the one. At the edge of the square, on the corner." Mrs. Lloyd looked a little sheepish. "It's not that I was spying on them, you understand. I was just waiting for a friend outside the post office."

"Of course you were. Well, that's very interesting." Penny checked her watch. "Sorry, Mrs. Lloyd, I've got to go and speak to the mine manager about a few details." She paused for a moment. "You know, Mrs. Lloyd, the musicians will be ready to break in about half an hour, so it would be really helpful if you'd station yourself just outside the café and let them know refreshments are waiting for them.

"I'll have to see if Karis needs anything. Rhian was supposed to look after her, but apparently her grandfather doesn't have much time left, so she's gone to be with her family."

"Yes, I did hear that about Dylan Phillips. Don't worry. I'll make sure the musicians find their way here," Mrs. Lloyd reassured her.

Penny picked up her hard hat and torch and left the café. She stepped out onto the gravelled walkway that led to the staging area where she found Bevan Jones. They had a few words about

226

media arrangements and then Penny continued on her way. The train should be waiting now at the deep level to bring the musicians to the surface. She checked her watch. Eight thirty. If she hurried down the stairs, she should just be in time to join them as they began to make their way to the surface during their rehearsal break, keen for a cup of tea, a chance to visit the lavatories, and to discuss the program's progress with their colleagues.

As she groped her way along the dark tunnel that led to the chamber where the concert would be held, someone spoke.

"No, not that way. This way. It's a more direct route to the exit."

She stopped, pressed herself against the rough, wet walls, and held her breath when she heard footsteps coming toward her.

"You seem to know your way around these tunnels," a second voice replied.

"I told you not to speak to me in front of other people," the first voice said in a low, urgent tone. A woman's voice, with a South Wales accent. That's got to be Karis, thought Penny. I wonder who she's talking to. "We've got to be careful so people don't connect us."

"But I was worried," said the second voice, which Penny now recognized as belonging to Rebeccah. "When I didn't hear from you I wondered if you were all right."

"Of course I was all right," snapped Karis. "Why wouldn't I be?"

"Well, it's just that . . ."

"Look, Rebeccah, this isn't the time to go into all that. I've got to focus on the performance. We'll meet up after the concert and work out where we go from here. But for now, just leave me to get on with my work. *Dyfal donc y dyr y garreg.*"

Rebeccah laughed. "'Steady tapping breaks the stone.' Very good, that, Karis, considering where we are." The two women stopped. "But listen, we don't have much time. People might ask questions and it's better if they don't know about us," said Karis.

Penny flattened herself further against the tunnel wall as the two approached her, a jagged piece of slate in the rough-hewn wall digging into her back. She let out a little gasp of pained surprise.

"What was that?" said Karis.

"Who's there?" said Rebeccah.

"Oh, hello," said Penny, taking a swift step forward that she hoped included enough momentum to indicate she had been walking toward them and had been further away than she really was. "I was just on my way to bring everyone upstairs for some refreshments."

The look Karis gave her, barely discernible in the dim light of the tunnel, was as hard and black as the slate walls that surrounded them. The moment passed when the rest of the musicians and singers flowed into the tunnel and the excited, chattering group hurried to the train to take them to the surface.

Mrs. Lloyd greeted them at the entrance to the caban and Florence gestured proudly at the table of freshly cut sandwiches, homemade biscuits, cakes, tea, and coffee. Penny and Victoria stood to one side as the musicians, slowly and politely at first and then, as they realized how hungry they were, eagerly helped themselves. They took their plates and cups to the tables and tucked in. Soon the room was filled with the ambient background hum of happy chatter in a partylike atmosphere.

Penny and Victoria were the last to make their way to the buffet table with its cheerful red-and-white gingham cloth.

"Unfortunately all the gingerbread loaf is gone," said Florence gloomily. "I'll have to remember next time to double the recipe. I hope you're not too disappointed."

"That's all right, Florence," said Victoria. "Everything you make is delicious so I'm sure we'll find something here . . . ooh, look, there's a bit of lemon drizzle cake left." The two helped themselves and then sat at an empty table near the serving counter. After a moment Florence and Mrs. Lloyd joined them.

"How's the rehearsal going so far?" Mrs. Lloyd asked Victoria.

"As you'd expect. A lot of starts and stops and from the top."

"And Karis Edwards. Did she sing?"

"She did," said Victoria.

"And?" Mrs. Lloyd prompted. "How did she sound? Are we in for a treat?"

"Well, she seemed a bit, how shall I put this? Out of practice? And I don't think she was giving it her best. Just seemed to be going through the motions. But some performers do that. They hold something back so they can give it their all on the night." She took a bite of egg salad sandwich. "Or, it may be that what she once had is starting to go. That happens, too."

"Did you say something to her?" asked Florence, looking over Penny's shoulder. She tilted her head and pursed her lips. "Has something happened? She seems to be looking in our direction and judging by her face, she's not a happy bunny."

Penny shuffled uneasily in her seat. She started to turn her head to look over her shoulder at Karis, thought better of it, and turned her attention to Florence. But as she did so, the memory she had struggled to capture since Doreen's death charged into the forefront of her consciousness. Now she remembered what she'd seen at the nursing home that had seemed significant at the time.

"She just seemed a little off, as I said, but everything's fine,

229

so far as I know." Victoria glanced at Penny. "Well, there is one thing. For some reason she wants to change one of the pieces from a major key to a minor key."

"Is that a big deal?"

"It is, rather. Sad songs or serious ones, like hymns, are written in a minor key. Upbeat happy ones are written in major. So if you change from major to minor, you're going to get a different sound. If you want to get technical about it, changing from major key to minor key alters the distance relationship between the degrees of the scale and therefore naturally changes the melody slightly—and I don't think our audience will take very kindly to that. It adds a touch of melancholy to the music. It doesn't seem necessary to me and all of us have now got to make the changes. You just don't do that at the final rehearsal. But she's insistent. So it's made for some heavy going. Ifan is trying to keep her in line, but he can't. Divas just don't like hearing the word 'No.'" She paused and exchanged a glance with Florence. "Do they, Penny?"

Penny started. "Sorry, what?"

"You were a million miles away, I think," said Florence. "But that's understandable. You've got a lot on here, and I expect you'll be very relieved when all this is over."

"Yes," agreed Penny. "Very relieved."

Victoria wiped her hands on her serviette, bunched it up, and set it on her plate. "I'm sure I speak for all of us, Florence, when I tell you that really hit the spot," she said. "Thank you."

Florence pinched her lips together and nodded in a low-key, satisfied way.

"I expect we'll be another hour, unless the Karis part of the rehearsal drags on, which it very well might do," Victoria continued. "If you don't mind waiting that long, we'd be happy to drive you home."

"That should work very nicely," agreed Florence. "We'll tidy away here, sort ourselves out for tomorrow evening, and be ready to leave when you come up."

The room was beginning to thin out as performers shuffled toward the door to return to the train and descend to the concert chamber for the second half of the rehearsal. Victoria stood up to join them, looking over her shoulder at Penny.

"I'll give Florence a hand and then be down in about an hour for one last check," Penny said.

"Right. See you then."

"I'll give you a hand with the clearing up, Florence," said Penny, "but I've got to make a quick phone call."

She stepped out into the area just inside the entrance and stood in front of the locked and darkened gift shop.

"Oh, good, you're there," she said when Davies answered. "I've just remembered something that happened at the nursing home around the time Doreen died. It wasn't after she died, it was before. I was sitting in the lounge with my back to the door and Doreen looked over my shoulder and saw someone. She looked as if she'd seen a ghost. She brushed it off, but seeing this person, whoever it was, shook her up. She asked me to leave soon after. And within a day or two, she was dead. I think someone she did not want or expect to see again turned up at the nursing home."

"I'll send Bethan over tomorrow to look into it," said Davies. "Thanks for this."

Thirty-nine

A n hour later, the last of the dishes had been washed, dried, and put away. Florence took off her old-fashioned apron with its cheerful pattern of blue pansies, folded it, and placed it in her bag.

Mrs. Lloyd looked up from her magazine. "Well? Is it time to go?"

"It is," said Florence. "In fact, I think I hear them. Yes, here they come," she said as the sound of voices came closer, passed the open-fronted sheds now shuttered for the night, then filed past the windows of the café. Their voices receded as they continued on their way to the exit. When the last of them had disappeared into the night, the two women turned to each other.

"Well, Penny and Victoria must have stayed behind for a few minutes for some reason," said Florence, checking her watch.

"They probably have some last-minute details to sort out. We'll give them ten more minutes."

Mrs. Lloyd made an exasperated little sound. "Ten more minutes and then what? It's getting late and I'm tired. Now we've probably missed our chance of a ride home. Everyone else will have left and the buses have long since stopped running. And we're practically in the middle of nowhere."

"Ten more minutes and then we'll see about getting some help," said Florence. "We can't just leave them down there all night and ring for a taxi, can we?"

By the time she finished her sentence, just two vehicles remained in the visitors' car park.

A frowning Victoria closed the zipper on her harp case. "I'm not sure the case will keep all the damp out. I hope my beautiful harp will be all right down here overnight with this humidity. To be honest, I'd be happier if I could bring it back to the surface. If the wood swells, even a little, the sound will be completely off and I don't know what kind of permanent damage that might do to it."

"I can give you a hand carrying it up the stairs, if you like," said Penny. "Or better yet, maybe he can help us." She gestured at one of Bevan Jones's assistants covering up the audio equipment with a blue canvas-type material. Victoria had a word with him and then returned to Penny.

"He's got some extra waterproof material that he can spread over my harp, and the keyboard, too. That should keep the damp out, so the instruments should be okay for one night. I hadn't thought about this, but I'm glad he can help."

"I wonder," said Penny. "There's something I'd like some help with. Now it's my turn to have a word." The lights had been turned up and the stage area was fairly well lit, but the sides and back of the cavern were bathed in absolute darkness. "Is Bevan not here?"

"Now that you mention it, I haven't seen him for a while," said Victoria. "He wasn't in the café, was he?"

"I'll have a word, then, with your man over there." Picking her way over cables and moving a couple of chairs out of the way, she reached the assistant who had just finished wrapping the sound equipment in waterproof material.

"No, he's gone home. His missus called. His son was having trouble breathing and she wanted him home."

"Trouble breathing? Is he . . . ?"

"Yeah, he has that condition where he gets very short of breath and he has to use one of those puffer things. Anyway, what was it you wanted?"

With her thoughts running in all directions, Penny told him.

While she was explaining what she had in mind, Karis approached Victoria and the two discussed last-minute concert arrangements as Rebeccah hovered nearby.

As she got closer to the three women, Penny breathed in a fragrance, heady and strong, as if it had just been applied. Sharp and over-the-top flowery. Overwhelming, even. Oh, what was it? The box. It came in a yellow-and-white striped box. She hadn't smelled that fragrance in many years and now she'd smelled it at least twice within the past few weeks. When? Where?

Forty

The night wrapped its cold, silent arms around them. Victoria, who'd reached the stage where she did as little night driving as possible, kept her eyes on the winding road ahead as she switched on the car's heater.

"That feels good," said Penny. "I didn't realize how cold I was." She stifled a yawn. "Or how tired." She turned to the pair in the backseat. "Are you two all right?" Mrs. Lloyd's eyes were closed, her head reclining against the back of the seat. Florence nodded.

A few moments later the ping of an incoming text message broke the silence. Penny checked her phone and then turned slightly in her seat toward Victoria so the backseat passengers could hear what she had to tell them.

"Rhian's grandfather has just died. The family has decided they'd like to come to the concert tomorrow as a way to honour him."

Mrs. Lloyd and Florence made little murmuring sounds of acknowledgement.

"We should mention the miners in our introduction," said Victoria.

"Agreed," said Penny.

"Absolutely," murmured Mrs. Lloyd, her eyes still closed.

Penny settled back in her seat and closed her eyes, too.

Eventually they came to the familiar few houses at the edge of town that couldn't properly be called the outskirts, but did indicate the separation of town and country. Sensing the car slowing down, Penny opened her eyes and looked out the window until she got a sense of where they were.

After dropping off Mrs. Lloyd and Florence, and waiting until the front door had closed behind them and the hall light switched on, Penny and Victoria drove off.

"It's been a long day," said Victoria. "If you'd rather not be alone tonight, you're more than welcome to stop at mine."

"Oh, home I think," Penny said. "I appreciate the offer, but there's no comfort on earth like your own bed. Especially when it's been a long day."

"True," said Victoria as they passed the Spa and turned down the road that led to Penny's cottage. A few moments later they pulled up in front of it.

"We'll talk about everything in the morning," said Penny. "I've got a lot to think about. Sorry I wasn't very good company on the drive home."

"A little quiet is a good thing. Everybody was tired and nobody was in the mood to talk. Good night and see you in the morning." Penny gave a little wave as she walked up the path and then let herself into the dark house. She switched on the hall light and heard Victoria drive off as she hung her keys on the little hook near the door.

"Harrison?" she called.

Her little grey cat padded out from the kitchen. The tip of his tail twitched slightly and he regarded her through narrowed eyes filled with reproach.

"Sorry," she apologized. "Got held up. I'll put some food out for you straight away." She filled his shallow dish and stood over him as he crouched over the bowl. After a few mouthfuls he looked up at her and then turning his back on her, walked away. She followed him into the sitting room and sat down on the sofa. A few moments later he jumped up, walked the length of the sofa, and then turned around and walked back to her. Finally, knowing he'd made his point, he snuggled up against her thigh and began purring. She reached down and began stroking his silky fur. She'd always thought herself more of a dog person, but loved having him to take care of. She let her head droop against the back of the sofa and closed her eyes. As waves of exhaustion washed over her she wondered if she had enough energy left to get herself upstairs to bed. She tucked her hand under Harrison's front leg and stroked his soft underside. She thought back to the woman who'd raised her, a cousin of her mother's. She'd been a hard, humourless woman and because she hated animals, everyone around her had to hate them, too. Except Penny hadn't.

Although she was exhausted, there was one more thing she had to do. She opened her laptop, and googled "perfume yellow and white striped box."

And there it was. Giorgio. That's the name of it. Giorgio. Hugely popular in the 1980s and so potent that some restaurants banned it. That was what she'd smelled tonight and . . . she couldn't remember. Leave it, she told herself. It will come to you. Probably someone at the Spa. That place was full of fragrance, which was why she and Victoria had decided that their house-brand skin-care products would be fragrance free.

Oh, so achingly tired. She thought how easy it would be to put her head on the pillow at one end of the sofa, cover herself with the light blanket draped over the armrest at the other end, and just drift off to sleep. How blissful it would be. But then she remembered the times she'd done that and how cold and uncomfortable she'd been, waking up at 3 A.M. and having to haul herself off to bed in an even worse state than she was now—stiff, groggy, and in a very bad mood. No, she'd be better to push herself for a few more minutes, get upstairs, and fall into her lovely bed. Harrison could take care of himself and sleep wherever he chose. With a sigh she stood up, turned off the lights, and lifted one leaden foot after the other until she reached the top of the stairs.

She switched on the electric blanket to give it a few minutes to warm her bed while she brushed her teeth, wiped her face with a cleansing cloth, undressed, and put on a nightshirt. As she slid into the comfort of sheets that were just beginning to warm, she was glad she'd made the effort to haul her tired bones upstairs to bed. As she stretched out, she remembered that she needed to tell Gareth what the mine worker had told her about Bevan Jones's son and his breathing difficulties in case it was connected to the incident that Peris had described of the angry man at the market shouting at Glenda about the toxic air freshener. But there would be time for that in the morning. It was too late now to ring him; he'd be asleep and anyway, it wasn't urgent. Longing for sleep herself, she turned on her side, closed her eyes, and drifted off.

———

DCI Gareth Davies picked up his watch off the nightstand and checked the time. He'd been asleep for a couple of hours and awakened, as people with a lot on their minds sometimes do, to find that the long night's journey into day had ended prematurely. He knew the signs. It would be two or three hours before he'd be able to get back to sleep, so he might as well use the time wisely.

He threw back the covers, pulled on his old green plaid dressing gown, and wandered into the kitchen. A few minutes later, a cup of tea in his hand, he sat at the kitchen table and opened the file he'd brought home. He went over the notes to see if anything struck him this time that he'd missed on previous readings. Was there a different way to approach this case that would lead him to the solution? After a few minutes of rereading the same paragraph without getting any sense out of it, he gave up, closed the file, and pushed it away from him. He took a long sip of tea and allowed his mind to focus on something he'd been thinking about a lot lately.

It wasn't so much that he resented the long nights that the job sometimes demanded, it was more that his body protested more loudly each time it was asked to do things that had come so much easier just a few years ago. The idea of retirement was becoming increasingly appealing. Not so long ago he had hoped that Penny would share the coming years with him, but he was starting to accept that she wouldn't. When someone tells you they don't want to get married, what they're really saying is they don't want to marry you. He'd seen that many times. The confirmed bachelor who met the right woman and that was that. Married within months, leaving a trail of broken hearts behind him. At least Penny had been honest with him, sharing her feelings, including her doubts that they had a future together. And she'd told him before he'd made a fool of himself asking her to marry him. He respected her for that, but he couldn't help wishing the outcome had been different. He thought they'd found something wonderful in each other, but apparently he wasn't what she was looking for.

Perhaps a change of scenery might do him good. Sometimes a bit of distance can provide much-needed perspective on a problem. He considered a few days in Liverpool with his son and daughter-in-law, but they had a new baby and wouldn't want him under their feet. And then he remembered a fairly recent acquaintance, Alan Nesbitt, retired chief constable for the county of Belleshire, who had married Dorothy Martin, a former schoolteacher from America. There were a lot of similarities between the two couples and at one time he'd hoped his and Penny's story would have the same happy ending as Alan's and Dorothy's.

When the Roberts case was wrapped up, and he expected it wouldn't go on much longer, he'd drive over to Sherebury and have a word with Alan. Maybe get in a few rounds of golf, a few pints down the pub. And since Penny had been the one who'd introduced them, he'd ask her if she wanted to go with him. He didn't think she would, but that didn't matter. If Alan and Dorothy could put him up for a few days, he'd go on his own. And depending on what advice and insight Alan had to offer, when he got back he'd request a meeting with the superintendent to discuss his retirement options.

Feeling better now that he had a plan and something to look forward to, he went back to bed and fell into a dreamless sleep.

Forty-one

"I've come to apologize to you, Jimmy."

"Me? What on earth have you got to apologize to me for?"

They were seated in the lounge of the nursing home, Jimmy in his wheelchair in his usual place and Penny beside him. The care aide would be here at any moment with the residents' cups of lukewarm midmorning tea.

"Because in making all the arrangements for the concert I forgot to invite you. And now that Dylan has died, we are going to mention the miners and their importance to the area, and his family will be there. You were his last friend, so you should be there, too."

Jimmy made a vague, dismissive gesture at his legs. "It's a mine, Penny. It's not accessible to someone like me."

"Tonight it is. I spoke to one of the guys last night. They've got a little chair that paramedics use to transport people on stairs and they'll bring it out for you. And your old friend DCI Gareth Davies has agreed to keep an eye on you to make sure you don't get into trouble. And we'll sort out your ride. So what do you say, Jimmy? Would you like to come?"

His smile lit up the room as he turned shining eyes to her.

"Best offer I'll get all day."

"Great! So you'll need to be ready about five thirty. We'll get you there early. Oh, and be sure to dress very warmly because it's cold and damp down there, as you'd expect. If you've got a rug of some sort for your knees, bring that." As she finished speaking, the care aide entered the lounge, handing out cups of tea to those who wanted one. Penny's eyes followed her for a moment, then turned to Jimmy.

"Did you notice a different care aide around the time Doreen died?" Penny asked. "Someone you hadn't seen before and who wasn't around very long?"

"Can't say as I did. I really don't take much notice of them. They're just here one day and the next day they're not, so what you've just described—someone 'who wasn't around very long'—sounds like all of them."

"What do you mean?"

"There's a pretty high staff turnover here. They're young women, they need a job, there's always work going in places like this, they take it and discover it's boring or a bit on the unpleasant side, so they quit. And then someone else comes along. For a while. But the real problem is that the pay is low and if they have a kiddie or two, they can get more money on benefits than they can earn here. So in effect the government pays them not to work."

He fell silent for a moment, looking at his hands.

"You know, I've been thinking about work, lately, ever since Dylan told us how boys who grew up around here felt there was no hope of escaping the mine. Well, it was a little like that for me, too."

Penny leaned closer.

"When I was a lad I fell in with the wrong crowd. We stole a few things, not real bad by today's standards, but I was sent away to Borstal. And that became a life sentence, you might say. All I ever knew was petty crime. And in those days, just like for Dylan, there was no one to say we could do better. Make something of ourselves."

"What would you do now if you had a chance to do it all again?"

"I came to have a real respect for the law, being as I was on the wrong side of it for so long. I saw how smart the lawyers were and I'm sure the work would have been interesting. So if young Jimmy were here today, he'd pull his finger out, borrow the money, go to uni, and become a solicitor. Maybe even a barrister."

Penny looked at him in admiration. "You know, Jimmy, I bet you would."

They exchanged a warm, companionable smile just as the care aide approached and held out a Styrofoam cup. Jimmy held up a "no, thanks" hand and Penny smiled and shook her head.

They watched her move on to the next resident, who raised trembling hands to take the tea and then they turned back to face each other. "Tell me, Jimmy, do you think someone could pretend to be a worker here and get away with it for a day or two before anyone asked any questions?"

Jimmy gave her a sharp look. "Well, yes, I suppose someone

could. If they had the right clothes and knew what they were doing. And didn't hang around too long." He raised an eyebrow. "You thinking of anyone in particular?"

A line of black, bare trees stood in stark silhouette along the top of the hills as Davies and Sgt. Bethan Morgan drove toward the mine. Unable to reach Davies, Penny had called Bethan first thing that morning and talked to her for a few minutes about the implications of Bevan Jones's argument in the market with Glenda Roberts over the toxic air freshener.

"This could be where everything starts to unravel," Davies remarked. "So far, this investigation's been all over the place and if Bevan Jones is in fact the man who was seen arguing with Glenda Roberts in the market the day before she died, we could be getting someplace. He'll have some explaining to do."

"Penny thinks . . ." Bethan began, but Davies interrupted her.

"I think we've had enough of what Penny thinks for now, Sergeant," he said. "What we need more of here is good solid police-detective work. For example, what about the lab results of the slate splitters? When can we expect them?"

"But I thought you . . ."

"I do value Penny's input. But just not right now."

Someone's very tetchy this morning. Well, that's me told, thought Bethan. Now clearly separated by rank, they drove on in awkward silence through the wild mountain pass, as the old keep of Dolwyddelan Castle, the only surviving fortress of the great Welsh prince Llywelyn the Great loomed into view. The views all around them of bleak, bare mountains in mournful shades of brown and grey were stunning in a cold, forbidding

246

way; trees and most of the plant life had given way to a rugged and inhospitable terrain.

"All right," Davies said, breaking the silence. "Go on, then. What did she say?"

"She can see how we'd want to look at Bevan Jones for Glenda Roberts's murder, but Doreen? The slate in the hands would seem to bind the two victims together, with one killer."

"That's where the detective work comes into it. If there is a connection, we'll have to find out what that is." Davies flicked on the turn signal and slowed down for the turn into the Llyn Du mine car park.

Bevan Jones was waiting for them at the reception desk. The greeting was formal and over quickly. "Is there someplace private we can ask you a few questions?" Davies said.

"There's seating outside the café. Would that do? There's no one around and we won't be bothered." He led the way along the covered walkway until they came to an outdoor seating area. He gestured at one of the tables and they sat down.

"Mr. Jones," Bethan Morgan began, "a man was seen arguing with Glenda Roberts in the marketplace the day before she died, apparently over some fake air freshener. He said his son had had a bad reaction to the product and had to be treated in A and E." She glanced at her notes. "The local hospital tells us that your asthmatic son was treated the night before for shortness of breath and wheezing." She looked up at Jones. "Were you the man seen shouting at Glenda Roberts?"

Bevan Jones ran his hand across his cheek and mouth and then nodded.

"Yes. I was very angry with her. She was responsible for this dangerous product. I took the can to the hospital and told them I thought it had to do with my lad's condition. He was very

247

poorly. Practically unconscious. They said they'd seen two or three similar cases in young children and the can was full of methanol. It could kill somebody! It harmed my boy and, yes, I was very angry. My wife was beside herself."

"As a father, I know how you must have felt," said Davies. "But I wonder if you can imagine how this looks to us. You have a heated argument with our victim and the next day, she's found dead, down your mine. And you're the one who finds her. And she's been killed by a slate splitter, a tool that you had easy access to."

"Which one?" Bevan asked.

"Which one what?" Davies replied.

"There were three slate splitters. Bryn Thomas has one, one was locked in the display cupboard, and the third one was in the mine as part of a display of tools that we use to demonstrate Victorian mining techniques. The tour guide would talk about it, but not actually use it because the splitting is done up here, as you know. Which slate splitter killed Glenda Roberts?"

"I'm afraid I can't tell you that," Bethan said. She glanced at Davies. "We're almost finished for today, Mr. Jones. Just a couple more questions, but we may need to speak to you again. Did you kill Glenda Roberts?"

"I did not."

"Why didn't you mention the argument earlier?"

"Because I knew what it would look like to you."

"But you must have known we'd find out about it."

Bevan Jones shrugged.

"I guess I was willing to take my chances."

"Did you know Glenda's mother, Doreen?"

He shook his head. "Never met her."

"And why didn't you tell us about the third slate splitter when we first asked you about them?"

"It slipped my mind," Bevan replied.

In the car on the way back to Llanelen, Bethan got the lab results.

"The third splitter from the Victorian demonstration contains traces of Glenda Roberts's DNA. The other two do not," she said.

"Interesting. So whoever killed Glenda used the slate splitter because it was handy."

"And that could have been just about anybody who was down the mine that day."

Forty-two

*P*enny reached into the wooden bin and pulled out two hard hats and in what was now becoming a familiar gesture, handed one to Victoria and fitted the other one on her head. "I'll be so glad when this concert is over," she said. "My stomach is positively churning thinking about all the things that could go wrong. And my to-do list is as long as your arm. Check this. Pick up that. Do this. Don't forget that."

"The great thing is you've got Florence in charge up here," said Victoria. "You know she'll make sure everything goes well. She'll keep Mrs. Lloyd on track and the food for the after-party will be brilliant. Don't worry. Everything'll be fine."

"And then there's Karis. She's a loose cannon, if you ask me. Anything could happen there. I hope she'll stick to the program you sorted out with her."

"She has to," Victoria replied, "if she wants to get paid."

"Well, let's get on with it." Along with the rest of the musicians, they climbed aboard the small train and began the steep descent into the mine. No one spoke as the dark walls of the mine closed in. The train reached its docking station and after reminding everyone in her compartment to mind their heads as they left the train, Penny ducked her head and stepped out onto the floor of the mine. The musicians stood in a small group, awaiting instructions.

"Right, everybody," she said. "Here's Bevan to lead us to our concert space so we can get everything set up. Be sure to stick together."

Carrying their bags of material needed for the concert, and as their eyes adjusted to the darkness, they set off one last time down the maze of dark tunnels that led to the concert area, pausing for a moment to gaze at the underground lake, its surface calm and the water cold and clear. The air was fresh, not stale or stuffy as you might imagine, and cool with a hint of dampness like an early October morning after a steady overnight rain.

In the great concert space, rows of folding chairs had been set out in straight lines with a narrow aisle down the centre. A separate row of chairs had been set up near the stage and at a right angle to the audience for local dignitaries and special guests. Penny had arranged for Jimmy to sit at the end of this row nearest the audience. Because Mrs. Lloyd, who was taking tickets would be the last to arrive, and because Florence, who was handling the catering would need to slip out early, chairs had been reserved for them.

Penny smiled to herself as she taped the seat card printed with Florence's name to the backrest of the chair beside Jimmy's—he admired her tremendously and seating her beside him would add to his enjoyment of the event. Mrs. Lloyd would sit beside Florence and Bethan Morgan beside her with Davies on Bethan's right. The extra four seats were reserved for media and the local councilor who had promised he would do his best to attend, which Penny took to mean he'd come if he had nothing better to do and didn't receive a better offer.

Because real burning candles were out of the question for safety reasons, hundreds of battery-operated tea lights lined each side of the aisle and had been placed on every small ledge, nook, and cranny that could hold one. Volunteers had switched them all on a few minutes ago and now their little white artifical flames flickered all around the massive chamber as a visual tribute to the miners who had once worked this space by the light of tallow candles they'd had to pay for themselves.

The fake candles looked real enough, Penny thought, as she admired them, and they certainly helped create the right atmosphere for a special event in such a unique setting.

A small area to the left of the stage, draped by black curtains that so blended in with their surroundings as to be invisible to the audience, had been set up as a kind of green room. Penny pulled the curtain back and peered in. A small lamp rigged up with a heavy-duty extension cord and fitted with a low-wattage bulb shone a pool of weak light over a small table. Karis Edwards sat beside the table, eyes closed, a bottle of water clutched with both hands resting in her lap. She seemed to be meditating or simply contemplating the performance ahead. If she sensed the curtain had been pulled back and someone was observing her, she gave no sign. She remained as she was, still and closed off.

As the sound of excited voices from the tunnel signalled the arrival of the first group of audience members Penny let the curtain drop and approached the volunteers who would act as ushers. "Right. Show time! Torches on and let's get everyone seated as quickly as you can. We want this lot seated before the next group arrives. And be sure to give everyone a program."

"How will they ever read the program in this light?" asked one.

"It's a souvenir for later," said Penny. "The choir leader will announce the songs as we go."

The first arrivals, many of whom were experiencing the mine for the first time and all of whom were wearing daffodils on their lapels, entered the concert space and exclaimed in wonder at the massive cavern lit by dramatic theatre-type lighting enhanced by twinkling candles. They took their seats and as the next group arrived, Penny's shoulders relaxed a little and she let out a long, slow breath of relief. Every seat was filled; this concert just might come together after all.

The last train brought the final guests to be seated in the reserved-seating row. As Penny led the way, Mrs. Lloyd acknowledged her friends and acquaintances in the front row with gracious smiles and nods. Jimmy was helped to his seat, and Florence tucked his blanket around his legs.

Penny stood to one side of the stage with Ifan Williams as an expectant hush fell over the concert chamber. A moment earlier she'd asked him how Taff was doing and was rewarded with a huge smile. Still wearing the smile, he walked to the edge of the slate stage, introduced himself, and welcomed the audience to this special concert on St. David's Day, the national day of celebration of all things Welsh. He paid a moving and emotional tribute to all the miners who had spent their working lives creating this majestic space that they were now enjoying; several audience members, descendents, perhaps of those very men, dabbed at their eyes. Penny was surprised by his eloquence and confidence. Where she hated public speaking, Ifan was thriving on it. He was poised and professional, completely unlike the somewhat awkward and ill-at-ease man she had thought him to be.

He kept his remarks brief and a few moments later he cued the audio technician and musicians to start the performance of the first song, "*Cwm Rhondda.*" This was followed by "*Ar Lan y Môr,*" a popular folk tune about the pleasures of the seaside, and then he invited the audience to join in the singing of the third song, the much-loved "*Calon Lân.*" A crowd favourite at Welsh national rugby matches, the song extols the virtues of a pure, clean heart.

Halfway through the song, Penny pulled back the curtain of the backstage area and gave Karis her three-minute stage call.

As the last strains of the song faded away, the crowd broke into applause. Ifan waited. Then, when the cavernous room was quiet, he introduced Karis Edwards and she glided onto the stage, greeted by polite clapping.

Dressed in a simple slate-grey, floor-length wraparound dress she stood in the spotlight, smiling, confident, and composed. As she sang the first few words of her song a capella, the music seemed to float in the air above the audience's heads and then soar upward to the slate ceiling. Her powerful voice filled the chamber with musical magic and a reverent hush fell over the audience as if they knew they were about to hear something extraordinary. She kept them waiting a moment longer than necessary and then the musical accompaniment filled in as she hit the well-known "And I will always love you" to rapturous applause. As the final note faded, the audience was on its feet, cheering wildly. Karis, who seemed a little surprised by the warmth of the applause, stepped back, bowed, blew them a kiss, and then began her second song.

Jimmy leaned forward in his chair staring at Karis. Davies

watched him out of the corner of his eye and then spoke in a whisper. "What is it, Jimmy?"

"I've seen her before. She was at the home the day Doreen Roberts died. She was wearing a blue sort of uniform. The others wear purple."

"Are you sure?'

Jimmy nodded. "Quite sure. Of course, it's a bit difficult to see properly in this light and at this distance. If I could get a closer look at her I might be more certain."

"After the concert we'll introduce you to her so you can get a closer look."

Karis performed her next two songs while Penny watched from in front of the curtain. With the end in sight, she could feel the tension in her shoulders starting to drain away.

And then, before she knew it, the concert was almost over. The choir performed "*Rhyfelgyrch Gwŷr Harlech*," inspired by the siege of Harlech Castle during the Wars of the Roses in the fifteenth century. The applause was rapturous and, finally, there was just the encore performance to go. Penny held her breath. She could almost feel the musicians starting to relax a little.

Karis stepped out from behind the curtain into the spotlight to be greeted by loud and sustained applause. Her face lit up and as the music began she raised her arms as if to embrace the audience. They loved her. The first notes signalled the start of the song Victoria had chosen to end the performance. It was another big song, "I Dreamed a Dream" from *Les Misérables,* and Karis was ready to give it everything she had.

As the song ended with its melodramatic yet haunting last line, Karis waited for the music to fade out, then smiled at the audience, accepted their applause, raised her arms to them, bowed, and then disappeared.

In the small, curtained-off space, technicians and a few musicians crowded around her to offer congratulations as Karis, flushed with excitement and on the adrenaline high of a winner, smiled and thanked them all. Penny and Victoria exchanged relieved smiles and then Victoria made a small "see you upstairs" gesture and turned back to her harp. Penny realized this was the first time she'd seen Victoria perform. The experience had been oddly moving, as if she were seeing an unknown side of someone she knew well. Penny wondered if Victoria felt the same way when she looked at one of her paintings. Penny gave Victoria a thumbs-up.

Karis took a swig from a water bottle just as the curtain parted and Davies entered, pushing Jimmy in his chair. The chair rocked and bobbed as it tried to negotiate the uneven ground.

Penny immediately went over to them, smiled her gratitude at Davies, and bent down to kiss Jimmy's cheek. He'd had a bath that afternoon and his hair had been washed and was neatly combed. She was glad to see him wearing a warm overcoat with a cheerful red plaid rug over his knees. As her lips touched his freshly shaven face, she inhaled an old-fashioned aftershave, something like bay rum, with a hint of lime. An uncle of hers had worn a similar type of cologne many years ago and smelling it now immediately transported her many years into the past and many miles across an ocean. As she straightened up, the smell of the Giorgio fragrance hit her again. She had smelled it in the mine tunnel after the dress rehearsal but she'd also smelled it at the nursing home. That was the smell that had been in Doreen's room when she'd discovered the body. And here it was again, right beside her.

Karis smiled at Davies and then lowered her eyes to Jimmy, who leaned forward, frowned, and reached back to touch Davies's arm. Her eyes flicked back to Davies, widened slightly, and her posture stiffened. She raised one hand in a small gesture and took a step back. Penny would later say that from that moment, everything seemed to happen in slow-motion and that events unfolded quickly—in confusion and in sharp, detailed relief at the same time. Karis gave Jimmy a dark, hate-filled stare and something unspoken crackled between them. *She knows*, Davies thought. *Karis knows that Jimmy's worked it out that he's seen her before. At the nursing home around the time Doreen died.*

Karis turned, brushed past Penny, pulled the curtain back, and melted into the first of the crowd of happy, chattering concert-goers who were being herded out of the concert chamber and into the tunnel.

"It's Karis you want," Penny said to Davies. "That heavy perfume she wears—Giorgio—it was in the room when I found Doreen's body. It's unmistakeable. Karis was there and I think she killed her."

Davies yanked the curtain aside and spotting Bethan, waved to attract her attention, and then called her name. The din of the crowd noise made it impossible for him to make himself heard. Penny hesitated a moment, exchanged a quick glance with Jimmy, and bolted after Karis.

"What is it? What's happened?" Bethan shouted, excusing herself and gently pushing people aside to reach Davies.

"Jimmy recognized Karis as having been at the nursing home when Doreen Roberts died," Davies said in a low voice, "and more importantly, she obviously recognized him. Penny thinks she can place her in Doreen's room at the time of Doreen's death. Karis is spooked and it looks like she's doing a runner. She'll try to work her way through the crowd, and knowing who she is, they'll be happy to let her through."

Bethan looked wildly at the area outside the chamber and could see only the crowd shuffling along in the semidarkness.

"Oh, Christ," she muttered. "Can we not ask them to let us through?"

"We have to be very careful here," said Davies. "We don't want to alarm the crowd or cause panic. The results of that would be disastrous. It's better to let her go than risk a crush."

By now the crowd was out of the chamber and into the tunnel, being led along to the train. As only about twenty-eight people could board the train at one time, and the rest would have to wait in the large open area nearby, Davies realized too late that for crowd-control purposes it would have been better to hold the crowd in the concert chamber, counting them out in groups of about twenty-five and escorting small, organized groups to the train. When the train reached the surface, the next group of twenty-five could then be brought forward ready to meet the train when it returned to the lower level. However, since no one had anticipated this kind of emergency, about a hundred people, two or three abreast, were now surging through the semidarkness of the tunnel. He didn't have a hope of getting through them and even if he did, he had no idea in what direction Karis had gone.

Davies turned back to Jimmy who said something that made his blood run cold.

"Penny's gone after her." Davies looked around wildly.

"What do mean? Did Penny . . . ?"

"She just took off after her. Why would she do such a daft thing?" Before Davies could reply, Jimmy continued. "Never mind. Don't answer that. Just get on it. You've got to do something. There's no telling what that Karis woman might do."

Forty-three

*I*n the now almost empty concert chamber, a few musicians and Bevan Jones and his team were clearing up. Davies approached Jones as workers stacked chairs and a technician dismantled the sound system. He placed his hand on Jones's arm.

"We've got a situation and I need your help. Now. A person of interest in our investigation has fled into the tunnel and the crowd's blocking the way. I have no idea what direction she went in and no idea where she's going. Tell me where the tunnels lead to from here."

Bevan straightened up. "If he turned right, he would have been headed toward the train stop and in that same area, the lake," he said. "If he'd gone the other way, he'll eventually come to a set of stairs that lead up to the next levels. And from there, he can make his way to the surface. He'll come out near the staging area where we board the train, or there's another way that

leads to the surface and comes out a few hundred metres west."
He made long, loops with the cabling in his hand. "Of course,
that's assuming he knows where he's going. If he's just running
blind through the tunnels, he's got about twenty-five miles to
get lost in and anyone who doesn't know where they're going
can get lost down here very quickly."

Davies groaned. "So she—and it's a *she,* not a he—could possibly get lost down here and we'd never see her again?"

"It's a mine, Inspector. Mines are dangerous places if you don't
know what you're doing. And, hell, they can be dangerous places
if you do know what you're doing. So, yes, for sure she could
get lost. Or if she ignores warnings and notices, she could find
herself headed down a tunnel that's due to be sealed off. The
ground is rough and uneven and the lighting is dim, as you know.
She could trip over something, fall, twist an ankle, or break a
bone and be unable to move. A lot of nasty things could happen."

Jones walked to the edge of the chamber and peered into the
tunnel, looking both ways. "The crowd is almost gone. Give us
a minute and the lads and I'll spread out, have a look in both
directions, and see what we can find. We've got the equipment
and there's nothing you can do to help, really. In fact, you'd
probably only slow us down. We'll give you one of our portable
radios and contact you if we find anything. So if I might suggest, sir, the best thing you can do is let us take care of this and
you wait to hear from us."

"I'll need to come with you," Davies said. "This is a serious
police matter. There's no way I can leave this situation to you.
The woman may be dangerous." And, he added silently, she
might have a hostage.

Davies turned to his sergeant. "You go back up. Get Karis's

vehicle registration and check the car park." He then returned his attention to Bevan. "I need one of your men to bring Sergeant Morgan to the surface, as quickly as possible. And I want him to stay with her and do whatever she asks him to do, and then bring her back down here to me."

"Who exactly are you after, Inspector?" Jones let out a low whistle when Davies told him.

In the tunnel, Karis grabbed Penny's arm and jerked her out of the line of concertgoers making their way to the train and pulled her down a dark side passage. "What the hell are you playing at?" Penny shouted at her as she stumbled on the rough ground. "Let go of me. I just want to talk to you." She tried to wrench her arm free, but Karis held her too tightly.

"Oh, really? You've been been asking a lot of nosy questions, I hear."

Before Penny could reply, someone called out. "Karis, where are you? It's me. Rebeccah."

"Down here."

Panting slightly and smiling, Rebeccah Roberts approached them.

"I thought I saw you go down here. What are you doing? This isn't the way to the train. We've got to stick with the crowd." Rebeccah looked from one to the other and sensing the alarm in Penny's face, took a step back as her smile faded. "Karis? What's going on?"

"Look, Karis," said Penny, finally freeing her arm. "You know this isn't going to work. Let's just get on the train and go up above and talk. It isn't worth it. Whatever happened, it's over." Aware that her tone sounded shrill and urgent, she tried to take it down to a calming timbre. "Doesn't it just feel over, Karis? Hasn't all this gone on too long?"

Karis grabbed her arm again and pulled her roughly further down the tunnel. Although Penny had spent very little time in the underground labyrinth, she sensed that she was being pulled deeper into the mine workings, away from the train that could take her to the surface. A set of stairs somewhere also led to the surface, but she was disoriented now in the semidarkness and had no idea where they were. After a few minutes of struggle as Karis pulled Penny by the arm while she tried to keep her footing, and Rebeccah trotted along beside them, they came to a small clearing, or open space, where a little pile of implements used in a demonstration of Victorian mining techniques was kept.

"Get the jumper," Karis snapped at Rebeccah. "And the rope. Bring them over here." A moment later Rebeccah approached with a long implement that looked like a javelin but with a more rounded, rather than pointed, tip. This was the jumper, used to manually drill a hole into the slate into which explosive material, often gunpowder, was poured to blast large boulders of slate out of the mountain.

Rebeccah handed the jumper to Karis, who waved it at Penny. "Start walking." The path underfoot was rough and uneven but the lighting had not yet been switched off, so dim though it was, they could see a little way in front of them. They passed a small glass sign that said EXIT in a rather fancy script that reminded Penny of an old theatre sign. The three stumbled on a few more metres and then Penny turned around and faced Karis.

"Where are we going? Do you know?"

"There's a small cavern ahead on your right. Get in there."

"You seem to know your way around these tunnels and caverns."

"My father worked here, a long time ago. In fact, he died down here. I come here often. Well, when I can. I know the emergency escapes. It's not hard to avoid being seen."

"So you do know your way around these tunnels?"

Karis shrugged. "You could say that. Now shut up and get in there."

Arms outstretched, Penny inched forward into the blackness of the small cavern. As her eyes adjusted to the darkness, an image emerged of what looked like rows of light-coloured boxes arranged on wooden shelving. They gave off a woody, earthy smell that was pleasant and comforting.

"What's all this?" asked Penny, referring to the boxes on the shelves.

"Yeah," said Rebeccah. "What's this all about? Why are we here? We're supposed to be at the after-party. People were looking forward to meeting you. Everyone will be wondering where we are."

"Shut up and let me think," snarled Karis. She pointed at Penny. "You're really annoying me. Just sit down and put your hands behind your back."

"Karis, the ground is cold, hard, uneven, and wet, for God's sake. I'm not going to sit on it."

Karis made a jabbing motion with the jumper. "All right. Please yourself. Just stand there, then. But put your hands behind your back." She motioned to Rebeccah. "Tie her up. Tight."

Rebeccah reached behind Penny and wrapped the short length of rope, which would have been used as a fuse in the blasting operation, loosely around her wrists. She gave Penny's arm a reassuring, steadying squeeze and then, with her back to Karis, she reached over to the shelf.

A moment later a box flew past an astonished Penny and struck

265

Karis in the forehead. With a piercing scream, she sank to the ground, dropping the jumper and clutching her head. "Give me the rope," Rebeccah said to Penny and when she handed it over, Rebeccah smoothly and efficiently wrapped Karis's wrists with it. And this time, she tightened and tied it.

"It's over, Karis," Penny said. "Give it up now." Karis moaned and struggled to sit up. Rebeccah placed a hand under her shoulder and heaved her into a sitting position. Karis winced at the roughness of the jagged slate beneath her and looked questioningly at Penny.

"So you're in charge now, are you? Well, what's next?"

"We're going to wait here until help arrives," said Penny. "We're not going to risk losing you in the tunnels. And we don't want this to get any more undignified than it already is."

Penny reached behind her and pulled a box from the shelf. It had NWD stamped on the top so she opened it and examined what looked like black bars. She sniffed the contents and then touched one. The bar felt smooth and waxy. She held it up to her nose again.

"Do you know, I think this is cheese? In a wax coating. Well, at least we won't be hungry." She stacked up four boxes and sat on them.

"How are you feeling, Karis?" Penny asked.

"What the hell do you care?"

"I do care." A moment later she added, "I'd really like to hear what this is all about. It all seems so desperate and sad. I know you were at the nursing home and I think you were involved in the death of Doreen Roberts. Am I right?"

"*Mam?*" said Rebecca, looking wildly at Penny. "What do you mean? Did she have something to do with *Mam's* death?"

Forty-four

I guess I stirred things up a bit, didn't I?" said Jimmy.

"You did just great, Jimmy," said Victoria.

"Except for the part where Karis bolted, but I don't think we could have predicted that. I didn't expect her reaction to be so, well, extreme. And to run off down the mine. It's not like she could have escaped. There's nowhere to go."

"And for Penny to take off after her like that! How daft can she be?" Victoria said, nervously.

"I don't think she thought about it. She just reacted."

They exchanged worried looks. "I hope she's all right," said Victoria.

"Me, too. This isn't good," agreed Jimmy.

Victoria scanned the cheerful, noisy crowd that had gathered in the café for the concert after-party. Davies had remained below, assisting in the search for the missing singer and Penny.

Bethan had been into the café a few minutes earlier asking if Karis had driven herself to the mine. When told she had, Bethan asked about Rebeccah. Victoria told her she hadn't seen Rebeccah in the crowd, but had seen her earlier at the concert. Bethan thanked her and left immediately before Victoria could pepper her with questions.

As the concertgoers enjoyed their glasses of wine with Florence's canapés, Mrs. Lloyd made her way over to Victoria.

"Well, Victoria, I'm sure you'll be very pleased with the way everything went. It was a wonderful performance and we couldn't have asked for a more enjoyable and may I say, unusual, St. David's Day event. And Florence has done herself proud with the refreshments."

"Thank you, Mrs. Lloyd. I'm glad you're enjoying yourself."

"I'm not sure everyone is, though. I noticed Rebeccah just as we were leaving the concert chamber. She seemed very upset."

"Did she? Was she with anyone?"

"Not that I could tell, but perhaps she found the music and the singing a bit too much after the deaths of her mother and sister. Or even being in a crowd. I'm sure people came up to her and told her how sorry they were. I haven't seen her at the reception, so maybe she left. Anyway, I wanted to compliment you on your playing. I don't think we've heard you perform since the Rhys Gruffydd funeral, and that was ages ago. Must be almost two years. You should play for us more often." She gazed around at the crowd and waved to an acquaintance. "And by the way, where is Penny? I would have thought she'd be up here overseeing this aspect of the event, and not leaving it to Florence and me to see that everything goes off all right."

"I expect she's been delayed clearing up down below," said Victoria. "She's probably waiting with Ifan for the mine crew to finish up so they can bring up the rest of our instruments and music stands and just making sure everything's done and dusted. Even when the event seems over, there are always so many things to do to get it wrapped up properly."

"Oh, there are," agreed Mrs. Lloyd. "Well, good job, both of you. Just going to have a word with Florence about the arrangements for our ride home."

Jimmy watched her go before speaking. "Speaking of getting home, I got a lift here with Inspector Davies and I'm not sure now how I'll get home. But it doesn't matter. I'm not leaving, I'll tell you that right now, until I know Penny's safe and sound. She's like a daughter to me and . . . well, I just hope she's okay."

"I'm sure Gareth is doing everything he can. But I agree, not knowing is awful. Let's just hope they're back soon."

At that moment, a mine worker opened the door to the café, and seeing Victoria, gestured to her. She went over and he pointed to her harp, in its case, leaning against the wall. "We brought that up for the lady," he said. "Is it okay to leave it here?"

"Yes," said Victoria. "It's mine. It's fine here. What's happening down there, do you know?"

"Don't really know. We've almost finished with the clearing up."

"Well, did you see the concert organizer down there? Do you know who I mean? Attractive lady. Red hair."

"No, I didn't see her. Everyone's left. Except the policeman. He's still there."

"Right, well just leave the harp there. Thank you."

With her stomach churning, Victoria went back inside the café. The reception was starting to wind down and several people came up to thank her for the evening. She smiled at them, trying to focus on what they were saying, but was beginning to feel such a rising sense of panic she found it difficult. She reached Jimmy and pulled up a chair so she could sit beside him.

"I think we've got trouble, Jimmy," she said. "Penny's still down there, but everyone's gone and no one's seen her. I think Karis has got her."

"Got her? You mean she's taken her hostage?"

"Something like that. Anyway, have a word with Florence. Tell her I've got a problem to sort and I've stepped out for a minute. Don't give her any details, though. You and Florence hold the fort here until I get back."

"What are you going to do?"

"I've got to find Bethan."

Forty-five

Karis said nothing.

"Right, then," said Penny. "Let's start with this. I know you were at the nursing home on the day Doreen Roberts died and I think at best you helped her die and at worst, you killed her. We found the helium balloon equipment in the cupboard. The hood."

Karis looked straight ahead into the dark nothingness. The depth of her expression was difficult to read in the dim light from the tunnel, but the air of dull despair that clung to her was unmistakable.

"Tell me!" demanded Rebeccah. "She was my mother and I mean to know how she died."

"How long have we got?" said Karis, finally.

"As long as it takes," said Penny.

"All night, if need be," said Rebeccah.

Karis took a deep breath.

"You could say I helped her die, I guess, but she didn't really want to go, so I'm not sure helping is the right word."

Rebeccah gasped. "Really? You killed *Mam*? Are you saying you killed *Mam*? Why would you do such a thing?" She let out a low, unearthly groan and inwardly, Penny did, too. This was now all going to go very badly.

"And it wasn't just Doreen, was it Karis? You killed Glenda, too, didn't you?" Penny asked.

Nobody said anything. The eerie silence was broken only by the gentle trickling of water down the walls of the mine. And then Karis raised her head.

"'I have no sense of being your mother.'" She spat out the words. "That's what Doreen said to me when I met her. 'I have no sense of being your mother.' What kind of woman says that to her child?"

"When did she say that?" Penny asked. "When did you meet her?" Ignoring the question, Karis continued.

"I'd always known I was adopted. I think most adopted children know without being told. They just do. They don't fit in. They look different. They act differently. Something just doesn't feel right. A feeling of belonging is missing. So I asked my adoptive Mum."

"What did she tell you?"

"She told me what she knew, which wasn't much. That I'd been put up for adoption as a baby. But these days the records are pretty much open and it didn't take much to find out who my birth mother was and with social media, you can find just about anyone. It wasn't hard to find Doreen. So I contacted her and I came to Llanelen about a year ago and we had a little meeting in a café over a cup of tea. It was so stilted and uncomfortable. She was very cold and dismissive. I don't know why she even agreed to see me. I asked her about the circumstances of my birth and she said she was married and had two daughters. Then she'd had an affair and fallen pregnant and her husband made her give the child up for adoption because he couldn't raise another man's kid. She said she wanted nothing to do with me, that she'd moved on years ago. Moved on! And then that's when she said it. That she had no sense of being my mother."

Rebeccah and Penny said nothing as the words sank in and they tried to imagine the unbearable emotional pain and devastation they must have caused.

Penny exhaled softly. "That must have been terribly difficult to hear," she said.

"Difficult to hear? It was more than that. I boiled over with hate and rage and I knew in that moment that I could kill her. That's how difficult to hear it was."

No one said anything. The trickling of water and, in the distance, the gentle splash of the waterfall filled the silence. And then Karis spoke, in a soft, ambient tone.

"We were on tour. You know, with The Characters. A huge group at the time. There was a reception in a fancy hotel. Can't remember exactly where it was, America, I think. Atlanta, possibly. The hotels all looked the same. Anyway, I overheard one of the waitresses telling another one that she was planning an away weekend with the women in her family. Sisters, cousins, aunts, daughters . . . all of them. They did it every year and had so much fun. Stayed in a hotel, all crammed into a couple of rooms, up half the night talking and laughing, drinking wine, and just carrying on. I would have given everything to be part of something like that. With my sisters and my mother."

Rebeccah started to weep softly.

"I had so much at the time, or so everyone thought. She was a waitress, this woman who was going away with her family. And yet she had the one thing I wanted more than anything."

"She was probably filled with envy for you because of all you had in your life," said Penny. "You achieved a tremendous amount, Karis."

"That's the funny thing," Karis said. "When I met Doreen that one time, she said she had a feeling years ago I might be her daughter when she saw me performing with the group on television. Wouldn't you think if a woman saw someone on television she thought was her daughter she'd be . . ." Karis made a vague gesture. "Interested? Proud even? But nothing."

"She wasn't much interested in me, either," said Rebeccah. "It was all about Glenda with her. Glenda this, Glenda that. There was the two of them, and then there was me. Oh, they invited me to the Christmas dinner and all that, but there was never closeness. I was always the outsider. They didn't take much notice of me."

"But at least you got to grow up with your own family," said Karis.

"Oh, if that's what you're thinking you missed, you should be glad you weren't there," said Rebeccah. "It was a horrible childhood. She was a vicious, controlling bully. I hated going home. I hated being there, listening to her fight with my dad. Different story for Glenda, of course. She got all the nice things, the new things. I got whatever was left over. Mum would ignore me at night, but she'd tuck in Glenda, sit on her bed, and they'd talk and giggle and I had to lie there and pretend to be asleep. It was awful."

Karis started to say something, but Rebeccah interrupted her.

"Look, Karis, it was a terrible thing they did putting you up for adoption and telling everyone you died. I'm so sorry for that and I wish it hadn't happened. I wish I could have got to know you before you did all these terrible things. I wish you'd told me sooner that you're my sister. Maybe if you had, *Mam* and Glenda would still be alive. But I don't want you thinking you missed out on a perfect childhood because you didn't. Dad drank too much, there were terrible fights, and *Mam*," she glanced at Karis, "our mother lavished everything she had on one daughter and ignored the other. Others. Me and you. So, yes, that might have been the family you were born into but let me tell you, you didn't miss much by not being there." Her voice was breaking up.

"Rebeccah, when did you learn that Karis was your sister? Was it on the market day when you left your stall and went to the café with Karis?" Penny asked.

Rebeccah nodded. "How did you know?"

"You two were seen going off together."

Rebeccah thought for a moment. A picture of a grey-haired woman in a burgundy-coloured coat crossing the town square flashed through her mind. Rebeccah let out a little groan.

"Of course. Mrs. Lloyd," she said.

Karis looked from one to the other. "Who's Mrs. Lloyd?" she asked.

"Where to begin," said Rebeccah, as Penny managed a half smile. For a moment, the atmosphere became calmer and a little more relaxed.

"You two will have a lot to talk about," said Penny. "But Karis, tell me. I'm curious how you came to be performing at this concert. Did you contact Glenda or did she contact you?"

"She contacted me. She didn't know who I was, at first, but I knew who she was. And I told her she was my sister just after

I signed the contract. She was shocked. And like her mother, our mother, she didn't want to know."

"But after she knew who you were, the concert plans still continued?"

"Well, they had to, didn't they? After the contract was signed she had to go through with it. So did I. I needed the money."

"And Glenda," said Penny. "Did you kill her, too?"

"I didn't plan to. I just got so enraged with her. I followed her here and when I saw the slate splitter lying there I picked it up, and . . ."

"But why?" Rebeccah shouted. "I don't understand how you could kill them!"

"I think I know why she killed Glenda," Penny said. "I think Glenda really brought all the feelings of loss and hatred that you had against Doreen into focus. And I think Glenda's rejection was a huge additional source of pain for you when you were down and vulnerable."

Rebeccah started to cry.

"How am I doing, Karis?" Penny asked.

"Really good," said Karis in a low voice.

"In fact," said Penny, "I bet you didn't even know why you hated Glenda. You just did."

Karis nodded. "Yeah. I just did. I tried reaching out to Glenda. A couple of days before the mine visit I went round to her house to talk to her. I wanted us to have a relationship but she didn't want to know me, either. We got into a fight and it got ugly. She started hitting me and I bit her on the arm. I'm not proud of that, but yeah, I guess you could say hated her. But I hated Doreen more."

"You hated her for some time, apparently," said Penny. "So why now? Why did you kill her now?"

Karis shrugged. "When my life was going okay I pushed all this to the back of my mind and didn't really think about it. But lately, I started thinking about Doreen. Thinking about her a lot. I was drawn to Llanelen and I wanted to see where Doreen lived. How they lived. So I started watching them, following them."

"The way you do," scoffed Rebeccah.

"And then she moved into the nursing home, so I went there, just to look around."

"Didn't anyone stop you or question what you were doing there?" Penny asked.

"No I just put on a pair of scrubs I bought at a charity shop that looked vaguely like the uniform they wear at the nursing home, except they were the wrong colour. But no one took any notice. I went wherever I wanted to."

"And why did you leave pieces of slate in Doreen's and Glenda's hands?" Penny asked.

"Oh, that was just a bit of fun to wind up the police."

"I thought you might have left them as a kind of calling card. A souvenir, almost. Something to remember you by."

Karis closed her eyes and turned away.

"Think whatever you like. Doesn't matter to me."

"Karis, why did you do a runner after the concert? You must have known you couldn't escape," asked Rebeccah.

"I could tell by the way that man in the wheelchair gestured to that cop that he'd recognized me from the nursing home. I recognized him, too. Nosy Parker. And I could have made it out of the mine through an emergency exit if you two hadn't got in the way."

A silence filled with sadness and hopelessness settled over them until Karis spoke.

"I'm very cold and I've had enough of your questions. How much longer do you think we'll be down here?"

"She can have my jacket," said Rebeccah. "I've got a jumper on."

"No," said Penny. "Don't untie her. They won't be long."

"You don't know that," said Karis. "Maybe they'll never find us."

"Oh, they will," said Penny. "They've got a device called a CO_2 detector. It detects the slightest trace of human breath. Border-protection people use them to scan lorries coming into the country for illegal migrants. If anyone goes missing down here they can find them, no matter how deep in the mine they may be."

"Listen!" said Rebeccah. "I think I can hear them now." She went out into the tunnel and called out.

"They're down this way," said a disembodied male voice. A moment later, the focused beam of a strong torch lit up the chamber and two men and a woman ducked their heads against the low entry and entered.

"Told you we'd find them," said Bevan Jones.

"Is everyone all right?" asked DCI Gareth Davies. He avoided looking at Penny for a moment and then stood in front of her, holding out his hand. She took it, and he pulled her to her feet.

"We're all right," said Penny. "Karis here has a lot to tell you about the deaths of Glenda and Doreen Roberts." Davies nodded at DS Bethan Morgan, who moved toward Karis with handcuffs.

"She's very cold," said Penny. "She's just got on stage wear. Can we fetch a blanket for her?"

Bevan Jones nodded. "Anyone else want one?" Rebeccah and Penny shook their heads.

"What's all this?" Davies asked, shining his torch on the stack of wooden boxes.

"Cheese," said Bevan Jones. "The ambient temperature down here is fifty-four degrees and it's perfect for maturing cheese, apparently. The North Wales Dairy stores cheese here for fourteen months while it ripens. It'll be on the market next year."

"What's that box doing down there?" His torch had picked up the box, now dented in the corner, that Rebeccah had hurled at Karis. Penny explained where it had come from and Bethan bent over to bag it.

"You must be hungry," she said to Penny as she straightened up. "The reception's over, but should we see if we can find you something to eat?"

Penny shook her head. "I'm tired and I just want to get home."

As they made their final journey aboveground in the little yellow train, Penny turned to Davies.

"I completely missed the reception. How did it go? And what about Florence and Mrs. Lloyd?"

"We weren't sure what we'd find down here, so they've been driven home. In fact, everyone's gone home. Except for Jimmy. He simply would not leave until he knew you were all right. He'll be happy to see you. He thinks the world of you."

As do I, he added silently. He longed to take her hand, hold her, tell her how desperately worried he'd been for her safety, and take her home and take care of her. Instead, he looked straight ahead and said nothing.

Forty-six

*P*enny slept late the next morning, pulling the bedclothes tighter around her shoulders to hide from an annoyed Harrison, who was pawing at her to tell her she was late with his breakfast and he wasn't best pleased. Finally, when he had made it quite clear that there would be no more sleep for her, she gave in, stretched, and got up. And then she noticed the bright light on the ceiling toying playfully with odd shadows and shapes.

She pulled the curtains back expecting to see the green hills beyond. The hills were there, all right, but they weren't green. In one of those late winter surprises it had snowed in the night and everything was covered in a light dusting of white. The winter had been unusually mild and this was the first snow she'd seen in months.

Downstairs, she opened the front door and peered at her garden. The recently opened daffodils, their trumpets bowed under a cap of snow, were toughing it out in a bitter wind as the bright red berries of the flowering quince ignored the snow and kept up their brave, showy display.

She closed the door, went to the kitchen and dished out Harrison's breakfast. Then, knowing she would now be left in peace, she plugged in the kettle and made herself a cup of coffee. Cradling it in both hands, she sat at the table and thought about how she would like to spend the day.

She hadn't been sketching for some time and the combination of a snowy scene that would likely be gone by the end of the day, fresh air, exercise, and time to think was just what she needed after the emotionally demanding events of last night.

Listening to Karis's account of her rejection by her mother and sister had been deeply troubling. It didn't justify murder, of course, but it was a terrible ending to a scenario that had begun many years earlier in a heartbreaking story of childhood loss and pain.

When her phone rang, she knew without looking that it would be Gareth. He'd said they'd want to take her statement today, if she felt up to it, and she was eager to get that out of the way. She went upstairs to get dressed.

He arrived with DS Bethan Morgan about an hour later.

"It all happened so fast," she began. She described everything that had happened down the mine, and related everything Karis had said.

"She didn't mention the break-in at Glenda's home, but I expect that was Karis," Penny said.

"We think so," replied Davies. "The only things taken were the mother's jewellery. In spite of everything, she wanted something that belonged to the mother who didn't want her."

"That makes sense," said Penny. "When I was doing her manicure she was wearing a pretty amethyst ring. I commented on it and she said it was her mother's."

"We'll ask Rebeccah to identify the ring," said Bethan. "Everything you've told us gives us good background detail for our interview."

"It seemed to me she gave up very easily," said Penny. "I wondered why that was. I thought she would have put up more of a fight."

"It's not that surprising," said Davies. "People who plan crimes focus all their attention on the committing of the crime and ignore the aftermath. They don't make an escape plan, they don't think about where they'll go, or what they'll do. But in her case, she just seems to have given up."

"So what exactly led you to Karis as the murderer, Penny?" asked Bethan.

"When I remembered the fragrance and where I'd smelled it, it pointed to her. It's such an '80s smell. She probably likes it because it reminds her of a time in her life when she had a lot more than she has now. And I found the pieces of slate in both Doreen's and Glenda's hands intriguing. Usually the killer takes something away from the victim, but in this case, she left something. I saw that slate as a symbolic calling card. To me, it was a clue that the reason for the killings was connected to the mine. And if we looked deep enough, and went back far enough, we'd find it. And we did. The slate connected the killings of Doreen and Glenda and tied them to a place. Of course, the two women were connected in life, too."

Bethan and Davies exchanged a quick glance. Davies made a little open gesture with his hands.

"Karis was connected to them in life, too," said Bethan. "In a terribly sad way. We got the DNA results back. Karis, Rebeccah, and Glenda are sisters."

Penny nodded. "Yes, we thought so."

Bethan leaned forward. "No, we thought they might be half sisters. But they're more than that. They're full sisters. Gwillym Thomas, the man Doreen had the affair with, wasn't her father."

As the meaning of this sank in, Penny leaned back and put her hands to her head.

"Oh, no," she moaned. "Of course. There was no DNA testing back then, so Aled Roberts forced his wife to give away their child because he thought her father was Gwillym Thomas. But he wasn't. The child was his. His and Doreen's. Oh, that's heartbreaking. Poor Karis."

"That's another thing," said Bethan. "We checked her original birth certificate. Her name is spelled C-e-r-y-s, not K-a-r-i-s. The spelling was anglicized probably when The Characters group was getting off the ground to make it easier for international audiences to pronounce it."

"Unbelievable. Cerys, of all names. It means love."

"I know. We're only just starting to unravel all the details, but the whole thing resonates with sadness and irony."

Doesn't it just, thought Penny, thinking about the deaths of Gwillym Thomas and Aled Roberts, who died down the mine so long ago. And now that Dylan Phillips was gone, she and Jimmy were the keepers of the secret. With no one left alive who'd played a part in that tragedy was there any point in opening it all up again? Should the dead be left to rest in peace? Or have they been waiting all these years for the truth to be revealed so they can rest in peace.

"Well, if there's nothing else," said Davies, "we'll be on our way and leave you to enjoy the rest of your day."

This was the moment. She hesitated.

"There is one more thing. I've got a story to tell you. It happened down the mine a long time ago, and I couldn't say anything about this until now because it wasn't my story to tell. But now that Dylan Phillips has died, I can tell you.

"It's about the death of Aled Roberts . . ."

"So it was murder, then," said Bethan when Penny had finished telling them how the miners had conspired to murder their much-hated boss.

"It was," said Penny. "And they would have got away with it, too, except Dylan Phillips decided he didn't want the secret to die with him."

Forty-seven

"Would you mind waiting in the car for me?" Davies said to Bethan. "Won't be long."

When they were alone, Davies gazed steadily at Penny. He'd been wondering what to say to her and in the end, decided to keep it simple.

"Haven't really told anyone yet, but I'm seriously thinking of retiring. I'm owed a few days leave—well, a lot, actually—so I'm heading over to Shrebury to talk things over with Alan Nesbitt and if I still feel like this when I get back, I'll put things in motion. It won't happen right away, of course, but I thought you should know."

Penny made a noncommittal murmur.

"At one time I'd hoped that you and I . . ." His voice trailed off.

"I'm sorry, Gareth, I guess I'm just not the marrying kind.

Some women aren't. It's just not right for me, not anymore. Once, maybe, but my life is in a different place, now."

"I know that and I appreciate how honest you've been. Not pretending to feel something you don't."

"I didn't mean to hurt you and I'm sorry if I did," said Penny.

He wanted to embrace her, but she stood just a little too far away and there was a hint of stiffness in the way she held herself that prevented him from touching her.

"Right, well, I'll be off," he said. "I'm guessing you don't want to come to Sherebury with me."

Penny shook her head, smiled, and he was gone.

She closed the door behind him, gathered up her sketching materials, and set off. She was troubled and she'd always found walking the perfect salve for an uneasy spirit. But it wasn't the exchange with Gareth that bothered her. Jimmy had said something to her last Christmas that she couldn't put out of her mind.

"Don't forget about us, Penny. We're still here."

She thought about the nursing home and its residents—once vibrant, contributing members of the community who had raised children, baked pies, walked dogs, sung in choirs, read bedtime stories to their grandchildren . . . done all the daily tasks, that woven together form the tapestry of a life.

And now most of them had been forgotten by families who lived too far away or couldn't make time to visit. Or perhaps there was just no one left.

She sped up and instead of heading into the countryside for a sketching session, she headed to the Spa and walked down the hall to Victoria's office.

"Hello," she said. "Who's in this morning?"

"Just me and Eirlys. We don't really have anyone on reception. Eirlys is running back and forth."

"Does she have a client with her at the moment?"

"I don't know. What's this about?"

"Come with me."

They walked down the hall to the manicure room where Eirlys was tidying up between clients. She looked surprised to see Penny.

"Oh, Penny. I didn't think you were in this morning. Do you want me to take over on reception?"

Penny shook her head. "No. I want to talk to the both of you. I need your help."

"What is it?" asked Victoria. "You seem wound up. Is something the matter?"

Penny shook her head.

"It's about the nursing home. We need to do something for the residents. They're bored and lonely. I've been thinking what we can do to make things better. I think we should start offering manicures to the ladies at a low price and me, personally, I plan to visit Jimmy at least once a week."

Eirlys and Victoria smiled and immediately caught her enthusiasm.

"I could do a little harp recital, just a few songs, say one afternoon a month," said Victoria.

"They'd love that!" said Penny. They looked at Eirlys.

"What if I helped them get on Facebook or showed them how to Skype so they could talk to their families?" Eirlys said. "Not everybody, of course, but the ones who want to."

"Perfect!" said Victoria and Penny at the same time.

"Look, let's form a little committee, and see what else we can come up with," said Penny. "Maybe we can speak to the local florist and see if she could help. I'd love to get rid of those dusty old fake flowers in the lounge."

"And maybe we could work with the owners to get the place painted and freshened up. It really needs to be brought out of the 1980s," said Victoria.

"I think it's a great idea to do something for them. After all, we'll be old one day ourselves." said Eirlys. "I'll see if I can think of something that would get some of the young people in town involved." She gave Penny a broad smile and returned to her work.

"We might organize a little roster of guest speakers," said Victoria, as they made their way down the hall to the front door.

"Mrs. Lloyd could discuss how to write a memoir!"

"Whatever happened with that?"

"I don't know," said Penny. "She hasn't mentioned it lately, so perhaps it just kind of quietly went away."

"You know, if she wrote it, I'd read it," Victoria said.

"So would I."

"So would everyone in town."

They looked at each other and burst out laughing.

Enthused about the new project to do more at the nursing home, Penny finally set off for her afternoon of sketching. The snow had almost melted away, leaving only patches on the hillsides, but enough to add a bit of visual interest.

But there was one last thing to do before she left the town behind her and began her countryside ramble.

"Hello, Jimmy," she said. "Just popped in to see how you are this morning."

He smiled up at her. "Let's sit over here for a few minutes, Jimmy. I'm off to do some sketching and I want to get out before the light changes, but I want to tell you that things are hopefully going to get a little better around here."

She explained the plans she and Victoria were hatching for the nursing home and then discussed the events of the night before.

"I was that worried about you, love," he said. "If anything had happened to you, I would . . ." He turned his head away. Penny gave him a moment to regain his composure and then touched his arm.

"I'm sorry I didn't come to see you as often as I should have," she said. "But I promise I'll do better. And you be sure to let me know if there's anything I can bring you."

"I will."

"See you soon." And she meant it.

A few hours later, tired, hungry, but happy, she opened the door just as the phone rang. She set her gloves down and picked it up.

"Hello?"

"Emyr Gruffydd here. Just wanted to say how much I enjoyed the concert last night and tell you what a brilliant job you did organizing it."

"Oh! Thank you!"

"Well, there's more to it than that. In fact, I'm calling to ask for your help, really. I've just been contacted by the BBC and they're hoping to bring *Antiques Roadshow* to Llanelen and they want to hold the event at the Hall."

"That sounds like fun."

"The thing is, you see, I'm going to need help organizing it. There'll have to be a marquee, and heaven knows what else. So I was wondering if you would consider taking it on."

Penny thought for a moment.

"Why not, eh? What could possibly go wrong?" She laughed. "And at least I'll be able to start this project with a clean slate."